Marsh chuckle ~~d. "I'm~~ ... **I just do my best to** ~~uphold it."~~

Maybe that was why he intimidated Sarah, because he was so good. He was the kind of man who ran into burning buildings and who wasn't afraid to take on dangerous criminals. He probably saw everything in black-and-white. So there was no way he would understand her past.

But she forced a smile and held up her hand as if she was being sworn in. "I promise that I haven't broken any..." She paused, distracted with the errant thought that maybe keeping her suspicions about the fire to herself was a crime of some kind. Or maybe the distraction was that he was smiling, too, his dark eyes as bright as the little twinkling lights dangling from the arbor over the deck.

"Any what?"

She blinked, trying to break the connection she felt. "Laws, of course," she said. "What did you think I was talking about?"

Dear Reader,

Welcome back to Willow Creek, Wyoming. Sadie March Haven-Lemmon isn't done matchmaking yet. Sheriff Marsh Cassidy, her grandson, is the last bachelor cowboy left, but he won't be for long if Sadie has her way. The sheriff has bigger things on his mind than romance, but somehow he can't stop thinking about his father's home nurse, single mom Sarah Reynolds. Sarah knows her patient no longer needs her, and she needs to start making plans to leave. But she's fallen in love with Willow Creek and with the Haven/Cassidy family.

She's not the only one. I've fallen in love with this series, too, and with this family. While Marsh is the last bachelor cowboy of the Haven/Cassidy family, there are some single Lemmons who are now Sadie's stepgrandsons. Their new cousins have already warned them to watch out for Grandma, so telling their stories is going to be a lot of fun!

I love writing about big families. I come from one myself, so I'm familiar with the dynamics and with strong women like Sadie who will do anything for the people they love. Sadie is one of my favorite characters of all of them I've written. While her meddling might bother her family, it's just proof of how much she loves them and wants them to be happy. I hope these books have brought you some happiness like they have me.

Happy reading!

Lisa

A MATCH FOR THE SHERIFF

LISA CHILDS

HEARTWARMING

Harlequin® HEARTWARMING™

ISBN-13: 978-1-335-05133-2

A Match for the Sheriff

Copyright © 2024 by Lisa Childs

For questions and comments about the quality of this book, please contact us at CustomerService@Harlequin.com.

TM and ® are trademarks of Harlequin Enterprises ULC.

Harlequin Enterprises ULC
22 Adelaide St. West, 41st Floor
Toronto, Ontario M5H 4E3, Canada
www.Harlequin.com

Printed in Lithuania

Recycling programs for this product may not exist in your area.

MIX
Paper | Supporting responsible forestry
FSC® C021394

New York Times and *USA TODAY* bestselling, award-winning author **Lisa Childs** has written more than eighty-five novels. Published in twenty countries, she's also appeared on the *Publishers Weekly*, Barnes & Noble and Nielsen Top 100 bestseller lists. Lisa writes contemporary romance, romantic suspense, and paranormal and women's fiction. She's a wife, mom, bonus mom, avid reader and less avid runner. Readers can reach her through Facebook or her website, lisachilds.com.

Books by Lisa Childs

Harlequin Heartwarming

Bachelor Cowboys

A Rancher's Promise
The Cowboy's Unlikely Match
The Bronc Rider's Twin Surprise
The Cowboy's Ranch Rescue
The Firefighter's Family Secret
The Doc's Instant Family
The Rancher's Reunion

Visit the Author Profile page
at Harlequin.com for more titles.

For Sharon Ahearne, my mother-in-law and
mother in my heart and my inspiration for
strength and resilience.

Love you!

CHAPTER ONE

THE OLD DESK chair creaked as Sheriff Cassidy leaned back and stared down at the lighter that lay cupped in the palm of his hand. Two horseshoes, turned on their sides to represent the initials CC, were engraved in the pewter, which was old and soot stained. Irony struck him that the lighter was in his possession now, since he was the only one of his brothers not to have those initials. Unlike his older brother, Cash, and his younger brothers, twins Colton and Collin, Marsh had been named after an uncle he hadn't even known existed until recently. Michael March Cassidy was his full name, but Cash's pronunciation of it, as a toddler, had stuck: Marsh. So that was what everyone called him now.

"Marsh?"

He glanced up to find his brother Cash standing in the doorway to his office. Whereas Marsh and the twins were dark haired and dark eyed, Cash was blond and blue-eyed. Now they all knew why: they didn't have the same biological father. But they did have the same *real* father, the man who'd lovingly raised them all. JJ Cassidy. Despite how much he loved them, or maybe because of how much he loved them, he'd also kept some secrets from them. Like his real name. He wasn't really JJ Cassidy; he was Jessup Haven.

If only Marsh could be certain that there were no more secrets that his dad or anyone else was keeping from him...

But since he'd gone into law enforcement, people often lied to him to protect themselves or people they cared about. He knew that, and he usually could tell when people were lying and figure out the truth. But this time...

"Hey, you're giving me that interrogation-room stare again." Cash held up his hands as if Marsh had drawn his weapon on him. "I swear I don't know anything about how my lighter got into the house. I absolutely did not burn down our childhood home."

Marsh believed him, but he wasn't certain that he should. Cash had spent nearly two decades estranged from the family. When he'd learned, as a hotheaded teenager, that his parents hadn't told the truth about his paternity, Cash had taken off. But now that they'd all reconciled, it felt as if they'd spent no time apart. Like they were as close as they'd always been.

Or maybe that was just the way that Marsh

wanted it to feel. He wanted his family to be together and happy. And they were now.

But for this.

For wondering how their old childhood home had burned down six weeks ago and who was responsible for starting the fire. Colton, the firefighter, had found the lighter in the cellar of the burned house and, knowing it was Cash's, had been hanging onto it before he'd recently turned it over to Marsh.

"No, I don't think you did it," Marsh said.

"Thanks for the vote of confidence, I think," Cash said. "But I wish that you *knew* for certain that I didn't."

Marsh sighed. "I'm not even sure something really happened. The Moss Valley Fire Department initially determined that it was because of poor maintenance of the property." He flinched with guilt at the thought of how the ranch had become run down while he and his brothers had all been so busy. He'd gone to college for criminal justice and started his career in law enforcement. Collin had gone for medicine and had become a cardiologist. Colton had been fighting fires and working as a paramedic for years, while Cash had just been gone.

Cash flinched, too, as if the thought and the guilt had crossed his mind as well. "I'm sorry…"

"Even those of us who were there couldn't keep up with school, then our jobs, as well as helping with Dad's doctor and hospital bills, not to mention all of his appointments and in-patient stays. Darlene did her best to take care of him and the ranch." He didn't know what they would have done without the woman they'd thought was their late mother's friend but was actually their aunt, the widow of the uncle they hadn't known they had.

"So, the fire could have been an accident," Cash suggested, his upbeat tone hopeful.

Marsh shrugged. He didn't know, but even though he'd left his job as a deputy in Moss Valley, and therefore the jurisdiction, to accept the interim sheriff position in nearby Willow Creek, Wyoming, he was determined to find out the truth. No more secrets.

"And if it was an accident, then the lighter had nothing to do with starting the fire," Marsh continued. That was what he wanted to believe—that it was just an accident. But he wouldn't be able to put his doubts to rest until he had proof.

"I hope it didn't start the fire," Cash said. "Because then it is my fault for losing it."

"But you weren't the one who used it," Marsh said. Someone else would have, if it had actually started the fire. But who? And why? "And even if they hadn't found your lighter, they probably would have found something else to start the fire, assuming it wasn't just an accident. But until I know for certain what happened, I can't give the lighter back to you."

"I'm not here for the lighter," Cash said. "And if it is what someone used to start the fire, I don't ever want it back."

It was a family heirloom. Their maternal grandfather's lighter. But they'd never met him or their maternal grandmother. They'd thought their paternal grandparents had died before they were born, too, but then they'd learned the truth.

Their paternal grandfather was gone, and that uncle, their father's brother, for whom Marsh had been named had passed away years ago, too. Just before Marsh and his brothers had learned they were really Havens, they'd also lost a cousin, when he and his wife had died in a tragic auto accident.

But they all suspected that cousin was still with them, in the heart transplanted into their father after years of a debilitating illness had destroyed his. Thanks to that heart, their father was the healthiest he'd ever been, and since Cash was back, he was happy again, too. He hadn't been happy in so long.

"Why are you here?" Marsh asked, and he tensed a bit with concern. "Any reason you need to be at the sheriff's office?" Had something happened?

Cash chuckled. "Like I said, I'm not turning

myself in for something I didn't do. I'm here to ask the sheriff for help with something, though."

Marsh narrowed his eyes. "Help with what?"

He had never met anyone as independent as his older brother. But then Cash had always had Becca, so maybe he wasn't as independent as Marsh had always thought he was. Cash was finally taking his friendship with Becca to the next level; just a couple of days ago, he had proposed to her.

"Help getting married," Cash said. "I'm here to ask you to be my best man."

Marsh had to blink hard for a second before he could focus on his brother's face. Squashing down the emotions threatening him, as he usually did, Marsh grinned and said, "Of course I'm your second choice."

"What do you mean?"

"You can't ask your real best friend since she's the one you're marrying," Marsh pointed out.

"Becca is my best *friend*," Cash agreed. "I'm asking you to be my best *man*."

"Dad is the best man I know," Marsh said.

Cash blinked hard now and nodded. "He is the best man I know, too. But you're a pretty close second, Marsh."

"I've always been second," Marsh said. "But that was to you." He was just teasing him; that was something that he had never minded. He'd idolized his big brother.

Cash shook his head. "You were never second to *me*."

"I'm two years younger than you," Marsh reminded him.

"And yet, we sometimes felt closer than the twins were to each other."

"Until you left," Marsh murmured with a pang as he remembered how hurt he'd been when Cash had left, how alone he'd felt. The twins had had each other, and Darlene had been there to help their dad. But Marsh...

He'd been alone then. Like he was alone now. All his brothers had found the loves of their lives, or in Cash's case, finally realized his best friend was his soul mate. But Marsh was still alone.

That was the way he wanted it, though. He was used to being alone; he preferred it. That way, he couldn't lose anyone else close to him like he'd lost his mom to cancer, and like he'd nearly lost his dad so many times, and then he'd lost Cash, too, for nearly twenty years. But Cash had attended the college that he'd had a scholarship for, and he had become a veterinarian just as he'd planned. Then, after traveling for a while as a rodeo vet, he'd settled close to home in nearby Willow Creek, near family that they hadn't even known they had—all the Havens.

"I'm sorry," Cash said, his voice gruff with regret over leaving.

Marsh sighed and shook his head. "No, I'm

sorry. And I won't bring it up again. I know we can't change the past."

"I wish I could," Cash said, his blue eyes glistening with unshed tears. "I wish I'd been there for you and Dad and the twins, and most of all, that I'd realized how I felt about Becca. I wasted so much time."

Despite being uneasy with emotion, Marsh stood up and hugged his brother. Then he pulled back and asked, "You know how to make up for that?"

Cash shook his head.

"Make the most of the time we have now."

"So, you'll be my best man?"

Marsh grinned and lightly slapped his brother's back. "Yes, I will."

"And then when it's your turn to get married, I'll be yours if you want me," Cash said.

Marsh snorted. "It's never going to be *my* turn."

"Yeah, that's what a lot of our cousins and even our own brothers said, and then Grandma Sadie got a hold of them," Cash noted with obvious affection.

She wasn't his biological grandparent, but she had claimed Cash as her grandson. Maybe because they were so much alike: both stubborn.

Marsh shook his head. "Not going to happen."

"She's got a great track record as a matchmaker," Cash said.

"And if she wants to keep her streak alive, she's

going to have to focus on someone else," Marsh said. "I'm never getting married."

"Ah…famous last words…" Cash teased.

At least, Marsh hoped he was teasing. But before he could make sure his brother understood that this best man thing was definitely going to be one-sided, his phone rang. Once his caller identified himself, Marsh waved his brother off. Cash left with a grin and a mouthed *thank you*.

"Sheriff Poelman," Marsh greeted his old boss from Moss Valley. "It's great to hear from you."

"No, you're not hearing from me," Poelman replied. "I never made this call. You know nothing about this."

Marsh let out a chuckle. Poelman wasn't as old as Marsh's grandmother and her new husband, but he was a lot like them in that he was quite the character. "Well, that's certainly true," Marsh agreed. "I have no idea what this is about."

"The fire."

Marsh's amusement turned to apprehension. "What about the fire?"

"The insurance company isn't accepting the fire investigator's determination on cause," Poelman said. "They want us to investigate."

"What? Why?" Marsh asked, and he closed his hand over the lighter, hiding it from sight as if Poelman could see through the phone line.

"For some reason, the adjuster has it in his head that it's arson," Poelman said. "I just wanted to give you a heads up. Your family has already been through so much."

"So, are you going to…?" Marsh couldn't bring himself to finish the question.

"Investigate?" Poelman's sigh rattled the phone. "We'll go over it all with the fire department, make sure there's nothing they missed."

Marsh tightened his hand around that lighter. "Well, uh, thank you for—"

"For nothing," Poelman interrupted. "This case isn't in your jurisdiction, and your family could be involved, so this call never happened." He chuckled then hung up.

With the way Poelman was joking around, he didn't seem to be taking the insurance company's request too seriously, but he was still a good lawman. He would investigate. And what would he find?

Marsh curled his fingers and stared down at the lighter in his palm. He couldn't hide it forever. He was going to have to turn over the lighter, but with the initial determination being that poor maintenance caused the fire, the lighter had nothing to do with anything. It was just like any other possession in the house. So hanging onto it wasn't breaking any laws. But, like Poelman had just pointed out, Marsh couldn't be part of the investigation because it was family and out of his jurisdiction, too.

But neither of those reasons was going to stop

him from investigating. He had to learn the truth no matter what it was, just as he hoped his brother understood he'd spoken the truth. While he would be Cash's best man, his brother would never be his…because he was never getting married.

SARAH REYNOLDS NEVER should have gotten married. She'd been too young and naive to realize that what she'd felt for her high school boyfriend had been puppy love and friendship and not the real thing. Despite her parents' objections, she'd married him anyway and had realized too late the mistake she'd made. But she knew now, because of her child, what real love was.

She loved her son so much. And if she hadn't married his father, she wouldn't have six-year-old Mikey now. So, as humiliating and painful as the end of her marriage had been, it'd also been worth it.

Mikey was worth every moment of pain she'd suffered and every sacrifice she'd had to make. But ever since the fire at the Cassidy ranch, he hadn't been himself. She'd tried to find out why—if the fire had scared him, or he was upset about leaving the ranch. But he kept shutting her down every time she asked.

She was so worried about him and about their future, but she couldn't let him, or anyone else, see that concern. So she stayed up after everyone else had gone to bed in the house that her patient,

JJ Cassidy, had rented in the town of Willow Creek after his ranch in Moss Valley had burned down. She sat alone on the back deck and let the tears of exhaustion and worry roll down her face.

During the day, for Mikey's sake and everyone else's, she hid her fears behind a bright smile. But at night…she felt so alone. And so scared…

She'd been working as a home health nurse for JJ for nearly seven months now, two months prior to his heart transplant and now five months after it. He didn't need her help any longer. He'd had no issues with rejection; his body had readily accepted the new heart as if it had always been his. Or maybe a part of him…if it had once truly belonged to his nephew.

JJ was healthier and happier than he'd been since she'd met him. From what she'd heard about his family tragedies, he probably hadn't been happy for a very long time. He was such a kind man—his entire family was—that she wanted to stay, but she felt like she was already taking advantage of his new heart, which was as compassionate as his old one. Maybe that was how he'd worn it out. Maybe loving too much and too generously had worn it out and not the lupus that had ravaged his body.

She uttered a shaky sigh. That romanticism had gotten her in trouble her entire life just as her no-nonsense father had warned her it would. He'd been right, but she wasn't about to admit that to him. Even after her marriage had ended, she'd refused to go back home and had worked hard to support herself and her son.

She'd figured it out then, and she would figure it out now. There was just one thing that she was afraid to figure out: how the fire, which had burned down the ranch, had really started. She'd thought it was an accident, but JJ was still waiting for his insurance company to settle the claim. For some reason, they were hesitating or still investigating. Why?

Because they suspected there was more to it? She wondered…

"I didn't realize anyone was out here," a deep voice rumbled.

Sarah jumped and nearly let out a scream despite recognizing that voice. Or maybe because she recognized it. She turned her head to find Sheriff Cassidy standing behind her, wearing the white hat he'd worn even before he'd gone into law enforcement. Not that she'd known him then. She'd just seen the pictures of him when he was a kid. Those pictures, those memories, were all gone now, just like the house where he'd grown up.

She was afraid that she might be at least partially responsible for that loss. Was it something she'd done—or hadn't done—that had caused the fire? If it was, she wouldn't be able to forgive herself, let alone expect him to forgive her.

IF ANYONE HAD told Sadie March Haven, now Lemmen, that she would be this happy again, she would have called them a fool. Would've said it wasn't possible, not after all the losses she'd suffered in the eighty years she'd been alive.

Lem, her new husband, had suffered some losses, too, so he understood. He understood her better than even her first husband had, and it wasn't just because they'd known each other since they were kids. While they shared so many of the same memories and experiences from life, they also shared something deeper, a connection that she'd never had with anyone else, as if they shared a soul, or at least a heart.

So she could feel the turmoil inside him that she felt herself. But her happiness wasn't dimmed at all. This was just a part of life—at least, a part of theirs. They loved so many people, and when those people were upset, they were, too.

She smiled as Lem poured some milk that he'd warmed in the microwave into her mug. She sat at the long stainless-steel-topped island in the enormous kitchen of the ranch house. Usually Taye, Sadie's youngest grandson's fiancée and also the cook Sadie had hired to help out after the tragic accident, was behind that counter, taking care of everyone.

But Lem was taking care of Sadie now, just as she took care of him. Even though she was sitting on one of the stools and he was standing, she was still a bit taller than him. She was six feet, or she used to be, and he was probably closer to five. With his pure white hair and beard and sparkling blue eyes, he looked a lot like Santa Claus, which was why he'd been playing him every holiday season in the town square of Willow Creek.

Since marrying him a couple of weeks ago, Sadie felt as if every day was Christmas. She reached across the island and covered his left hand with hers. Her hand was bigger, her knuckles swollen with arthritis. They'd chosen tattoos instead of rings, and the infinity symbol wrapped around their ring fingers.

Lem turned his hand over and entwined their fingers. "If we want to sleep, we should probably skip the sugar."

But he'd set out a plate of cookies anyway. Snickerdoodles. Her favorite. Taye baked them perfectly every time, so they were kind of crunchy on the outside and perfectly soft inside. With her right hand, Sadie picked up a big one and took a bite. Cinnamon and nutmeg exploded on her taste buds, and she couldn't help but murmur, "Mmmmm."

Lem grinned. "Is Caleb right? Do cookies make everything better?"

She grinned, too. Five-year-old Caleb was one of the great-grandchildren new to their family, but it felt as if the young boy had been forever a part of it, and of her. Just as Lem had been. "You tell me," she said.

Lem hadn't touched the cookies or the warm milk he'd poured into his mug after pouring hers. A call from his oldest grandson had awakened them and their little long-haired Chihuahua earlier. While Feisty had fallen back asleep, they hadn't been able to.

"Are you okay?" she asked.

He nodded. "Yes, I'm just not sure if giving Brett what he asked for was enough or if I should do more…"

"And if you do more, you'll be accused of meddling," she finished for him. They often finished each other's sentences and thoughts. She sighed again but with regret, not bliss. "I'm sorry. That's my fault. I'm pretty sure that my grandsons warned yours at our wedding about my…"

"Penchant for matchmaking," he said. "It was my grandsons' father who warned them about my penchant for being overly involved, as Bob says, in the lives of my family."

It was one of the many things they had in common, loving their families so much that they wanted the best for them. They wanted them to be happy and healthy. But wanting that too much had driven away Sadie's oldest son, so she'd learned to step back when it was necessary. Or so she hoped.

"You gave Brett the phone numbers he asked

for, for Ben and for Genevieve." Ben was the mayor of Willow Creek, but he was also a lawyer, like Genevieve, who had recently married one of Sadie's other grandsons, Dr. Collin Cassidy. Brett, Lem's grandson, needed legal advice. After the wedding, he and his two brothers had returned to the ranch they ran in nearby Hidden Hollow to turmoil and tragedy; their boss and friend had passed away while they were gone. "But we can go to Hidden Hollow, if you want to personally check on them," she said.

Lem sighed then took a long sip of the now cooled milk. "I think we should wait, at least until I find out what Ben has to say." As well as now being his grandson, Ben was Lem's friend and his boss. Ben was the mayor, and Lem was the deputy mayor. Roles they'd served in reverse before.

Just as Ben had turned Sadie's matchmaking back on her when he'd started bringing Lem around the ranch. That stinker…

She smiled with affection.

"What about your text?" Lem asked.

And her smile slid away. When Brett's call had awakened them, Sadie had automatically reached for her cell as well, and she'd seen the text Marsh had sent her: We need to talk.

That message filled her with dread because it usually did not mean they needed to talk about good things. But there had been more to it, something that brought her smile back now: Love you, Grandma.

Marsh was such a good man. With his sense of honor and his calm demeanor, he was so much like the man after whom he'd been named, his uncle, her younger son Michael. The two of them never having the chance to meet was yet another tragedy.

Marsh's text hadn't been the only one she'd found on her cell. Jessup had sent her one as well, with nearly the same message about needing to talk.

"If you're worried, you should just call them now," Lem advised her. "Then maybe you'll be able to sleep."

She was more worried about Lem and her new step-grandsons than she was about her son and Marsh. She sighed again. "I'm sure they both just want to warn me not to subject Marsh to any of my matchmaking." She shrugged, just like she would shrug off their warnings.

They had to see how happy the rest of their family was now. Marsh's brothers, Jessup's sons, had found the loves of their lives, or in Cash's case, realized his best friend was his soul mate. Marsh's cousins, Jessup's nephews, were all happy now, too, despite their recent loss.

So were she and Lem.

They'd all found love and happiness. That was all she wanted for Marsh and for Jessup. Now she just had to figure out how to make them want that for themselves.

CHAPTER TWO

MARSH COULD HAVE stepped back from the open patio door when he'd noticed Sarah Reynolds, the home health nurse, sitting outside on the deck, her curly dark blond hair blowing softly in the night breeze. Then she'd turned her face slightly, and he'd noticed the tears sliding down her cheeks.

He really should have backed away then and left her alone. That was what he would have preferred if someone had caught him in a vulnerable moment—that they would pretend they hadn't noticed and just walk away.

But because she was taking care of his father, he needed to know why she was crying, in case it had anything to do with the man he loved most in the world. So he stepped through the open door and joined her. Not that he expected her to stay. Since he'd moved into the house his father was renting in Willow Creek, she'd been as skittish around him as that bronco they'd had out at Ranch Haven. The one that rodeo champ, and his cousin, Dusty Chaps, had won in a bet. The horse's owner had bet Dusty that he couldn't stay on the bronco for the required eight seconds. That day, Dusty had. But nobody else had before or since that day, not even Dusty. The owner had been so sure of himself that he'd wagered the horse, and he'd honored his bet, giving Dusty the bronco. Midnight. He was a beautiful animal. But he was a beast to those who didn't know him, pawing at the ground and making threatening noises.

Sarah, with her delicate features, big dark eyes and curly hair, was a beauty, not a beast, but she seemed jumpy around him. Like how she jumped when he spoke to her seconds ago, saying that he hadn't known anyone was outside.

He was lying, but only a little bit. When he'd headed toward the deck, he'd figured everyone else in the house was already asleep. He'd stayed late at the office, going over everything he knew about the fire, which wasn't much.

The day his family home burned down, he had arrived at the ranch after the fire had already started, after Dad had gone back inside to try to find Sarah's kid. The little boy hadn't been in the house, though; he'd been in the barn. Mikey was even more skittish than his mother. Marsh was pretty sure the kid had never uttered a word around him. Sarah hadn't uttered many herself.

But maybe their reticence was more about him

than them—or more about his badge. A lot of people tended to be quiet around officers of the law, probably because the only time he saw them was when he was investigating a crime or assisting at the scene of a traffic accident. But even before he'd pinned on his badge, he hadn't been great with kids. Of course, he hadn't really been around them before, and after, he'd only seen them in the line of duty except for dropping in at the ranch after Sarah and Mikey had moved in with his dad. Now he'd moved in with them in the house his dad rented in Willow Creek.

"Are you all right?" he asked. And he wasn't wondering just about this night.

She rubbed her hand over her face, wiping away the tears he'd already seen, and nodded. "Yes."

"Is my *dad* all right?" he asked, his voice gruff with a rush of his own emotions. His father's health had been up and down for so many years. But he'd thought that had all changed now, with the new heart, which had put his lupus into remission. He'd thought that he could finally quit worrying about him.

Sarah jumped up then and touched his arm, as if she was the one comforting him now. "Yes, he's doing great. Better, I think, than anyone expected."

Marsh released a shaky breath of relief. "Good."

"Yes," she said. "He's doing so well that he really doesn't need me anymore."

"Is that the reason for the tears?" Marsh asked, and he reached out but pulled his hand back before he touched her face. He didn't want to make her any more skittish than she already was, and the thought of touching her made him a little skittish, too. Uneasy. Too aware.

Ever since she'd started working for his dad, he'd been interested in her. He'd wondered about her past, why she was raising her son alone. Why she'd chosen to be a home health nurse and not work at a hospital.

But he'd never asked her those questions, feeling that they were too intrusive. All that mattered was how well she took care of his father; she was a good nurse and clearly a compassionate person. And beautiful.

He'd dealt with his interest in and awareness of her the way he dealt with all his uncomfortable emotions: he just ignored them. But ignoring her wasn't as easy now that they were living in the same house.

Ignoring her was also counterproductive. To learn more about the fire, he should have talked to her about it sooner. She'd been there when it had started and had been living at the ranch in the months before it happened.

She swiped at her face again, as if worried that

she'd missed a tear. "No tears. I'm just tired," she said.

Marsh had an innate ability to determine when people were lying to him, but he didn't need it with her. She was easy for anyone to read. In addition to lying to him, she seemed anxious to get away from him; her gaze kept darting away from his to the house behind him. But he remained where he was standing between her and the open sliding door.

"I need to get some sleep," she said.

He did, too, especially since he'd asked for a meeting with Sadie tomorrow. He had to be sharp to keep up with his grandmother's quick mind, or he might find himself getting talked into something he didn't want. Not that he would let even Sadie talk him into risking a relationship.

He had his family to worry about, like always, and now he had an upcoming election to worry about since he definitely wanted his interim sheriff position to become permanent. It wouldn't be fair to a romantic partner to come so low on his list of priorities.

"I don't want to keep you up," Marsh said. "But I don't often have the chance to talk to you alone. And I'd really like to talk to you, Sarah."

A pang of guilt struck him because he hadn't made more of an effort to have a conversation with her before, and now he just intended to question her about the fire. He had the excuse that he'd been too busy, but she was the one caring for his dad, so he should have talked to her. Instead he'd just talked to his dad and to Darlene, who'd hired her. And he wasn't sure why he'd avoided her except that he tended to avoid things that unsettled him.

And Sarah Reynolds, with her big soulful eyes, unsettled him, especially as she was staring up at him with those eyes now. And in that moment, he couldn't tell if she was scared or if *he* was.

SARAH WAS SCARED for so many reasons. It wasn't that she didn't trust Marsh Cassidy; he was the sheriff after all. If he hadn't scared her even before he became the sheriff, she might have thought that he frightened her *because* of his position. But there was more that intimidated her than the badge and the gun. He was so big, well over six feet tall, with broad shoulders. Yet his brothers were tall and broad as well, and she was comfortable around them.

JJ, their dad and her patient, was a big man, too. And she loved him like he was *her* father and really wished that he was. JJ was so kind and upbeat despite all the years of illness he'd suffered. Other patients with similar health challenges had been bitter and resentful and had lashed out at her. But he never had. After recently meeting his mother, Sarah knew where he got that strength and resilience. But unlike her son, Sadie Haven was an intimidating woman; maybe she'd passed that trait onto her grandson Marsh.

All edgy with nerves, she wasn't the least bit sleepy, but she feigned a yawn. "It's really late. Can we do this another time?"

"It won't take long," he said. "I just have a couple of questions for you."

"Questions?" She'd been working for his father for months, and he had never acknowledged or addressed her with anything other than a nod. "I've probably said more than I should have about your father's health."

She wouldn't have done that if JJ hadn't already assured her that it was fine to answer whatever questions his sons asked about him. He'd confessed that he'd already kept too many secrets from them, and he wanted them to be certain he wasn't holding back any longer, especially about his health. He'd told her how scared they'd all been, pretty much their entire lives, that they were going to lose him.

But then they'd lost their mom to cancer instead. Sarah couldn't imagine growing up like the Cassidy brothers had, and a pang of sympathy for them, and maybe especially for Marsh, struck her heart. Obviously they had inherited their grandmother's strength, just like their father had.

She released a shaky breath and asked, "What do you want to know?"

"About the fire," he said.

Another pang struck her heart, this one of pure fear. "I... I doubt I know any more than you do." And she didn't know anything for certain, but she'd recently started having suspicions, horrible suspicions that she felt guilty for even considering.

"You were there when it started," he said. "I didn't get there until after the house was already ablaze."

Ablaze. She and JJ and Darlene had been out in the barn, admiring Darlene's mare, when they'd smelled the smoke. When they'd stepped outside to see what was burning, they'd seen that the house was on fire. She and Darlene had rushed inside to get JJ's oxygen tanks out before they could explode. She shuddered as she remembered the heat of the flames devouring the worn wood of the old farmhouse. Once they were out with the tanks, she'd realized that Mikey was missing. And she'd been scared, so very scared, that her son was inside.

She'd tried to go back in to rescue him, but Darlene had held her back while JJ rushed inside to find him. Her patient could have died. He was more than a patient, though. And she'd been so scared for him, too. Then his sons Marsh and Collin had arrived, and they, too, had run into the fire to find Mikey and their father. They'd all come out except for her son. And in those moments, when she'd thought she'd lost Mikey, she'd nearly lost her mind. Just remembering it now made her tremble, tears rushing to her eyes again.

Marsh's big hands cupped her shoulders. "I'm sorry, Sarah. I didn't mean to upset you."

"It's just… I thought my son was in the house, in the…" Tears choked her now, making it impossible for her to voice her greatest fear aloud.

Marsh closed his arms around her, holding her gently as the tears rolled down her face. She could have pulled away from him. She should have pulled away from him. But it had been so long since anyone had held her like this…since she'd had anyone she could lean on like she was tempted to lean against him now, to slide her arms around him and hold on and…

Then he asked, "Why did you think he was inside?"

She tensed with fear, again, that he suspected the same thing she was beginning to, that her son might have…

No. She couldn't let herself go there, and she definitely couldn't let the sheriff go there, either.

She stepped back, pulling away from him, and his arms dropped back to his sides. "I guess I just panicked," she said. That had to have been why Mikey was so apologetic and tearful when she'd found him. He'd just been sorry that he'd upset her. "I should have known he was in the barn." That was where she and Darlene had found him, in the loft, with that stray cat who'd started coming around the ranch. "Mikey was *always* in the barn."

So he couldn't have had anything to do with the fire starting. But she didn't say that last thought out loud. If Marsh hadn't considered that someone might have started the fire, she didn't want him to consider it. And she certainly didn't want him to suspect her son; she didn't want to suspect him either. But he'd been even more upset than she'd been when she'd found him, and as he'd clung to her, he'd kept whispering, "I'm sooo sorry. I'm sooo sorry."

And every time she'd tried to talk to him about the fire since, he'd completely shut down and not spoken at all until she dropped the subject.

"It was good that he was in the barn," Marsh agreed, and a slight grimace crossed his handsome face.

She flinched as she remembered that Marsh had been hurt, along with his dad and brothers, while trying to find her son that horrifying day. "I'm not even sure I thanked you for going back into the house that day. I owe you my gratitude and an apology as…" Her voice cracked as she remembered the burns and smoke inhalation they'd suffered. It hadn't been too bad, but it could have been so much worse.

"It wasn't your fault," Marsh said, but he seemed to stare at her for a while, as if he was now considering that *she* could be a suspect.

"It was just an accident," she reminded him. "That was what Colton said the fire investigator had determined. That it was bad wiring or poor maintenance or something…" And the arson investigator would know better than she would what had caused it. Maybe the fire, and her reaction to not knowing where Mikey was, had scared her son so much that he'd apologized for upsetting her and didn't want to talk about it now.

He'd enjoyed living at the ranch, playing in the barn, but he hadn't wanted to go back the other day when the Havens had planned an impromptu excursion to the Cassidy ranch in order to find that stray cat and make sure it was all right. Mikey had loved that cat and the mare Darlene had in the barn, but he'd refused to go back with the others. No. He had more than refused; he'd seemed to panic at the thought. And that was when she'd started thinking that horrible thought she'd been thinking…

But maybe he'd just been traumatized from witnessing the fire and the destruction and the fear and also from the ambulance taking away the Cassidy men.

"I'm sorry that you and your father and your brother got hurt looking for my son," she said, clarifying her earlier apology. "I should have known where he was." And that was why this was more her fault than anyone else's. Mikey was her responsibility—hers and hers alone.

"I don't think my parents ever really knew where my brothers and I were," Marsh said. "We pretty much ran wild around the ranch."

"They didn't worry about any of you getting hurt?" she asked.

"We got hurt wrestling in our bedrooms," he said with a slight smile. "We were safer running around with the animals. And on the ranch, the animals were really just animals, not like some of the people I've arrested over the years."

She sucked in a breath. Did he know...

Heat rushed to her face with embarrassment and dread that he might know about her past.

"Not that there's a lot of crime in Willow Creek or that there was in Moss Valley," he added, as if he'd sensed that he'd scared her. "They're both safe places to live."

"Because you've been the law in both places?" she asked with a slight smile.

He chuckled. "I'm hardly *the* law. I just do my best to uphold it."

Maybe that was why he intimidated her, because he was so good. He was the kind of man who ran into burning buildings to rescue people and who wasn't afraid to take on dangerous criminals. He was the kind of man who probably saw everything in black and white. So there was no way he would understand her past.

She'd been there, and even she didn't understand it. But she forced another smile and held up her hand as if she was being sworn in to testify. "I promise that I haven't broken any..." But before she could finish, she got distracted...with the errant thought that maybe keeping her suspicions to herself was a crime of some kind. Or maybe the distraction was that he was smiling, too, his dark eyes as bright as the little twinkling lights dangling from the arbor over the deck.

"Any what?" he asked when she trailed off.

She blinked, trying to break that connection she felt to him through their gazes. "Laws, of course," she said. But then she couldn't help but ask, "What did you think I was talking about?"

"Hearts, Sarah," he replied, and his grin slipped away.

Her heart started pounding then, fast and hard. She had no idea how to respond. Was he flirting with her? Sarah wasn't even sure she knew how to flirt back if she was inclined. But she was not at all inclined to flirt with Marsh Cassidy, or with anyone else. She had to focus on her son, and she couldn't risk making another mistake that affected him.

Marsh said, "I have a feeling that you might have broken a few of those."

She wanted to laugh off his comment. But there was some truth to it. Hearts had been broken just as promises had been broken. But she hadn't been the one who'd caused the damage, who'd broken the promises.

She had learned from that damage, though. She'd learned never to risk that pain again, for herself—or for her son.

MIKEY REYNOLDS STOOD behind the frilly curtains at the window of the bedroom on the second story, where he'd been sleeping since the fire at the ranch. Except he really wasn't sleeping much, not since that fire.

So through that filmy lace, he tried to study the people standing on the deck below. He couldn't see much through the boards of the peek-a-boo roof thingy over the patio, but the twinkling lights dangling from the boards made his mom's golden hair even shinier, and made the sheriff's white hat glow in the dark.

His stomach ached, and it wasn't because he'd eaten too much. Like sleeping, he hadn't been eating that much since the fire, either. Not even when they'd gone to Ranch Haven for that end-of-summer party a few days ago. And there'd been a lot of food there, cookies that the other kids swore were so good.

But, like then, he felt sick over the thought of trying to eat. Of trying to sleep...

Of trying to talk to anyone...

He wanted to listen right now instead. He needed to know what the sheriff was saying to his mom, so with a shaking hand, he turned the lock and pushed up the window. But as he did, it squeaked, and both people tipped back their heads and stared up at him.

He jumped away from the window. But it was too late. He was pretty sure they'd seen him. So he left the window open and rushed back to his bed and climbed into it and pulled the light blanket over his body. Then he pressed his head into the pillow and squeezed his eyes shut. And he held his breath.

The stairs creaked first and then his door as someone turned the knob and opened it. Was it the sheriff or his mom? He wasn't sure which one it was, but he resisted the urge to open his eyes and look.

He had to pretend to be asleep, especially if it was the sheriff. He didn't want to talk to the guy, and he'd made sure that he hadn't. Not that the sheriff had ever really tried. They usually just nodded at each other. That was it.

And that was enough to make Mikey's stomach hurt, just like it was hurting now, probably because it was full of the air he was holding in.

Maybe he should have pretended to snore instead, but if he let out the breath now, it was going to be loud. But if he didn't, he might pass out. So the air escaped him in a heavy gust that stirred his blanket.

A soft laugh tinkled out. His mom's laugh. He didn't hear it that often, but when he did, it made his heart warm, and he smiled.

She touched his hair, brushing it back from his forehead. "Why are you awake?" she asked. "Are you nervous about starting school?"

He didn't feel like smiling now. He groaned. "Can't you just keep teaching me?" he asked.

"You'll like school here in Willow Creek," she said. "And you already know so many kids."

"Who?"

"All the Haven boys and Bailey Ann and Hope."

He'd met them at that party a few days ago, but he hadn't really talked to them. They'd tried talking to him, though, and they hadn't said the things the kids at his old school had. These kids had been nice, and he wasn't used to that.

He didn't know what to say when someone was nice to him or even when they were mean to him. So he never talked much, even before the fire.

"You're going to make so many more friends," his mom assured him.

He didn't make friends, though. Not with people. He made friends with animals, like Miss Darlene's horse and that cat that had hung around the barn—just like he'd hung around the barn. He'd rather be with animals. So would Miss Darlene. She'd told him that she got a job working with them now.

"Can't I just go to work with Miss Darlene?" he asked. "At the vet's office?"

Another chuckle reached his ears, a deep one.

And he jumped and turned toward the open door. A big shadow blocked it. A big shadow with that white hat. "You sound like my brother Cash," the sheriff said. "He's one of the veterinarians who Miss Darlene's going to work with, and all he ever wanted to do was be with animals. But he knew he had to go to school first and get his high school diploma and then his degree so that he could take really good care of the animals. When Cash was in school, he found his very best friend, and they're still friends all these years later."

A best friend. Something inside Mikey yearned for that, for a really close friend, someone he could tell everything to…like…the secret he'd been keeping.

He sucked in a breath.

"You need to go to sleep, honey," Mom said. "You have to get up early tomorrow for school."

He got up early every day, usually because it was so hard to sleep lately. Tonight it was going to be even harder. Because of school starting, and because of the sheriff.

"Good night, you two," the man said, his voice just a low, deep whisper. Then his boots lightly struck the wood floor of the hall as he walked away.

Mikey thought for a minute how it might be to have a guy around to tuck him into bed like his

LISA CHILDS 43

mom did now. He couldn't remember his dad. Had he ever done it?

Or had he just done bad things and nothing good?

"Are you going to be able to get to sleep, honey?" his mom asked. "Do you want me to stay with you until you do?"

"No, Mom," he said. "I'm tired now." Then he yawned and closed his eyes and pretended that he'd fallen asleep. And this time, he made sure he breathed normally so that he didn't blow out all that air again. And finally, Mom walked away like the sheriff had.

But, unlike with his mom, Mikey hoped that the sheriff didn't come back. He didn't want to see him again.

CHAPTER THREE

IF MARSH HAD had the time, he might have pulled over a couple of vehicles along the road to Ranch Haven. One was a big van that was speeding just a bit, but when the driver, a tall woman with a thick blond braid, saw him, she slowed down and waved.

Taye Cooper, probably driving the Haven boys to school for their first day. He waved back. Then, moments later, a red Cadillac sped past him. It stayed in its lane, but it was going much too fast. He flicked on his lights for a second, just as a warning, and in his rear view, he noticed the brake lights as the Caddy slowed down for him. That vintage Cadillac was pretty distinctive and belonged to the deputy mayor and Marsh's new stepgrandfather, Lem Lemmon.

Having seen both those vehicles leaving, he shouldn't have been surprised when he arrived at the house a few minutes later and was greeted with silence. He'd been told, several times, not to knock or ring the doorbell, that only strangers or salespeople did that.

Family walked right in. He wouldn't have believed, when he'd first learned that he was a Haven, that he would ever feel at home here. But it hadn't taken him long to feel that he fit in, maybe because he looked so much like his cousins. Or maybe because the ranch was also in his blood like it was for the people with whom he shared some DNA. Or maybe it was just because of Sadie…

It was through the sheer force of her iron will that he hadn't had a choice but to feel like family because that was what she'd wanted. He wanted that, too, which was why he was here, stepping through the patio doors from the courtyard that opened onto the kitchen.

For once, the kitchen was empty, almost eerily so. But he'd passed Taye on the road, so he understood why the cook wasn't at her usual spot behind the long kitchen island. And the kids were with her in that van instead of gathered around like they usually were.

Lem had left, too, in that red Cadillac Marsh had passed. But where were the others?

Toenails scratched across the brick floor, and then a little yap cut through the silence. And Feisty, his grandmother's long-haired Chihuahua, rushed up to him. Her little teeth snapped, and she growled despite the wagging of her fluffy black tail. She climbed over his boots and tugged on the bottoms of his jeans. By now, he knew what she wanted, so he leaned over and scooped her up in his hands, bringing her toward his face. She snuggled close, kissing his chin until he pulled her away and grimaced.

Then, from upstairs, came the cry of a baby. And another cry chimed in with the first, echoing and almost harmonizing with it. "Shh," he said to Feisty. "We woke up the twins." His cousin Dusty and his wife, Melanie, had just welcomed their babies into the world a few days ago.

He grimaced again, but this time, it was at the thought of having infants around, totally dependent on him. He wasn't good with older kids because he somehow unsettled or intimidated them. He couldn't imagine how bad he would be with babies.

"If the boys getting ready for school a little while ago didn't wake them up, you certainly didn't," Sadie said as she walked into the kitchen.

Feisty wriggled in his grasp, and he leaned down to put her back on the floor, which she rushed across to dance around Sadie's well-worn boots.

Despite being eighty years old, Sadie still worked the ranch a bit. And it showed in those worn boots and the arthritis that had swollen every knuckle of her big hands. Maybe that was why she and her new husband had chosen tattoos instead of rings as the declaration of their love and commitment.

Marsh admired their commitment, but it was something he was never going to risk himself. He knew nothing lasted forever. Even if the marriage didn't fail, people died. Like Lem's first wife and Sadie's first husband, the grandfather Marsh had never gotten the chance to meet.

"I suspect their empty stomachs are what woke them up," Sadie said. Instead of being bothered by the crying, she smiled with affection. Nothing seemed to faze the woman; she was so strong.

Marsh was counting on that strength, or he wouldn't risk sharing his burden with her. He was also hoping her strength would shore up his, so that he could figure out what was the right thing to do for his family and for himself.

"How's your stomach?" Sadie asked, and she reached out as if she was going to pat it. But then she hugged him instead.

Marsh closed his arms around her and hugged her back. She was nearly as tall as he was so he was able to rest his cheek against her head for a moment. Her long white hair was bound in a thick braid that reached almost to her waist. And she wore jeans and a Western shirt like he did.

"I'm not hungry," he said. Thinking about the fire investigation being reopened had killed his appetite. He held her one more moment, borrowing her strength, before pulling away from her.

She gave him a speculative look, as if trying to figure out what was going on with him. Not that he hadn't hugged her before, but he wasn't as comfortable expressing affection as his younger brothers were. Which was another reason that he'd determined it was better for himself and everyone else that he remain single.

"Taye saved some fresh cinnamon rolls and banana nut muffins for us," she said as if trying to tempt him. Then she opened the microwave and pulled out a covered dish. Despite the cover, the scent of cinnamon and banana wafted over to him.

And his stomach growled.

Sadie grinned. "There's fresh coffee, too."

"Sold," he said. "But just be aware that I'm not this easily manipulated when it comes to other things."

She blinked and widened her eyes, obviously feigning innocence. "What things are you talking about?"

He chuckled. "I think you know. But I didn't come here to talk about that." Then he released a heavy sigh with the tension that had been gripping him.

"You didn't?" Sadie asked with another speculative stare.

"No," he said. "That's the least of my concerns right now. I'm worried about something else."

"Your dad?" she asked with a slight gasp. "Is he doing all right? Is his heart—"

"He's fine," he assured her, just like Sarah had had to assure him the night before when he'd found her crying on the deck.

Why had she been crying?

She hadn't actually told him because she hadn't even admitted she'd been crying.

He suspected there was a lot she hadn't told him. And he wanted to know…*everything*…about her. He wasn't about to ask Sadie for help with that, though, knowing that she would get the wrong idea entirely.

He didn't want himself to get the wrong idea, either. He didn't want to be interested in Sarah for anything more than finding out what had caused the fire at the ranch. Despite how pretty and compassionate she was, he didn't want to get involved with her—for his sake and for hers. He wasn't family man material; his family had always been so much of a mess growing up, with the health and financial strains, his mother dying and Cash running away.

Family life was too hard for him to risk for himself or to inflict on anyone else, especially a young mother raising her son on her own.

Sadie waved a mug in front of his face, the scent of coffee wafting from it. "You seem very distracted, Marsh," she said as she handed him the mug and a plate with a cinnamon roll and a muffin on it. She pulled out a stool from the counter and settled on it, in front of another plate and mug.

Marsh put his on the counter and pulled out a stool to join her. "Distractions that I don't need right now," he murmured. He needed to concentrate on the upcoming election, not on the fire and certainly not on Sarah Reynolds.

"Can I help?" she asked.

"I don't know," he admitted. "I'm not sure what to do myself."

"About the election?"

"No, I want to run," he said. "I like being sheriff." And it wasn't a role he was going to give up without a fight. He just hoped it wouldn't be a fight.

"I can definitely help you with the election," she said. "I've helped Ben in the past."

"It's not about that," he said. "It's about the fire at the ranch."

"What about it?"

"It hasn't been settled yet," he said.

She narrowed her eyes and nodded. "So that's what this is about…"

He nodded, too. "Yes, the Moss Valley sheriff gave me a courtesy call to let me know the insurance company wants a more thorough investigation."

"They think it's arson?"

"I guess…"

"Do you think it's arson?" she asked.

"I don't know…" he murmured again. "But Colton shared something with me…"

"That same something that had him so anxious to find your brother Cash?" she asked.

"You know about the lighter then," he said. He should have known that she would know. Some of the tension drained from his shoulders as he expelled another sigh.

"Of course I know about it…" she murmured around a mouthful of cinnamon roll.

"Cash swears he doesn't know how it got into the house. He lost it somewhere else on the property. And I'm not even sure it started the fire, but where Colton found it…"

"He's worried that it did," she said when he trailed off.

But she didn't sound that certain, more like she was guessing. Or maybe she just couldn't bring herself to think someone had deliberately set the fire, either.

"I don't know what he thinks anymore, but with the insurance company wanting the fire investigator to take another look…" He shrugged. "I don't know what to think…"

"It still could have been an accident," she said. "Maybe that lighter had nothing to do with it."

"But maybe it did," he said. "So, should I turn it over to the fire investigator or the Moss Valley sheriff?"

"You don't know that it started the fire," she reminded him.

"But I don't know how it got in the house, either," he said. "Cash swears he hasn't set foot inside it since he ran away all those years ago, so how did the lighter get there? And did whoever brought it into the house start the fire?"

"Why don't you find out?" she asked.

"It's not my jurisdiction," he reminded her. "Someone got me hired here in Willow Creek after she got the former sheriff to retire early."

She snorted. "Early? It was way past time for him to retire. You're smarter and harder working than he ever was. And you'll figure this out faster than the fire investigator or sheriff in Moss Valley will."

He smiled at her praise. "But what do I do if I don't like what I learn?"

"You'll figure that out, too," she said.

Torn between law and order and loyalty to his family, he wasn't as confident as she was that he would. But maybe that was why he'd come to her for advice.

"How can you be so sure?" he asked. Especially when he wasn't. "It's not like you've known me very long."

She smiled, etching lines by her mouth and dark eyes. But her eyes sparkled and her face lit up with a glow of happiness. The lines didn't detract at all from her beauty; in fact, they somehow added to it, as proof that she'd earned the wisdom she had. "I know you like I know myself. You're a part of me Michael March Cassidy, and I'm a part of you."

That was what family was and why this was so difficult. He didn't want any of his family to get hurt. But for some reason, when he thought of family, he also thought of Sarah and her son. They weren't family. Nobody had even known them that long or that well.

But maybe it was because of what they'd gone through together—his dad's heart transplant and the fire—that they felt closer than simply a nurse hired for medical assistance and her child. While Sarah had taken excellent care of his father before and after his transplant, Mikey had been unobtrusive and sweet. He was a sensitive, empathetic little kid, totally unlike how Marsh and his brothers had been at his age.

Sadie chuckled. "Are you all right, Marsh? Is the thought of being like me too horrible to comprehend?"

He chuckled now. "No. It would be an honor to be like you, Grandma." It really would. The woman was incredibly strong to have survived all the losses that she had. She hadn't just survived; she'd thrived.

She blinked furiously at the tears that momentarily brimmed in her dark eyes. "And here I thought you wanted to meet up today to warn me to back off..."

He chuckled again. "From your matchmaking?"

She nodded.

"I don't need you to back off because I'm not worried about that," he said. "Whatever scheme you concoct isn't going to work on me."

"Why not?" she asked. "You must see how happy your brothers and cousins are now."

"Yes, and I'm happy for them," he said. "And for you. But as much as I may be like you and them, I wouldn't be happy in a relationship." He would be on edge, like he'd been growing up, worried that he might lose someone, or worse, put them through the stress that he'd endured growing up. With his job, it was even more likely that whoever loved him might lose him.

As Sarah found a spot in the nearly full parking lot at Willow Creek Elementary School, she wasn't sure which of them was more nervous: her or Mikey. She gripped the steering wheel tightly to still the trembling in her hands. But she had to remove one to shift the vehicle into Park and then shut off the ignition. As she did, she drew in a breath that was as shaky as her hands.

So many other parents were also driving their children to school on their first day. Mothers and fathers together, as well as other single parents like her, except that they probably weren't all single parents like her. The other parent was probably just at work, not where her ex was. Because of where he was, the other parents at Mikey's old school in their hometown hadn't treated her very well. They'd judged her by the actions of her ex, making it difficult for her to even find work because people hadn't trusted her in their homes. And with the way some of the people had talked to her, their kids had probably overheard the comments and judged Mikey as harshly as she'd been judged. And he was just a child. A sweet, loving child.

She glanced into the rearview mirror and studied his tense face. With strawberry blond curls and big blue eyes, he was so cute. And he was a good kid. He really was.

She knew it, and she felt so guilty that she'd even considered that he might have had something to do with the fire. And even if he had, it would have been an accident. He wouldn't have purposely done that, which could have been why he'd been apologizing so tearfully the day it had happened.

The one question she hadn't already tried to ask him that day was if he'd started the fire, and she didn't know if she could actually ask him that. She knew he struggled with self-esteem from the bullying at his old school, so she didn't want him to feel even worse about himself if he had accidentally started it. As a nurse, she could care for any of his physical wounds, but she wasn't certain how to care for that kind of injury, for the emotional and mental ones.

She cleared her throat of the emotion affecting her and said, "We're here." Then she turned around and forced a big smile for her son.

From his booster seat in the back, Mikey glanced out the side window. But he didn't make a move to release his seat belt or reach for the door.

"It's going to be fun," she said encouragingly as she secretly hoped she wasn't lying. Mikey looked at her with suspicion, like he thought she was. "You already met a lot of kids at Ranch Haven last week, and you know how nice they all are."

"At Ranch Haven," he said.

"You don't think they'll be nice when they're at school?" she asked.

His bony shoulders lifted in a shrug. "I dunno..."

"There's one way to find out," she said. "Let's go inside..."

She wasn't sure that she would be able to walk in with him, though, or if she would have to leave him outside the doors to the lobby at the center of the T-shaped school. She'd been in the building when she'd signed him up and knew the layout and how seriously they took security. All of the doors were kept locked, and there was even a retired deputy who acted as a security officer.

Her son would be safe here. After the scare she'd had at the ranch, when she hadn't been able to find him, she was happy she would always know where he was and that he wouldn't be in any harm. But she wanted him to be happy as well.

Yet the mention of going inside had his mouth pulled down at the corners in a frown and his blue eyes widened with fear. "I don't feel—"

Someone tapped on the glass of the driver's side window, and they both whirled toward it. Becca Calder stood next to their vehicle. Becca was a real estate agent in Willow Creek and Moss Valley. She was tall and beautiful with black hair and dark eyes. And her daughter, Hope, who stood next to her mother, was a mini version of her, with longer dark hair. She tapped on Mikey's window.

"We gotta get going," she told him. "The bell is going to ring soon." Then she tugged on the door handle.

Sarah pressed the button to unlock the doors, so that Hope could get it open. And as the door swung out, Mikey unclicked his belt and scrambled out of his booster seat as if he was embarrassed that he still had to use one. It was a struggle to get him into it because he protested that he was too big. But, legally, he wasn't.

He was actually small for his age. So much so that Hope was taller than him when he stepped out to stand next to her. "Do you have your backpack?" Hope asked him. The second he hooked his hand through it, she tugged on him, pulling him toward the school.

Another little girl called out to her from the sidewalk. "Hurry up!" The girl had a profusion of dark curls and held the hand of a blond woman who wore a suit jacket, skirt and heels like Becca and looked as put together and professional as the Realtor was.

Sarah, in her faded scrub pants and shirt, felt hopelessly out of place and out of class in the presence of the other women.

But then Becca opened her door and held it for her. "Come on," she said. "I know how hard this is." And she took Sarah's hand just like her daughter had taken Sarah's son's hand. She squeezed it. "We're just as scared on their first day of school as they are." She smiled. "Or maybe we're more scared than they are."

Sarah smiled. "You must be more scared than Hope." Because her daughter had tugged Mikey along toward that other little girl, who was jumping up and down on the sidewalk. "And certainly everybody is more afraid than she is."

"Bailey Ann," Becca said. "She's thrilled to finally go to school like other kids."

Sarah had briefly met the little girl and her

parents at Ranch Haven. "She had a heart transplant?"

Becca nodded. "Yes, like JJ."

But she was just a child, probably just a year or two older than Mikey. "That's so sad."

"You can't be sad around Bailey Ann," Becca said.

Sarah fervently hoped that was true, that the little girl could cheer up her son.

Like her daughter, Becca nearly dragged Sarah along down the sidewalk toward the other parents standing outside those double steel doors to the lobby. Their children stood closer to the doors, waiting for them to be opened, so they could rush inside toward their classrooms.

Well, Bailey Ann and Hope looked ready to rush inside while Mikey turned back and stared at Sarah, as if silently begging her to let him go back home.

But JJ's house wasn't their home. They hadn't had one for a while. Maybe it was time to put down roots somewhere. To make a life for them that wasn't moving from place to place anymore.

That was what she wanted for him, for them.

But what if…

She couldn't fixate on the fire anymore. He couldn't have had anything to do with it. As she'd told Marsh the night before, Mikey had been in the barn. And that was the only reason her son had apologized to her, because he'd scared her when she hadn't been able to find him.

He looked scared now.

But he wasn't the only one. The blond woman looked deathly pale as she stared at Bailey Ann. Becca let go of Sarah's hand to grab the other woman's. "Are you all right, Genevieve?"

The woman released a shaky breath. "Yes, it's just that I'm worried about her medications and her overdoing it."

"Is she still on three daily doses of her anti-rejection medication?" Sarah asked.

Genevieve nodded. "Yes, she has to take one of them at lunch, with food. Collin went over it all with the nurse, but he has concerns. He actually asked to speak with her again this morning." She bit her lip.

Sarah would have offered to speak with the nurse, too, but Collin Cassidy wasn't just a concerned father. He was a cardiologist. He could explain his daughter's situation better than anyone else.

"Hurry up! We're late!" Little bodies rushed through the crowd of parents. One belonged to a blond-haired boy, and the other had darker blond, almost brown hair. An older kid, with sandy hair, limped after the younger boys.

"Please, excuse us," he said with a long-suffering sigh. Miller Haven, at seven, seemed much older than his younger brother and step-cousin. But then all of the kids went through so much when Miller, his brother Ian and their toddler brother, Jake, were in an accident with their parents earlier that year. They had survived, but their parents hadn't. And the other child, Caleb Morris-Haven, had lost his dad a year or so before.

Tears of sympathy pricked the back of Sarah's eyes. She hated to see anyone suffer, but especially children. They looked good now, though. Happy.

Taye Cooper, who had started out as the cook at the ranch and was soon to be the Haven boys' aunt and co-guardian, joined them on the sidewalk. She held a toddler on her hip, and his head was snuggled against her, his dark curls mussed and his dark eyes bleary with sleepiness. "I forgot how far the ranch is from town," she said.

"You're not late," Becca assured her.

"Tell them that," Taye said with a chuckle as she watched Ian and Caleb move through the crowd of children now. They stopped by Mikey and Hope and Bailey Ann, and they greeted him with big smiles just like Hope had. Miller's smile slid away when he met Bailey Ann's though.

Sarah released a shaky breath. Hopefully, Mikey's and her fears were unwarranted. It looked as though these kids would be as nice to him here at school as they'd been at the ranch.

Then the big steel doors opened, and the children poured into the school. All but Mikey.

He turned back and stared at her again. Even though there was some distance between them, Sarah could see the panic on his tense face and in his eyes. And she could feel his fear pounding frantically in her heart, too.

She was tempted to rush forward to rescue him, to pull him out of the crowd and into her arms. But then Hope tugged on him, and he turned around and disappeared inside the school with the little, dark-haired girl.

"They will be okay," Becca said.

Sarah wasn't sure who she was talking to—her or Genevieve or Taye. They all released shaky breaths like she had.

"I'm glad I pushed back my appointments this morning," Genevieve said, "because I need to go back home for a while and recover from this. Please don't make me go back alone." She reached out and touched Little Jake's back. "Please, Taye, you can commiserate with me." Then she turned toward Becca and Sarah. "And you two have done this before, so you both need to come and assure us that it will get easier."

Becca chuckled. "So you want us to lie to you?"

Sarah laughed, too, despite herself. "That would be a whopper."

"Yes, lie to us," Taye said.

Becca made a tsking noise with her tongue and teeth. "No, Genevieve says we always have to be open and honest."

"Would have saved you a lot of trouble," Genevieve pointed out.

Becca sighed. "You're right. It is the best pol-
icy."

Sarah didn't feel like laughing now; she felt
like crying. Because she knew that if she was
open and honest with these women, they wouldn't
be as welcoming as they were now being to her
or her son.

WHEN JESSUP PASSED the Willow Creek Sheriff's
Department SUV on the road to Ranch Haven,
he beeped his horn and waved even as tight knots
formed in his stomach. What was Marsh doing
out at the ranch?

He could probably guess. A short while later,
when he walked into the sun-drenched kitchen
where his mother was sipping coffee from a big
mug, he asked, "Did you summon Marsh out here
for more of your scheming? Even after I warned
you not to push him?"

Her throat moved as she swallowed. Then she
smiled at him, but only with her lips. "I did not
summon him. He requested a meeting."

"A meeting about what?"

Her forehead furrowed. "I can't quite remember…"

He snorted. "Don't try that with me."

"I am getting older, you know," she said.

"The hearing is the first thing to go," he said.

"And that seems to be your problem. That you can't hear people telling you not to meddle."

She smiled. "I heard Marsh."

"He told you not to meddle?" So that was his reason for coming out to Ranch Haven. How typical of Marsh to be proactive and upfront. Just like his uncle, Jessup's younger brother, had been.

Sadie nodded.

"Are you going to listen?"

She held her hand up to her ear and leaned toward him. "What? What did you say?"

"Exactly," he scoffed then laughed and wrapped his arm around her shoulders. "I love you so much." How had he stayed away as long as he had? Because he'd been so convinced he was going to die and hadn't wanted to put her through that…

For her to feel helpless like she'd felt every time he'd gotten sick growing up. He knew how frustrating that feeling was because he'd felt helpless so many times in his life.

"I love you, too, my darling oldest child," she said as she wrapped her arm around him. "But I suspect that you're here to tell me to back off."

"Like father like son…at least about that," he said. He wished he was as honest and aboveboard as his son the sheriff. But every secret he'd kept had been for what he'd considered a good reason, to save the people he loved from pain and stress, but in the end, he'd just caused them more.

"Who do you think I would try to match you up with?" she asked, as if it was just out of idle curiosity.

But he knew better.

"You know Darlene is my sister, in my heart as well as by marriage," he reminded her. He doubted his mother considered Darlene a possible match for him, and that she was probably thinking of the same woman he couldn't seem to stop thinking about, the one currently staying at Ranch Haven to help out her daughter during her pregnancy and with the twins she'd just recently had.

As if thinking about her had conjured her up, Juliet Shepherd descended the back stairwell to the kitchen. Her auburn hair bounced around her shoulders, and she wore no makeup, but her face glowed. In one arm, she cradled an infant, and she stared down at the baby with such a look of love and fascination.

He lost his breath for a moment as something happened to his brand-new heart, something that wouldn't have happened to the old one, which had been too broken and worn out.

"Hi, Juliet," he said, when he was finally able to breathe again.

She glanced up from the bundle in her arm and smiled at him with that smile that lit up her whole face. "Good morning, Jessup," she said. "I didn't know you were coming out to the ranch."

But she seemed happy to see him, as happy as he was to see her. Juliet was his nephew's mother-in-law and a new grandmother to those twins, though she didn't look old enough to be anyone's grandmother. She looked so young, and something about her made him feel so young again.

So young and hopeful. Feeling like he did, he wasn't certain that he would mind his mother meddling…just this once. For him…

And if he wanted that happiness for himself, shouldn't he want it for Marsh, too?

Maybe it wouldn't be so bad for him or his son if his mother refused to listen to their requests for her not to play matchmaker with them.

CHAPTER FOUR

SARAH WASN'T ENTIRELY sure how she'd wound up at Genevieve and Collin Cassidy's home with Becca, Taye and Little Jake. But when Genevieve had invited her, she hadn't had a reason to say no.

JJ didn't need her; he'd left her a note that morning that he was going out to Ranch Haven to see his mom. Marsh, as usual, was already gone when she'd awakened. Last night was actually the first time they'd ever really had a conversation.

A conversation that she couldn't get out of her mind, just as she couldn't get the man out of her mind. But he had actually been stuck in her head from the first moment she'd met him at the Cassidy ranch. His big build, the white hat, the intensity of him that she found intimidating, but also his love for his father and his camaraderie with his brothers, which she'd witnessed during his visits to the ranch and while he'd been staying with them in Willow Creek. And she would never forget how fearlessly he'd gone into that burning house for the people he loved.

A lot of the people he loved were in the house she'd been invited to. Of his immediate family, only his dad and his brother Colton, the firefighter, were absent. His brother Cash had stopped in to join Becca. His brother Collin was there. He'd been at the school, too, touching base again with the school nurse.

Another nurse was also at their home, an older woman who usually worked at Willow Creek Memorial Hospital. "I wish you were the school nurse, Sue," Collin said to her. "I wouldn't be so worried about Bailey Ann being there without me or Genevieve."

Sue's icy blue eyes widened as if horrified. "Not me. I'm not good with children."

Genevieve snorted. "Yes, you are. Bailey Ann loves you."

"Bailey Ann is different," Sue said with a slight smile. "I love spending time with her. But a whole school of kids…" She shuddered slightly and shook her head. "No." She turned toward Sarah. "You're a nurse. You should apply for the job."

"I thought someone was currently in that position," Sarah said. After struggling to get jobs herself, she didn't want to take anyone else's from them if they needed it.

"Mrs. Howard would have retired years ago if

there was anyone else willing to take her place," Sue said.

"She mentioned to me today that she'll be putting in her notice soon," Collin said.

Cash chuckled. "Was that because of a certain overprotective father?"

"Overprotective?" Collin repeated and shook his head. Unlike his brothers, he didn't wear a hat, but maybe one wouldn't go with his white doctor's coat. Collin's twin, Colton, always wore a black hat unless he was in his firefighter gear. Cash, a veterinarian, wore a brown hat, while Marsh wore a white one, maybe because he was the sheriff.

Cash held up his hands. "I know, I know. You have every reason to be protective of Bailey Ann."

From what Sarah had heard, the little girl had come close to death many times in her young life. Just the thought of that made Sarah's heart ache. She couldn't imagine losing a child, though there were times lately when she felt like she was losing Mikey. He'd always been a quiet and shy kid, but since the fire, he'd shut down even more and was shutting out everyone.

Even her, despite all her efforts to get him to talk to her.

Then she remembered how sweetly Hope had taken his hand and led him into the school. Maybe he wouldn't be able to shut her out just as Sarah hadn't been able to refuse her mother's urging to join them here to commiserate over their kids' first day of school.

"Will you consider applying for the position?" Collin asked Sue.

She shook her head. "I can't. I'm near retirement myself at the hospital. Sarah would be better suited to the position. She has a child of her own there, too, so it would be a great job for her."

Sarah felt a tug of yearning to take the job to be able to spend more time with her son. She'd happily homeschooled him during her time at the Cassidy ranch, so she was already missing him. But after how withdrawn he'd become after the fire, she'd worried that maybe he'd been too isolated out there and that he needed to be around kids his own age for socialization.

"It really would be a great job for you, Sarah," Becca said.

Did they all know JJ didn't need her anymore? Maybe they were trying to find her a new position, so that she would move out of their father's house.

"But what about Dad?" Cash asked, his face going a little pale, probably with fear over JJ's health. "He just recently got his transplant, and if his lupus flares up again, he's going to need medical help."

"He's doing really well," Sarah assured him. "I am sure that he would be fine without me." She really needed to find another job and a place for her and Mikey to move to. But would the school hire her?

While her professional record was exemplary, her personal life wasn't. She'd made a mistake that had cost her so much, and she was afraid that it would wind up costing her son, too. It already had since he'd been bullied at his old school. If she applied for that position and someone found out about her ex-husband, Mikey's father, the little boy might start getting teased and bullied here.

And given how fragile he'd seemed since the fire, she wasn't sure how much more he could take.

A TEXT HE'D sent had brought him to Ranch Haven that morning, but a text he received brought him to Collin and Genevieve's house in Willow Creek. Swing by. Cash and Becca are here along with Taye and Little Jake. Baker and Colton might stop in, too.

Marsh should have headed right to the sheriff's office, but the chance to see his brothers together drew him to Collin and Genevieve's. Cash had been gone too long, so any chance to see him again felt like a gift, kind of like seeing Dad healthy and happy was.

But Dad wouldn't be at Collin's. Marsh had passed him on the road to Ranch Haven. He trusted that Sadie wouldn't share his concerns about the fire with her oldest son; she would protect him like JJ had been trying to protect her during all the years they had been estranged.

Marsh wanted to protect his family from any more estrangements. He had to find out the truth about that fire and make sure that, whatever the truth was, it didn't hurt anyone he loved.

His grandmother was right; he would figure out what to do. But first, he had to figure out what happened. Hopefully it was just an accident and there was no point in worrying his dad about the lighter.

When he pulled up to the large ranch house in town, he couldn't help but notice the small car parked in the driveway behind Becca's SUV. Was it a coincidence that Sarah was here, or had his grandmother already enlisted his brothers to help throw them together? Was this the match she was going to try to make next? Him and Sarah Reynolds?

The nurse was single and beautiful and sweet. She deserved to be with someone, but she and Mikey deserved someone who would have more time and attention to give them. He assumed Mikey's dad wasn't in the picture at all anymore. She didn't wear a wedding ring, and nobody had come to visit her and Mikey at the ranch or at the house in town. And Mikey hadn't gone anywhere for visitation with his dad either.

Was he dead?

Or had he just abandoned them?

Or was there some other reason, something that Sarah wasn't willing to share? Maybe that was why she was so skittish around him; she was keeping secrets of her own.

And why was Marsh so interested in her?

All that should concern him about her was what she and her son knew about the fire. While she claimed not to know very much, he still needed to talk to Mikey.

With no other places to park in the driveway or along the curb, Marsh pulled the sheriff department SUV behind her car. He didn't intend to stay, especially if his brothers were just trying to aid and abet Sadie's matchmaking scheme.

Once he stepped out of his SUV and approached the house, he could hear the deep rumbles of his brothers' chuckles drifting out through the open door and windows. His heart warmed from hearing them all together, laughing like they used to, when they weren't squabbling over something. The squabbling had happened when they were teenagers; they were adults now. Not that they hadn't squabbled a bit with Cash's return. But that had been over that stupid lighter.

He wished he could get rid of it and never see it again. But it was potentially evidence, and he couldn't bring himself to destroy it even though it might implicate someone he loved. He wasn't as convinced as his grandmother was that he would know what to do with the truth once he learned it. Yet he still had to find out what it was, whatever it was.

He drew in a deep breath and stepped through the open door. He wasn't sure if he was bracing himself for whatever teasing his brothers might do or if he was bracing himself for *her*. With the way his heart jumped a little the minute he saw her, he had his answer. Last night…her tears…

Touching her shoulders to comfort her, holding her close as she relived the terror she'd felt when she hadn't been able to find her son the day of the fire…

It all rushed over him again, making his fingertips tingle and his head a little light.

What in the world is wrong with me?

Maybe he just wasn't getting enough sleep with all his worries about the fire and his family and the upcoming election. Maybe that was the reason he felt lightheaded when their gazes met.

Her face flushed a little, and she looked away from him. Maybe she was embarrassed over getting so emotional the night before.

He wanted to look away from her, too, but she was so pretty with her dark blond hair pulled up in a clip, a few curls escaping to frame her heart-shaped face. Her eyes were so big and dark with dark circles beneath them. She must not have got-

ten any more sleep than he had after she'd tucked
her son back into his bed the night before.

"Hey, everyone, simmer down now," Cash
said. "The sheriff might be here to write us up
for disturbing the peace."

They weren't the ones disturbing his peace.
Or, at least, he hoped none of them had started
the fire. But it wasn't just the fire disturbing his
peace. For some reason, he couldn't stop thinking about Sarah.

But he forced himself to grin at his older
brother. "You're right. I got a call about some
disorderly conduct at this address."

"Good thing we have a lawyer in the family
to defend us," Collin said as he wrapped his arm
around his wife's slender shoulders.

Marsh still couldn't get over his shock that his
younger brother was married. He knew that Collin and Genevieve had initially wed so that they
would be able to foster and adopt Bailey Ann, but
they had fallen in love quickly and deeply. Very
quickly and very deeply.

Which was something Marsh wouldn't have
believed could happen if he hadn't witnessed
it himself. They not only loved each other very
much, but they loved their daughter, too. Despite
Collin's teasing, he looked tense.

"So, what is this party about?" Marsh asked.
He glanced around and noticed that Collin wasn't
the only one who looked tense. Taye and Baker

did, too, and they cuddled Little Jake between them as if unwilling to let him go.

And Sarah seemed unwilling to even look at him. Not that that was unusual. She usually didn't spare him any more attention than he did her, even though they'd been living in the same house for weeks.

Becca and Cash were the only ones who actually looked happy and relaxed. "We're supposed to be celebrating the kids going back to school," she said. "But it's hard not to be with them as much as we're used to."

"Cab," Little Jake murmured. "Cab..." The toddler was obviously missing his favorite cousin, Caleb.

Marsh felt bad for the little guy as he had a sudden memory flash through his head of watching Cash go off to school when they were little. And then again, when Cash had left home for good.

He'd missed him so much. He glanced at his older brother, still hardly believing that he was here with them again after so many years apart. Cash's return was almost harder to believe than Collin marrying as hastily and happily as he had. But Cash wasn't just back in their lives; he was engaged as well, just like Colton was engaged to Livvy Lemmon.

All their lives, Marsh and his brothers had sworn they would never get married, probably because of the heartache their parents had suffered over their health and financial issues. Mom had always worried so much about Dad that she hadn't taken care of herself, and so it should have been no surprise when she'd gotten sick and passed. But it had still been a shock, one that Marsh suspected none of them, his dad nor his brothers, had fully recovered from. He was pretty sure he hadn't. And maybe that was why he was so reluctant to get in a relationship.

"I'm happy, though, that Hope is thrilled to be back at school," Becca said. "As an only child myself, I always loved being in school."

"Or at the ranch with us," Collin reminded her.

"Sadie said you were heading out to the ranch this morning," Taye said to Marsh.

He nodded. "Yes, and thank you for saving some cinnamon rolls and muffins for me. They were delicious."

"There were more?" Baker asked, his light brown eyes wide with shock.

Taye chuckled and nodded. "Of course there were more."

"I should have known," Baker said. "My fiancée cooks enough for an army."

"She pretty much *is* cooking for an army, one of Havens and Cassidys," Cash said with a chuckle. Then he turned toward Marsh. "So, why were you out at the ranch, Sheriff? Were you cautioning our grandmother about disturbing the peace, too? Or about her matchmaking?"

"That would disturb my peace," Marsh muttered beneath his breath.

Cash and Collin heard his comment because they both laughed. Even Sarah glanced at him, and heat climbed into his face.

"The first time that you guys came out to the ranch, we warned you about her," Baker reminded the Cassidys. "She loves playing matchmaker."

"I don't think it's turned out too badly for any of us," Collin said as he pulled Genevieve a little closer.

"It's still meddling," an older woman said. Marsh recognized her from the hospital and from prior visits to Genevieve's house. She was a nurse. "And my saying so is as well, which is my cue to leave."

"Me, too," Sarah said, her face flushed.

"I'll walk both of you out," Genevieve said as they started toward the door.

Knowing he was blocking them in, Marsh started out, too, with an, "I'll need to—"

But Cash caught his shoulder. "So, who is Sadie trying to set you up with?"

Collin's gaze followed Sarah out the door, and he wriggled his eyebrows.

Marsh shook his head. "No…"

"Sadie casts a wide net when she sets couples

up," Baker said. "She found Dusty's wife when he couldn't. So it might not be Sarah."

"Dad loves Sarah and Mikey," Collin said.

"Dad won't let Sadie push Marsh into a relationship," Cash said.

Marsh was getting irritated with how they were talking around him like this was going to happen, so he spoke of himself in the third person, too. "*Marsh* isn't going to let anyone push him into a relationship."

He needed to make it clear to them because he wasn't sure whether Sadie had enlisted his brothers to help her scheme or maybe even his dad. But it didn't matter who she had helping her; her plan wasn't going to work. Especially if Sarah was the match she intended for him. She'd slipped away from Genevieve and Sue and rushed right to her car as if she couldn't wait to get away from him. She was obviously not interested in getting to know him any better, or maybe she didn't want *him* getting to know *her* any better.

GENEVIEVE HADN'T MISSED how quickly Sarah had rushed off, either. But she wasn't sure if that was because of the Cassidy brothers' teasing or for another reason. After waving at the young nurse who was already in her vehicle, she turned back to the older one. "Sue, I know the reason you gave for not applying for the job at the school, but you're great with kids. You'd be great as the school nurse. You were very sweet to encourage Sarah to go for it instead." She'd probably realized that Sarah's job was about to end; JJ was doing so well.

"I'm not great with kids," Sue said. "Bailey Ann isn't really a kid."

Collin came up behind Genevieve where they were standing in the doorway and chuckled. "No, she's Grandma Sadie in a child's body."

Becca and Cash, who were also on their way out, laughed. "Hope is, too. Sadie's getting to all of them, so we should be glad they're back in school."

"I think she's getting to all of you, too, with the meddling," Marsh said. He had already walked past them, but he turned back now to ask, "Why are you all encouraging Sarah to apply for a job at the school? Is it just because of Bailey Ann?"

Genevieve nodded. But clearly the sheriff was suspicious of their motives and worried that they were matchmaking, too.

"Will she?" he asked.

Genevieve shrugged. "I don't know. She seemed interested but apprehensive."

"Apprehensive?"

She shrugged again. "I can't say for sure. I don't know her very well."

"Nobody does..." he murmured as he turned back to where the young woman sat in her vehicle, which his sheriff's department SUV had blocked into the driveway. Then he started toward the street, but as he approached her car, his steps slowed. He was clearly going to stop and talk to her.

And Genevieve had a feeling he was going to try to get to know Sarah better. But after insisting that he wanted no part of Sadie's matchmaking, why would he? Because he was interested in her as a man, or as a lawman?

CHAPTER FIVE

So far, school wasn't as bad as Mikey had thought it would be. It was nothing like his last school. Nobody called him names. And when they talked to him, they were pretty nice. Hope was the nicest, though.

At recess, she didn't run off to meet up with Bailey Ann, who waved at her from the swing set; she stayed with him. "Grandpa JJ said you took really good care of that stray kitty from the Cassidy ranch," she said. "You left her so much food that she was able to take care of her kitties until me and Cash found her in the loft."

"She's okay?" he asked, remembering how she'd rubbed against him and purred. Her fur was so soft, and even though she was gray, the pattern of it had reminded him of a tiger or a leopard or some big cat. And when she'd stalked the mice in the barn, she'd looked like a big cat.

She nodded. "And she has the cutest kittens. I want to keep every one of them, but my mom says it's not fair to keep them all to myself. That we really need to share them with other people who would love to have one of them as a friend."

A friend. The mama cat had been his friend. Both she and Miss Darlene's mare had kept him company on the ranch. He missed them. He missed the ranch.

But it was his fault that it was gone. It must have been his fault...

He closed his eyes for a minute at that awful thought and the rush of guilt it brought him.

"Are you okay?" It was Bailey Ann who asked the question. She must have rushed up from the swings when he'd closed his eyes.

He opened them to stare at her.

"You look like I did before I got my new heart," she said, her voice all serious.

"What?" he asked uneasily.

"Really tired," she said. "I was tired all the time." She was breathing a little heavy now, like that short run from the swing set to where he and Hope stood by the slide had worn her out. She touched her chest. "But my new heart fixed me. Do you need a new heart?"

Did he need a new heart? Was there something wrong with his old one? It seemed to hurt a lot, especially when he thought about the fire. Or his old life at his old school...

Or his dad.

"I dunno," he replied.

"My daddy is a heart doctor," Bailey Ann said. "He can find out."

"He doesn't need a new heart," Hope said almost defensively. "He needs a friend."

Bailey Ann nodded. "Everybody needs friends."

He'd never really had any before, though. He wasn't sure how to be a friend.

"And everybody needs a best friend," Hope said. "Like my mom and Cash were best friends all through school."

"Aren't you going to be *my* best friend?" Bailey Ann asked.

Hope nodded. "Yeah, but I think maybe you can have more than one best friend. Like how Caleb has Ian and that horse that Dusty Chaps won."

Bailey Ann laughed. "Which one of us is the horse?"

He liked the sound of her laugh. It made him smile. "I want a cat," he said. He'd loved Miss Darlene's horse, but she hadn't purred and snuggled like that cat had.

"Come to my house after school," Hope said. "And you can pick one out."

"I want one, too," Bailey Ann said.

"You both have to ask your moms," Hope said. "I know my mom will be really happy to have some of the kitties go to other homes."

Would his mom let him have a cat? She'd never let him have any animals before, but that was because they were always moving, just staying with people for a little while until they were better.

Mr. JJ was better now. Were they going to have to leave again soon?

If they were, Mikey would need that cat even more than Bailey Ann would. Because she would have Hope, and he would have nobody once again.

Nobody but his mom. For as long as he could remember, it had only been the two of them. Hopefully, she would let him get a cat.

SARAH'S STOMACH MUSCLES had knotted the second she'd seen the sheriff's department SUV parked behind her car, blocking her from leaving. She'd felt trapped in that house with all the Havens and Cassidys joking around.

But she still wasn't able to escape. Instead of going back inside, she got in her vehicle and waited. He would probably be leaving soon. But when he stepped out of the house, he stopped to talk with the others who were slowly departing. And she closed her eyes and lowered her head a bit, not wanting to get caught staring at him like she'd probably been staring at him inside the house.

All of the Haven and Cassidy men were good-looking, but she'd never been tempted to stare at any of them the way she'd stared at Marsh. But he had more than an attractive appearance; he had a presence, too, one that drew her attention.

And after he'd comforted her last night, she couldn't stop thinking about him. And staring at him...

She closed her eyes more tightly, trying to shut him out of her mind as well as her sight. But then a tap on the glass startled her, and she jumped and whirled toward it to find him leaning down so that their faces were level with only that glass separating them.

He tapped again, and she rolled it down and leaned back a bit so that he wasn't too close.

"I'm sorry I startled you again," he said, his voice deep with what sounded like genuine remorse. "And I'm sorry I blocked you in."

Not wanting him to feel bad, she smiled and said, "I didn't mind having a minute to..." Try not to think about him. But she couldn't say that, so she just trailed off.

He smiled and glanced back at the people standing outside the house. "My family can be overwhelming, and this is probably only about half of them."

"I know," she said. "I met them all at Ranch Haven." That had definitely been overwhelming for her and for Mikey. He'd clung to her hand. Like her, he'd never seen that many family members in one place. Even before she'd been disowned, she'd just had a dad and mom, with no siblings. Like Mikey.

Like Hope. But unlike Hope, who seemed eager to go to school to be around other kids, Mikey was always reluctant to go. Like she was reluctant to leave now. But the morning was slipping away. "I should really get back to your dad's," she said.

"You don't have to rush off. He's probably still at Ranch Haven," Marsh said.

JJ hadn't asked her to go along with him. He didn't need her anymore; unlike Bailey Ann, he had no problem taking his medications correctly. And he always made sure to get his rest and try not to do too much too soon.

Except for the fire.

He could have died in it, trying to find her son. And that would have been her fault because she should have known where her child was.

"If you'd like to stay and visit with the others, you should," he said.

She shook her head. "No, I really need to get some things done around the house." Since she and Mikey lived with them, she insisted on doing most of the housework and cooking to cover their room and board, especially now that JJ was so healthy he didn't need her medical help. At least she could do something for him. But she owed him more than housework, especially if…

"The house is spotless, Sarah," he said, and

his dark eyes narrowed a bit as he studied her face, which was too close to his with how he was crouched down next to her car. Maybe he suspected she just wanted to get away from him.

He wasn't wrong.

"I need to figure out what to make for dinner, so I have to get back," she said.

"It's not even lunch time yet," he pointed out with a slight grin, like he knew she was looking for an excuse to get away from him.

"Still, I have work to do," she said. She should probably get her resume together just in case that job did open up at the school.

"I understand that," he said. "I need to head to the sheriff's office, too." But he seemed reluctant to head to his SUV. Then he asked, "How was Mikey this morning about going to school?"

Her heart softened a bit with his concern. "Nervous. I had to keep reminding him that he knew some kids already, the kids in your family."

"So he knows a lot of kids then," Marsh said with a smile. "My head's still whirling from how we went from being a family of all bachelors with Mikey as the only kid in our orbit to all of these little Havens and Bailey Ann and Hope now, too."

"They're all very sweet kids," she said with a smile, thinking again of how kind and welcoming Hope had been toward her son.

He nodded. "I don't know a lot about kids, but they seem like really good ones. Like yours…"

Was she just being paranoid or did he not sound quite as certain of Mikey's goodness? Did he know about Mikey's father?

Then he added, "Would it be okay for me to ask Mikey some questions about the fire?"

And her stomach dropped as fear gripped her. "Why?" she asked.

"I'd just like to question him about what he remembers about it, about things that had been happening around the ranch around that time..."

She nearly shivered at his mention of questioning her son, like he was a criminal, like the child was like his dad. The sheriff definitely wasn't convinced yet that her kid was as good as his relatives.

She shook her head. "That's not necessary." And it wasn't going to happen. "He was in the barn when the fire started, and he was always in the barn. He wouldn't have seen anything around that time that wasn't in the barn." She drew in a shaky breath, trying to steady her voice before she continued, "Can you please move your vehicle? Now."

He stood there for a moment, still leaning over to meet her gaze, before he finally nodded and started walking toward the street.

She held her breath until he started his SUV and backed up. She held that breath until she was able to back out and speed away from him.

But she wouldn't be able to escape him for long. They lived in the same house. With her son.

Her son whom a sheriff wanted to question about a fire.

She had been concerned last night that Marsh suspected her son might have had something to do with it. Now she was terrified that he did and that maybe he had a good reason to be suspicious.

She had to talk to her son before the sheriff did. She had to make sure that, when she'd found him in the loft, he had only been apologizing for scaring her and not for…anything else.

When Marsh backed up his SUV, Sarah wasn't the only one who exited the driveway. Collin drove off, too, and Cash and Becca as well. Yet Sarah was the one he was tempted to follow; she'd gotten too defensive over his questions. Both last night and just now, like she was hiding something.

Like he'd pointed out to Genevieve, nobody really knew that much about her. And that seemed pretty remiss of him and his brothers since she'd been hired to care for their sick and vulnerable father. Surely one of them must have checked her references or ran an employment check on her.

So despite needing to get to the office, he followed someone out of the driveway, but it wasn't her.

When he pulled in behind Collin's car in the

hospital parking lot, his brother stepped out and asked, "Was I speeding, officer?"

"I don't think you could in that old hybrid," Marsh admitted.

Collin almost lovingly patted the roof of the vehicle with its faded paint and assorted dings. "She carried me through college and med school and my residency and fellowships," he said. "She's been faithful."

Collin was faithful as well, to his career and to his patients and especially to his family. Although he'd never admitted it aloud, it was pretty clear that Collin had become a cardiologist because he'd wanted to help their father. Surely he would have had Sarah checked out before hiring her to care for him.

"Speaking of faithful," Marsh said, "there's something I should have asked you a while ago about Dad. Actually, it's not so much about Dad as about someone close to him, maybe too close to him…"

Collin's brow furrowed. "I know Dad kept some secrets from us, some major ones, but he's still faithful to Mom's memory even though she's been gone nearly twenty years."

"What are you talking about?" Marsh asked.

"Dad dating," Collin said. "Isn't that what you wanted to ask me about?"

"No," he said. But he actually wished his father would find someone, especially now that

Darlene was moving on and starting a life of her own. Not that she didn't deserve it. She'd helped them all so much with Dad and with the ranch. They would never be able to repay her for all she'd done for them and for all she'd sacrificed. "But if that's what you thought, I guess I worded that awkwardly."

"Thinking of Dad dating anyone is awkward," Collin agreed. "But it is overdue. Cash thinks he might be interested in Dusty's mother-in-law, Juliet."

Juliet was also the mother of Cash's half sister; they shared the same father. Poor Juliet had been through a lot thanks to her philandering husband. Marsh wasn't sure she would take a chance on romance again. Or that Dad would either, for that matter.

The only thing he knew for certain was that *he* wasn't about to take a chance on romance, no matter how much scheming Sadie did.

"I didn't follow you here to talk about Dad's love life," he said. Or his own. "I have some questions about his health care."

Collin's brow furrowed again. "He's doing well. Actually, with the transplant putting his lupus into remission, he's thriving. The transplant surgeon and his cardiologist are the best in their fields."

"What about his home health nurse?" Marsh asked.

"Sarah's an excellent nurse," Collin said, and

he sounded a bit defensive. "She's taken excep-
tional care of our father. If he hadn't had her
helping him before the transplant, I'm not sure
he would have made it until his new heart became available."

Marsh sucked in a breath. He knew she was a
good nurse, but he hadn't realized that she might
have actually saved his father's life. He owed
her his gratitude. But instead of thanking her,
he'd upset her. However, he also had to know
the truth.

"So you knew her before you hired her?"
Marsh asked. "You worked with her or something?"

Collin shook his head. "I didn't know her, and
I wasn't the one who hired her. Darlene did."

He nodded. "Okay, so she probably ran a background check on her. Hopefully, she'll know
more about her."

"And now you're going to grill Darlene?" Collin asked. "Why?"

"You don't think we should know more about
this woman who's been living with our dad?"
Marsh asked. And he felt foolish that he hadn't
thought about that when Sarah and her son had
first moved to the ranch. But with his job, he
hadn't gotten out there as much as he should
have. And he'd just assumed Collin knew her.

"Darlene lived with our dad a lot longer, and
we never knew she was our aunt," Collin pointed

out. "She took care of him and us. That's all that matters. Just like Sarah has been taking care of Dad."

"I know, but..." He felt like there was more to Sarah Reynolds, like his dad wasn't the only one who'd been keeping secrets. Sarah was, too. But what kind of secrets?

"Instead of interrogating Darlene, why don't you just ask Sarah about Sarah?" Collin asked. "You seem very interested in her all of a sudden."

It wasn't all of a sudden, but he wasn't about to admit that to his brother. Until now, he'd been able to ignore his interest, until he'd started investigating the fire.

"And what does it matter now?" Collin asked. "Dad doesn't actually require help anymore; I just think he doesn't want Sarah or her son to go. I also think she's aware he doesn't need her anymore, so if she applies for the job at the school, which I hope she does, the school will thoroughly vet her before hiring her."

That was true, but it didn't negate the fact that they should have known more about her before letting her move in with their father and Darlene. While she was a good nurse, it didn't mean that she was a good person. Yet, he could hardly bring himself to think that with how sweet and compassionate she always was.

But she seemed defensive and a little secretive,

too, now that he'd started asking her questions.
Like she had something to hide...

And he was determined to find out what that
was and, however unlikely, whether it had anything to do with the fire at the ranch. But he
didn't know if his motivation was just to protect
his father or to protect himself.

CHAPTER SIX

EVER SINCE LEAVING Ranch Haven, Jessup had had a smile on his face. As he drove back into the city limits of Willow Creek, he kept thinking of Juliet fawning over her grandbabies and of how happy and vivacious she was.

And beautiful.

He had a granddaughter now himself since Collin was adopting Bailey Ann. He already loved that little girl so much, and he probably understood her better than anyone else did since they'd both had their health struggles and heart transplants. Now Hope was joining their family as well; just seeing her reminded him so much of her mother, of how Becca had spent every moment she could at the ranch with them. She'd always loved animals and his son. She already felt like his daughter.

So he had every reason to be happy. But all the changes made him uneasy as well. Darlene was leaving. When he pulled into the driveway next to the two-story brick traditional, he saw the boxes loaded into her vehicle. Not that she had much to move. She'd lost everything in the fire like he had. Well, they'd lost everything but what really mattered: family.

In fact, the fire had inadvertently reconnected them with all of their family. But Darlene wasn't moving to the ranch with her sons; instead, she was going to be working for Jessup's oldest son, Cash, and his partner at Willow Creek Veterinarian Services.

He parked his vehicle, stepped out and asked, "Do you need any help?"

She closed the back door of her little SUV and shook her head. "No. That was pretty much the last of it. I feel bad, though, like I'm booting Cash out of his home."

Jessup snorted. "His home is with Becca. The studio apartment connected to the barn of the veterinarian practice isn't his home."

"Yes, and I could have waited until he and Becca were married before moving into it," Darlene said.

But Jessup doubted that; he knew she'd been looking for a job and a place of her own since shortly after they'd moved to Willow Creek from Moss Valley. After reconciling with her sons, she had a new lease on life, like he did with his heart, and clearly she wanted to live it to its fullest.

"Instead, Cash moved out for me," Darlene

continued, "and he's staying in the house with Dr. Miner until his and Becca's wedding."

"That's because he's going to marry Becca as quickly as he can," Jessup said. "Something he should have done years ago."

Darlene smiled. "You're starting to sound like your mother."

"Bite your tongue," Jessup teased.

She laughed.

That wasn't a sound he'd heard often from her. Eighteen years ago, she'd shown up at the Cassidy ranch as broken as a person could be and still survive—as broken as he'd been. And without her, he wasn't sure he would have survived. He'd needed her, and she'd needed to be needed.

"Sounding like Sadie isn't a bad thing," she said. "I idolize your mother."

That was why Darlene had tracked him down, to bring him back home to Sadie after his brother had died. But he'd been in no shape to reconcile with his mother then. He hadn't thought he would survive much longer, and he hadn't wanted to put her through the death of another child.

But he had survived. So now he had to figure out what to do with this second chance of his.

Darlene had already figured out hers. She'd gotten a job that he had no doubt she was going to love. And with the look that came over her face whenever she talked about Dr. Miner, Jessup wondered if she might come to love more than the job.

"I wish I could be more like her," Darlene said.

"You are," Jessup assured her. "If you're talking about her strength. As for the meddling, you don't have it in you."

"I don't dare meddle with my children," Darlene said. "I just want to be part of their lives again."

"What about mine?" Jessup asked.

"Of course I want to be part of my nephews' lives, too," she said.

"You are. They adore you," he assured her. "I meant about the meddling. Would you help meddle with mine?"

"Sadie hasn't asked me to," she said.

"What if I asked you to?"

She narrowed her hazel eyes and stared at him like he'd lost his mind.

Maybe he had. Maybe spending so much time with his mother was making him think like Sadie. Or maybe just seeing his other kids so happy made him want that happiness for all of them—for Marsh, too.

"What are you talking about?" she asked. "Colton is engaged. Collin is already married and Cash will be married soon. And Marsh... oh..." Her mouth dropped open slightly as she must have concluded what he had.

"Marsh deserves to be happy, too," he said.

She nodded. "I know…"

"And Sarah…"

"Sarah?" The sound of a car drew their attention to where the nurse was parking at the curb outside the house. Darlene smiled and nodded. "Yes, Sarah and Mikey deserve happiness."

"Want to help me help them find it?" he asked.

She shook her head. "I don't want to meddle."

He knew how much Darlene had suffered over thinking that anyone was unhappy or resentful of her. For years, she'd thought her own children, and Sadie, had hated her after her husband's death. She wouldn't risk being resented again.

But Jessup figured Marsh's happiness was worth the risk.

WHEN SARAH STEPPED out of her car and walked up to the house, she caught the look that JJ and Darlene exchanged before they turned toward her. The bright smiles they flashed made her even more uneasy. "Everything all right?" she asked.

They both nodded quickly. "Yes, of course," JJ said.

"How did the school drop-off go this morning?" Darlene asked.

"There was a lot of anxiety," Sarah admitted.

"Yours and Mikey's?" Darlene asked with a gentle smile. As a mother herself, she undoubtedly understood.

Sarah nodded. "And Collin's and Genevieve's

and Taye's," she said. "I think the only one who wasn't worried about their child was Becca Calder." Sarah envied her that. Becca was a single mother like she was, but she'd instilled confidence and kindness in her child while Sarah must have instilled shyness and insecurity in hers.

"Hope is Becca's mini-me, so I'm not surprised she loves school, just like her mother did," JJ said. "I can understand why Taye might be concerned with the boys returning to school for the first time since the accident. But why were Collin and Genevieve anxious?"

"Because of Bailey Ann," Sarah said. "They don't think the current school nurse understood the schedule or the importance of her anti-rejection meds."

JJ gasped. "That is a concern."

"Collin is going to check on her throughout the day," Sarah assured the new grandfather. "He's also hoping that the nurse will retire soon and someone else might apply..." She saw the sudden widening of his dark eyes, and the slight easing of the tension in his body.

"You?" he asked.

And her heart sank a bit. He didn't need her anymore, and he had pretty much just confirmed it. She forced a smile and nodded. "I was second choice to Sue, but she didn't want it."

"Do you?" Darlene asked.

She glanced over at the older woman and noticed the boxes in her vehicle. She was moving out. She was moving on. Sarah needed to do that, too. But she'd never met anyone as kind as the Cassidys and Darlene. Tears pricked her eyes at the thought of leaving them, but she quickly blinked them away and forced a smile. "I think I might—" she turned back to JJ "—if you don't think you need me anymore."

JJ smiled back at her. "At my last follow-up, Dr. Bixby said I'm doing so well that he couldn't believe this isn't my original heart." He touched his knuckles to his chest, where she knew all too well he bore a big scar. "He thinks I'm doing really well."

Meaning that he didn't need her anymore, and he probably hadn't for a while. But being as sweet as he was, JJ hadn't had the heart to dismiss her.

"Then I think I will apply for that job," she said. "It would be good for me to be close to Mikey during the day, too, after having home-schooled him for a while now." She'd done that because other kids had been bullying him just as their parents had been bullying her. If she could get this job, she might be able to make sure that didn't happen again.

If they gave her the chance.

JJ's head bobbed. She didn't think he was eager to get rid of her, but it was clear he'd known before she had that it was time for her to move on. "That would be good for both of you," he said.

"And I hope you know that you can stay here as long as you'd like."

She glanced again at those boxes in Darlene's vehicle. Then she heard the rumble of an engine and turned toward the street, where the sheriff's SUV was pulling up to the curb behind her car. Was he going to block her in again?

That was why she couldn't stay here. Marsh was everywhere lately. And she needed some distance between them for Mikey's sake and for hers. He was entirely too good-looking for her peace of mind.

"I appreciate that," she told JJ. But she had no intention of staying here any longer than necessary; she just had to find another place to live.

Becca Calder was a real estate agent. Hopefully, she also handled rental properties and could help her find another place for her and Mikey.

A place far away from the sheriff.

SHE PROBABLY THINKS *I'm stalking her.* That was Marsh's thought when he saw the paleness of Sarah's face and the widening of her dark eyes as he walked up from where he'd parked his vehicle behind hers. He probably should have driven past when he saw her car parked at the curb, but then that might have looked more suspicious, like he was just checking up on her.

Which was exactly what he was doing, but he didn't want her to know that. So he just spared her a nod, which was all he'd ever given her until that conversation the night before, and he turned toward Darlene. "You're moving already? Do you need some help?"

She shook her head. "Like I told your dad, I'm all loaded up already."

"Do you need help unloading? I can follow you back to your new digs at the veterinarian practice," Marsh offered. Thinking of that reminded him of the night before, and he found himself adding, "You probably shouldn't have told Mikey you're going to live in a barn. Last night, he was trying to convince Sarah to let him go to work with you rather than go to school."

Darlene and JJ glanced from him to Sarah. Sarah's face flushed, her cheeks pink. Was she embarrassed to admit they'd been talking?

The way JJ and Darlene looked at each other next, with slight smiles and bright eyes, had him flushing a little, too. Did they think he and Sarah had done more than talk last night? Or were they just surprised they'd talked at all?

Marsh had certainly not made any effort to talk to her before last night. Maybe that was why he was embarrassed, because he felt bad he hadn't at least thanked her for all she'd done for his father. As Collin had pointed out, he might not have survived until his heart transplant without her medical care.

But instead of thanking her, Marsh had interrogated her. While he felt bad about that, he also needed to find out what really happened with the fire so he could protect his family. Ever since he was a kid, that was all he had ever wanted to do, but he hadn't been able to protect them from bad health and accidents.

Hopefully that was all the fire had been. He couldn't imagine anyone wanting to purposely burn down the place.

Sarah cleared her throat and said, "Yes, it's Mikey's dream to live in a barn."

Darlene chuckled. "It was mine, too. I've always loved animals just like Mikey and apparently Becca and Hope, too."

"And Cash," Marsh added.

"That's how Marsh persuaded Mikey that he needs to go to school," Sarah said. "So that he can become a vet like Cash."

"I'd love to introduce him to Dr. Miner, too," Darlene said, and there was a slight catch to her voice when she mentioned Cash's partner's name. Then her face flushed. "He's funny and great with the animals."

"How is he with you, Darlene?" Marsh asked. He wasn't sure if he should be concerned or not, but after everything his aunt had done for them, he felt awfully protective of her. He had felt that way even before he'd learned how much she'd already lost in her life.

Darlene's face flushed a deeper pink. "Dr.

Miner is very professional or, at least, as professional as he probably knows how to be."

Marsh's dad looked at her with concern then, too. "You know you can continue to live here, right? You can work for the veterinarian practice without living there."

She shrugged and sent a furtive glance at Sarah, as if trying to signal to Marsh and his father that they shouldn't talk about moving in front of her, and maybe they shouldn't. Then she smiled. "It's past time for me to be a part of the real world again," she said. "I think I was hiding from it out at the Cassidy ranch."

"So selling it was a good thing," JJ said. "For both of us. We needed to leave there."

"The fire wasn't a good thing, though," Marsh said, thinking again of how he, his father and Collin had been injured. It could have been so much worse. Sarah could have lost her son, too, if he'd actually been in the house instead of the barn that day. His heart ached at the thought of that little boy losing his life before it had even really started.

As if she was thinking the same thing, the color drained from Sarah's face.

"Of course it wasn't," his father said. "We lost so much. The photographs of your mother and all of you kids. Your school awards and yearbooks. And the ribbons and souvenirs from your mother's days of traveling with the rodeo." He touched his heart then as if it hurt at the thought of what they'd lost.

Or maybe of her, his late wife.

Sarah cleared her throat. "I'm sorry... I just remembered I forgot to pick up a prescription..." And she turned and almost ran to her vehicle, as if desperate to get away from them.

Or to get away from him?

Or talk of the fire?

CHAPTER SEVEN

SARAH HADN'T FORGOTTEN a prescription. She wished, however, that she could forget all about the fire, but Marsh seemed determined to keep bringing it up for some reason. She could guess what that reason was.

He thought someone was responsible for it. And with the way he was suddenly focusing on her and Mikey, she could guess who he thought that was.

Nerves fluttered in her stomach, making her feel ill and anxious. She had to move out of that house. Maybe even out of Willow Creek.

But she would need a job to support herself and Mikey, and if the school would consider hiring her, and Mikey was already making a friend in Hope and maybe the other Havens and Bailey Ann, then it would be better for him if they stayed in Willow Creek. While they could stay here, they couldn't stay in the house anymore with the sheriff and JJ.

JJ didn't need her, and with Darlene leaving, it

would be even more awkward than it had already become since the night before. Since Marsh had started talking to her.

Or interrogating her?

She had to find a place of their own for her and Mikey. And she had to do it as soon as possible. Since she had no need to stop at the pharmacy for something she hadn't forgotten, she headed to Becca Calder's real estate office instead.

With the money she'd saved, she could pay rent and take care of her and Mikey for a while. Then, if she couldn't get another job, they could leave town. Of course, she would rather buy a house, but she knew it wasn't smart to count on anything or anyone.

She had to take care of herself and her son on her own, like she always had. She found a spot near the real estate office, parked and then headed toward the building. At the morning drop-off, Becca had been dressed like she was going to work, so hopefully she was here now and not busy.

Sarah pushed open the door, and an older woman looked up and greeted her with a warm smile. "Hello there, my name's Phyllis Calder," she said.

With her dark hair and eyes, she looked a lot like Becca, so she was probably her mother. Sarah smiled back at her. "Hi, I'm—"

"Sarah!" Becca said as she stepped out of a

doorway that must have led into her private office. "I'm so glad you stopped by. Mom, this Sarah Reynolds, who's been taking such wonderful care of JJ Cassidy."

Sarah smiled and shook her head a bit. "He really doesn't need *anyone* taking care of him anymore. He's doing so well."

"That's good," Mrs. Calder said. "He's always been such a kind man. He never minded how much my daughter hung around his ranch."

"He's a sweetheart," Becca agreed. "And was always like a second father to me."

"And he will be that officially as soon as we can get this wedding together," Phyllis said as she waved her hand over the bridal magazines spread across her desk.

"If we just did the city hall thing, there would be nothing to get together," Becca said.

Her mother gasped as if appalled. "My only daughter getting married—"

"I know, I know," Becca said. "We'll have a wedding, but it's going to be on my ranch, Mom. Low-key and casual."

Sarah had done the city hall thing with Michael, with no family present, because nobody had approved of their marriage. She hadn't realized until it was too late that they'd had good reason not to approve.

"Just don't muck out the stalls in your wedding

gown," Phyllis said, and she winked at Sarah to show she was teasing.

Sarah laughed.

Then Phyllis Calder sighed. "The sad part is that she probably will."

"I'm sure Sarah isn't here to talk about weddings," Becca said. "Unless Sadie is already working on you…"

Sarah shuddered. "Oh, no. I'm not here about weddings," she said. After being so wrong about a man she'd known since they were kids, she didn't trust her judgement enough to date anyone else, let alone marry them, especially while Mikey was so young and impressionable yet.

"Are you here about kittens?" Becca asked.

Sarah looked around, wondering where they were and why they would be at the office. "Kittens?"

Phyllis Calder laughed. "Becca is fostering the mama kitty from the Cassidy ranch, and she has a bunch of babies that Hope would love to keep."

"But those babies will grow up, and my house and my ranch will be overrun with cats," Becca said. "They should be ready to go to their new homes in a couple weeks."

"I need a home first," Sarah said. "JJ—Mr. Cassidy really doesn't need me anymore."

"Do you want to buy?" Becca asked.

Sarah sighed. "I would love to, but I'm not sure where I will find my next job."

"Hopefully at the school," Becca said. "I think Collin and Genevieve would feel a lot better about Bailey Ann being away from them if you were there to make sure she got her medication correctly."

A little jab of fear struck Sarah's heart at the thought of that sweet girl having a medical emergency while at school. She'd seemed so excited to be there that morning, unlike Mikey. "Collin said he was going to check on her," she said, as much to reassure herself as to reassure Becca.

"Yes, but he's also busy at the hospital," Becca said. "And if you don't get the school job, I'm sure you could work there, too."

So she had options in Willow Creek as long as no one found out about her past and started judging her and Mikey as harshly as they had in their old hometown. As interested as the sheriff suddenly seemed in her and Mikey, it was probably only a matter of time before he found out, which meant that she should probably just tell him herself.

Sarah shrugged. "I would hate to buy a house and then have another opportunity come up..." Or so many opportunities taken away that she had to leave.

"I hope that you'll stay in town," Becca said. "My daughter seems to really like Mikey."

Her son having a friend meant so much to Sarah. She smiled. "Hope is so sweet."

Becca smiled, too. "Yes, she is."

Phyllis sniffled even though she smiled, too. "She's a beautiful girl inside and out."

Sarah nodded in wholehearted agreement. Because Hope was so kind, maybe it wouldn't matter to her if people started talking about Mikey's father. Maybe she would still be his friend no matter what.

"Although, in this market, it will probably be easier to find you a place to rent rather than purchase. There's just not much for sale right now," Becca said.

"It's probably easier to find a good man than a good house," Phyllis said with a laugh. "At least, it seems that way with all the bachelor cowboys finally settling down."

"Thanks to Sadie," Becca said with a laugh of her own.

"It was probably the only way her grandsons would have settled down," Phyllis said. "And if I remember right, there's one left single, isn't there? The sheriff?" She gave Sarah a significant look, like she was implying…

Sarah nearly shuddered again. "I'm sure Sadie isn't going to try to match me up with one of her grandsons." Especially if she knew about the mistake Sarah had made all those years ago. "And even if she did, I'm only interested in a house. Not a man." Good, bad or otherwise.

Becca gestured for Sarah to come into her office. "Let's get some specifics and get away from my mother, who's been spending too much time with Sadie."

"I'm sorry," Phyllis said. "I'm so happy that Becca is finally marrying her best friend that I just want everybody else to be that happy."

Becca and Cash were happy. Sarah had seen it herself at Genevieve and Collin's that morning. The lawyer and the cardiologist were also very happy. And Taye Cooper and Baker Haven as well. If she hadn't seen it for herself, she might not have believed it was possible. But even though she'd seen the love between those people, she didn't believe a love like that was possible for her.

"I'll be happy with a nice place for me and my son to live," Sarah said. That was all she wanted. Security for her little boy. She turned then and followed Becca into her office, where she filled out a rental application.

"You have more than enough money for a down payment," Becca said as she read what Sarah had filled in as her bank account balance. "If I can find a suitable house for sale, you really wouldn't be interested? You'll have more freedom in a house that you own. You won't have to abide by the landlord's rules."

"Like the no-pet one some of them have," Phyllis Calder called out through the open door. "Becca really wants to get rid of a kitten."

Despite going into Becca's office, they really

didn't have much more privacy than they'd had in the reception area.

"A kitten or two," Becca called back to her mother. "Unless you want them all, Mom."

"I can't hear you," Phyllis said.

"Sorry about that," Becca said to Sarah. "We get a little carried away around here. Ignore us. Let's focus on what you want."

"Well, I'd just feel safer renting," Sarah said. Like she had an escape plan in case she needed it.

Becca nodded. "I understand. Then the landlord is responsible for maintenance and repairs. Unfortunately, there isn't much more available for rent than there is for sale."

Panic gripped Sarah again. What if she couldn't find somewhere for her and Mikey to live? Of course JJ had said they could stay as long as they wanted. But with Marsh there, too, Sarah couldn't wait to leave.

"I really don't care what it is," she said. "I don't mind sleeping on a couch if there's only one bedroom."

"We'll find you something," Becca promised. "Some landlords have gotten really picky. But I'll do my best to find someplace that allows pets."

Sarah laughed at her persistence. "Like I said, I really don't care what it is as long as it's a safe place for me and my son."

"I think pretty much everywhere in Willow Creek is safe," Becca assured her with a smile.

But Sarah didn't smile back at her. She didn't feel safe staying with JJ anymore because of the sudden interest his son, the sheriff, had taken in her and in Mikey. About the fire…

"Are you okay?" Becca asked, her voice a whisper now as she leaned across her desk.

Sarah nodded.

"I don't know what your situation is…" Becca said, and she glanced at Sarah's bare ring finger. "But I've been a single mom, too. I was fortunate enough to have a lot of support from my parents and my best friend. But even then, it wasn't easy. If you ever need anything, let me know."

Emotion rushed up the back of Sarah's throat. She hadn't had the support that Becca had; her parents hadn't been there for her. And the person she'd thought was her best friend had let her down more than anyone else.

But to have Becca make the offer she had, to know there were people here who genuinely cared about her and her son, moved Sarah to tears.

She furiously blinked them back and forced that smile. "Thank you."

Would she have this care and support though if she told the truth? Since JJ's doctors had so highly recommended her, he and Darlene probably hadn't dug any deeper into her past. But with the sheriff asking his questions, it would probably come out, either through him or through the in-depth background check a school or hospital might run. So she needed to tell everyone the truth.

But first, she had to talk to her son. Or at least get him to talk to her before she or he talked to anyone else, especially the sheriff.

"SHE DIDN'T REALLY forget a prescription, did she?" Marsh asked as he looked at all the pill bottles on the kitchen counter.

His dad looked at the bottles and shook his head. "Nope. They're all here."

So she probably was worried Marsh was stalking her or, at least, that he had some suspicions. And those suspicions were obviously spooking her. Would she react that way if she didn't have something to hide?

"What were the two of you talking about last night?" Darlene asked. Even though her vehicle was all packed, she hadn't left yet for her new place. Maybe because she'd realized it was lunch time. She flipped a sandwich on the griddle, and melted cheese oozed out between the grilled slices while steam and the scents of tomato and basil rose from a pot of soup simmering on the back burner.

Marsh shrugged. "Not much. Just Mikey...the first day of school..." The fire. But for some, reason he didn't want to broach the subject yet with his dad and Darlene. He didn't want to worry them if there was nothing to worry about, if the fire had truly been an accident. And no matter what or who had caused it, he really believed that it hadn't been intentional.

His dad narrowed his dark eyes and studied his face. "That was all?" Being that he was a man who'd kept secrets of his own, maybe he had an uncanny ability to detect when someone else was keeping secrets.

Marsh shrugged again. "I might have asked her about the fire."

JJ tensed. "Why?"

"I'm just trying to figure out everything that happened that day."

JJ snorted. "You and the insurance company. Even though the fire inspector ruled it an accident, they're still dragging their feet on the final payout, but maybe that's because I'm not going to rebuild. I'm just trying to close the sale with Dusty, but the title company won't sign off on the final sale with an open claim on the property."

"So what did happen that day?" Marsh persisted.

"We were all out in the barn when we noticed the smoke coming from the house," Darlene said. "Sarah and I ran inside to see what it was and get the oxygen tanks out. And then once we were outside, we realized we didn't know where Mikey was. She tried going back in, but by then, the fire was going strong, flames everywhere…" Her voice cracked as emotion overwhelmed her.

"And you ran inside to look for him," Marsh said to his dad, his stomach sinking as he thought of how close his father had come to dying. Again.

"We should have realized he was in the barn," Darlene said.

"But you were just out there and hadn't seen him," Marsh pointed out.

"We were by the mare," she said. "Mikey was in the loft with that cat."

Marsh nodded. And maybe it was as innocent as that. But why was the insurance adjuster so convinced that there was more to it?

And why was Sarah so reluctant to talk to him?

"What do you know about Sarah?" he asked.

"That she's an incredibly sweet, compassionate person," JJ said.

Marsh smiled. "I understand why you're a fan." For what she'd done for his dad, he was, too. "But I mean, what do you really know about her?"

"What are you asking about?" JJ asked, and again, he stared at Marsh as if he suspected he had ulterior motives for his questions.

"I mean like where she came from, if she has a record, that kind of thing."

"Record? Like police?" JJ asked, horrified. "That's ridiculous."

Marsh turned back to Darlene, who was flipping the grilled cheese sandwiches onto plates. "You ran a background check on her before you hired her, right?"

Darlene laughed. "I wouldn't know how to run a background check on anyone. No. I take that back. If I needed one run, I would ask you."

"Why didn't you?" he asked.

She shrugged. "The cardiologist highly recommended her. She had great references, too, from other patients and doctors. And when we met her..." She smiled.

"She just clicked," JJ finished for his sister-in-law. "She felt like family, her and Mikey. He's such a sweet kid, and he loved the ranch."

"She never told you about his dad?" Marsh asked.

"What about him?" JJ asked.

"Like why he's not involved," Marsh said. "Like why it's just her and her son and nobody's come to visit them and they've not gone to visit anyone."

"Some people aren't as lucky as we are to have so much family," JJ pointed out.

"Even more than we realized we had," Marsh shot back at him. But he grinned. He'd forgiven Dad long ago for the secrets he'd kept. His health and his happiness were much more important.

JJ grinned back at him. "And some people we meet become family to us," he said. "Sarah and her son seemed like a great fit for us."

"As your in-home nursing care," Marsh said.

JJ shrugged. "Maybe not just that." He winked. "Maybe she would be a great fit for someone else in our family. Like the last bachelor..."

Marsh groaned. "Has everyone caught Sadie's matchmaking bug?"

His dad chuckled. "You can't dispute that your brothers are happy."

No. He couldn't. "But that's them. They have more time for romance than I do. I have an election coming up," he said. "The last thing I have time for is dating."

But dating would be a good way to get to know Sarah and Mikey better. Maybe once he knew what she was hiding and everything they knew about the fire, he wouldn't be so fascinated with her anymore.

SADIE HAD PLANNED on meeting her husband for lunch today, so Taye had packed her a picnic basket before she'd left that morning to take the kids to school. Lem would appreciate that Taye had prepared it and not her. He certainly hadn't married Sadie for her cooking skills; maybe he had married her for Taye's, though.

But when she carried the basket into his office at city hall, he reached for her first instead of it. He closed his arms around her in a warm hug. "Hello, my blushing bride," he greeted her with a grin and love sparkling in his blue eyes.

She was certainly too old to be called that, but the strange thing was that her husband could make her blush like she was a young girl again. He made her feel like a young girl again.

"Hello, my…" Sadie wasn't good at endearments, especially with Lem. She'd called him an old fool longer than he'd actually been old. But he was always so sweet to her even when she hadn't deserved his sweetness. "…my heart," she finished, her voice a little gruff with emotion. Because that was what he was to her: her heart, her soul—her sanity, sometimes.

Tears glistened in his blue eyes until he blinked them away. "You're my heart, too, Sadie March Haven-Lemmon."

Tears rushed to her eyes. She waved them away with a shaky hand and swung the picnic basket onto his desk with her other one. "You are going to need to retire soon," she told him. Because at their ages, they couldn't waste any of the time they had left.

"I agree," he said. "I've already told Ben he needs another running mate for the next election."

"Who's he thinking of asking?" she wondered aloud.

"I think Genevieve."

His new cousin-in-law was a lawyer who'd worked in DC for a while. "She's perfect," Sadie said. "Did your grandson Brett contact her?"

Lem shrugged. "I'm trying to stay out of it," he said. "How about your meetings this morning? Is that what you were told?"

She shook her head. "Surprisingly not. I think

Jessup might actually appreciate my meddling. And Marsh…he had something else on his mind."

"What?"

"The fire."

"What about the fire?" Lem asked, his brow furrowing beneath a lock of white hair that had fallen across his forehead.

She brushed it back, marveling at how soft it was. "He says the insurance company thinks that it may have been deliberately set."

"By whom?" Lem asked, clearly appalled.

She sighed. "I don't know. But Marsh doesn't want his father getting upset when he's finally doing so well." The way Jessup had been looking at Juliet that morning had Sadie hopeful that he was ready to enjoy the second chance at life his new heart had given him.

"We'll make sure that doesn't happen," Lem assured her. "Should we hire a private investigator? Or have Ben talk to the insurance company as Jessup's lawyer?"

Sadie smiled at how quickly he'd come up with solutions to their families' problems. "I am so lucky to have you," she said.

"And I am so lucky to have you," he said.

"I don't think we need to do anything yet," she said. "Marsh is working on it." She had faith in her grandson, or she wouldn't have instigated his becoming the interim sheriff of Willow Creek.

She had to make sure that he secured that position in the next election. "But we'll keep an eye on the situation and step in when we need to," she added. "Just like with your grandsons."

Lem smiled. "Yes. We will do whatever we need to..."

"To ensure the happiness of our family," Sadie finished for him.

"Ohhh," a deep voice murmured. "I just got chills."

She turned to find Ben standing in the open doorway to her husband's office. She smiled at her grandson.

"It's like I stumbled into a secret meeting of a crime family."

Sadie chuckled at his silliness even as she felt a little uneasy. Surely that fire had not been a crime. "We are just a family," she said.

"A family you two will apparently do anything for," he said. "Why does that scare me?"

"You don't need to be scared," Sadie assured him. Ben was happy. Settled. "Before this year is over, you're going to win the next election and marry your perfect mate." Just like she'd married hers.

"Yes, you have all of us partnered off now except for our sheriff," Ben said, and his dark eyes narrowed. "So Marsh is the one who needs to be scared?"

After their meeting that morning, Sadie was

pretty sure her last single grandson was already scared, but it wasn't over her matchmaking. He was worried about their family, too.

CHAPTER EIGHT

SARAH PACED NERVOUSLY on the sidewalk in front of the house. She should have picked up Mikey from school. Letting him ride the bus home on his first day had been foolish. Drivers were too busy focusing on the road and their stops to notice all the bullying that took place on buses, so they wouldn't be able to stop it.

But after lunch, the school had sent out a mass email addressing the traffic congestion from that morning and advising that all children on bus routes would be sent home on buses that afternoon unless there were extenuating circumstances that prevented them from riding.

Sarah's fear and overprotectiveness probably weren't valid extenuating circumstances. Not like a doctor's appointment or a sudden illness. She felt sick with anxiety, though, as she waited outside for the bus to appear.

It was later than the time that had been indicated in the registration packet she'd received after she'd signed him up for school. Due to their proximity to the school, Mikey didn't have a long ride, which was good. But their address was going to change soon.

It had to; Becca had to find them someplace else to live, someplace far away from the sheriff. But not the school.

Was that possible?

Was it even possible for her and Mikey to stay in Willow Creek? If Mikey liked the school, if he was making friends, she would get another job here; she would stay if he was happy. He hadn't been happy in so long.

Before she saw it, she heard the loud engine of the bus and the soft squeak of air brakes as it slowed to turn onto their street. Sunshine glinted off the yellow paint and the glass windows. Then its lights blinked as it stopped right outside the house. The doors opened, releasing a rumble of voices and laughter and, finally, a little boy. He skipped down the steps, but instead of walking up to her, he turned around and waved at all those windows as the bus moved, driving off down their street.

He was waving?

Sarah stared at her son through wide eyes, shocked at his friendliness. Then he turned toward her with a bright smile. "Hey, Mom…"

"How was your first day?" she asked.

"Good. Can we go to Hope's house now?" he asked.

"What?"

"Hope asked me to come over after school and see the mama cat I took care of at the…" His smile slipped away then, and he stopped as if unable to even bring himself to say the word *ranch*.

"That was nice of her," Sarah said.

"She is really nice," Mikey said. "She told me I can pick out a kitten to take home when it's ready to leave its mama. Can I have a kitty, Mom?"

She wanted to say yes, especially because she'd had to deny him the last thing he'd wanted, to go to work with Darlene instead of going to school. But after her conversation with Becca just a short while ago, she wasn't sure that would be possible. "There are a lot of things up in the air right now, Mikey. And I'm not really sure that we'll be able to take care of a cat."

And themselves, if she didn't find a place and a job to support them so her savings didn't run out. But she didn't know how to explain that to her son without potentially frightening him about their future. She wanted him to feel secure and as happy as he'd looked when he'd first gotten off the bus.

There was no hint of a smile on his face now. Instead, his lips had pulled down into a frown, and he wouldn't meet her gaze.

But she could still see the hint of tears in his eyes, and pain gripped her. "Oh, Mikey, I wish I could say yes…" She wanted so badly to get him everything he wanted, but she didn't want to be another parent who made promises they didn't keep. "I'm sorry…"

As she said that, she remembered him saying those words over and over when she'd found him in the loft the day of the fire. Since he was already upset, she forged ahead, desperate to get answers to questions that she knew the sheriff was going to eventually ask. "Mikey, we need to talk about some things."

He shook his head and turned toward the house. But before he could open the front door, she stepped in front of it. Then she drew in a deep breath, determined to have this talk with him.

"I told you school was good," he said, but he was mumbling, his head down.

"Good," she said. "I'm glad. And I hope you can keep going to that school, but we're not going to be able to stay here."

He glanced up at her then, his eyes wide.

"Mr. JJ doesn't need me as a nurse anymore," she said.

"He's all better now."

She nodded. "So we have to find a new place to live, and I'm not sure they'll let us have a cat."

He released a shaky sigh, and tears pooled in his eyes.

"I'm sorry," she said again. "I know you really love animals, like Miss Darlene's horse and the cat from the ranch."

He gasped at the mention of the ranch.

"What happened at the ranch?" she asked softly like he was that wild barn cat he'd befriended. "Why don't you want to go back there? Why have you been so quiet since the fire?"

He shrugged his shoulders then and stared down at the front steps. And a tear dropped from his face onto the concrete.

Her heart ached for upsetting him, and she crouched down to try to meet his gaze. "Is there something you need to tell me about that day?" she asked.

He shook his head.

"Mikey, you can tell me anything," she promised, and she started to close her arms around him.

But he dodged her hug and darted around her. Then he pushed open the front door and ran into the house. And she didn't know if he was upset about the move or the kitten or about the fire.

Instead of getting answers, she just had more questions.

ONCE HE FINALLY got into the sheriff's office, Marsh did what he should have done before she moved into the ranch with his father and Darlene and ran that background check on Sarah Reynolds. It took a while to get enough information to discern which Sarah Reynolds she was of the several women with the same name. But by tracing her through her nursing license and her son's birth certificate, he found the right one.

He was also right to think she was keeping secrets. But he understood why she would. And instead of feeling more suspicion about her, he felt sympathy and respect.

She'd fought hard to support herself and her son. She probably could have chosen a different career, one that wouldn't have required as much education or as long hours. But clearly she hadn't wanted to just help herself and her son; she'd wanted to help other people as well.

Like his dad.

And she had. According to Collin, who would know, JJ might not have made it if not for her care.

Guilt gripped Marsh, bowing his shoulders slightly. He shouldn't have been so intrusive into her personal life. He already knew she was a good nurse, so there had been no reason for him to run that background check on her. Sure, he'd been concerned that she had a secret. And after all the secrets kept in his family, he had no patience for them anymore. But, with the way she'd taken such great care of his dad, he was more curious than concerned about her.

She intrigued him as no one ever had. And now, after finding out what he had, he was even more intrigued and impressed. Sarah Reynolds was a strong woman and an incredibly fierce mother.

And now he owed her his gratitude and an apology for prying into her life. But if he showed up at the house again, she might take off like she had earlier.

Obviously, she didn't want to be around him anymore. Maybe that was the best way he could apologize, by going back to ignoring her like he had been. He just wasn't certain that he could do that anymore, not after talking to her and, last night, holding her.

He wanted to hold her again, especially after what he'd just learned about her. And he wasn't sure that he would be able to stay away from her.

Maybe Darlene shouldn't be the only one moving out; maybe he should as well.

He released a heavy sigh and leaned back in his desk chair. It creaked beneath his weight and another creak echoed as the door to his office opened.

"Marsh, Mrs. Little let me come back," his dad said. "I hope that was all right."

Marsh nodded. "Yes, of course." Then he quickly signed off of his computer, not wanting his father to see what he'd done, that he'd run that background check on Sarah. When he turned his attention from the black screen to his father's face, he noticed the tension in it and in his shoulders. And he jumped up from his chair. "Dad, what's wrong? Are you all right?"

Had something horrible happened?
Again?

JESSUP WANTED TO smile and reassure his son, but
he was too upset to do that now. Marsh had always been the strongest of his children, the one
with the widest shoulders to help carry Jessup's
burdens. He knew that hadn't been fair when
Marsh was young. That he'd probably done that
parentification thing to him that caused so many
issues for people even after they grew up and left
home. That caused so much resentment, too.

But Marsh had never seemed to resent him
then or now. He'd jumped up from his chair so
quickly that it had bumped into the wall behind
him. "Dad? Are you all right?"

Jessup nodded. "Yes, physically, I'm fine."
Emotionally, he was kind of a wreck right now.
He was just so mad and frustrated and confused.

"What's going on? What's happened?" Marsh
asked. "Is everyone all right?"

Jessup released a shaky sigh and reminded
himself while answering his son, "Yes, everyone's fine. After we talked about the fire again,
I called the insurance company to find out why
they haven't settled yet. I hate that they're holding up the sale with Dusty because the property is
still in escrow. I also borrowed money from Darlene, from the sale of her mare, and I want to pay
her back. She shouldn't have to stay in a barn."

Marsh smiled slightly. "You know she prefers that. And I have some money you can have."

"You can't have much," Jessup said, "because you've helped me out so much already. I'll be fine with the sale of the ranch. But the insurance adjuster said they've asked the fire inspector to reopen their investigation. They don't believe the fire was an accident."

And that was what really upset him.

But Marsh had no visible reaction. He didn't even blink, just like he'd reacted when Jessup had revealed that Cash wasn't biologically his son. Marsh had already known that somehow, just as he seemed to already know this.

"You're not surprised," he concluded.

"My old boss gave me a head's up last night," Marsh said. "I knew the insurance company has concerns, but I didn't want to worry you if nothing came of it."

"But why would they have concerns?" Jessup asked. "There was no one in the house at the time the fire started. It had to be an accident."

"You and Darlene and Sarah were out in the barn?"

"Yes, Sarah would still hover when I'd walk around on my own in those days. She didn't want me to overdo it."

"And moments later, you ran into a burning house."

"To find a child," Jessup said, and he shuddered

as he remembered that horror of thinking the little boy could be inside the smoke-and-flame-filled structure.

"Why would you think he was inside?" Marsh asked.

"We just didn't know where he was," Jessup said. "And the smart thing to do was to make sure that the house was empty."

"The smart thing to do was wait for the fire department to show up."

Jessup chuckled. "Something you didn't do, either."

"You were inside," Marsh said. "Collin and I weren't going to risk losing you…"

"Again," Jessup finished for him. They'd nearly lost him so many times. "I'm sorry for putting you through that scare. And I'm sorry for coming here to dump this on you." He wasn't even sure why he had except that *he* was scared now. "If they manage to blame someone for starting this fire, it's going to be me, isn't it?"

Marsh tensed. "What do you mean?"

"Well, I'm the only one who would have something to gain," he said. "Which is stupid, really, because I would gain more if the sale were to go through than whatever they were going to pay me for our destroyed personal property and a run-down building that nobody intends to replace. Dusty only cares about the land and the barn."

"And you've given him free reign of the property already," Marsh said. "He's not going to back out of the sale. And I am sure Darlene isn't worried about getting that money back. And I will give you everything I have—"

"No!" Jessup said, his pride smarting as well as his conscience. "I've already taken too much from you. I feel like I've always relied too much on you."

"I'm glad that you did," Marsh said. "I was happy to help out however I could. And I want to help you now."

And that was why he'd come to Marsh. "Whatever you can do to convince them that it was just an accident..."

Marsh nodded. "I'm working on it..."

"What do you mean?" Jessup asked. "Were you already looking into it?"

"I told you, my old boss already called me," Marsh said. "Don't worry about this, Dad. I'll take care of it. I'll take care of you."

And that guilt Jessup had been feeling intensified even more. "You reminded me earlier today that you're too busy to date because there is an election coming up."

Marsh's head bobbed in a nod so quick that the brim of his hat slipped down a bit over his face. "That's different, though."

"Not really. If you're too busy to date, you're too busy to take on any more of my problems. You need to focus on your future. You need to win to keep this job that I think you love. I don't want you to risk losing it because of me."

His boys had already sacrificed and suffered too much because of him. He didn't want to cost them anything else. He wanted them to be happy, even if that cost him...

CHAPTER NINE

ONCE SARAH HAD followed Mikey into the house, she hadn't immediately looked for him. Instead, she'd checked on JJ, who'd just been wrapping up a phone call in the kitchen. He'd looked pale after putting his cell away. And before she'd even been able to ask him what was wrong, he'd rushed away from her like her son had.

Knowing how Mikey shut down when he was upset, Sarah gave him some space. But she wasn't sure why he was upset. Because she'd asked him about the fire? Or was he just tired after his late night and early morning? Or did he really want that kitten?

She felt like an ogre for not taking him to Hope's ranch to pick out a little furry friend. Or at least check on the cat he'd cared for at the Cassidy ranch.

But if she did that, it would be even harder to deny him a kitten—if he saw all of them. It would be hard for her not to take one as well. Mikey wasn't the only one who wanted a pet. She had always wanted one, too, but with how often she'd moved in with patients while caring for them, she hadn't thought it appropriate to ask them to house an animal as well as her and her son.

That was another reason they needed their own place now; she didn't want to move in with strangers again. Not that JJ and Darlene had ever felt like strangers; they'd felt like family. But Darlene moving out was the signal to Sarah that it was time for her to do the same. Then there was Marsh and his sudden interest in her...

She had to leave, and until she knew if her new landlord would allow pets, she didn't want to get Mikey's hopes up about having one. So there was no sense in going to Hope's home, but maybe they could have the little girl over here to play or meet her at the park.

She wanted Mikey to have friends—human friends. And he seemed to be off to a good start with Hope. She wanted him excited to go back to school tomorrow. So after giving him some time alone, she fixed a snack plate of apple slices, cheese and pretzel sticks and called out to him.

"Mikey?" Her voice seemed to echo in the empty house that had gone almost eerily quiet since JJ had left.

Darlene had already been gone when Sarah had returned from the real estate office. She'd texted that she was coming back later this afternoon to talk to Mikey about his first day of school and to show him where she was going to work and live at the veterinarian practice.

Darlene and Mikey had formed a bond over their shared love of animals. Sarah was so grateful that the older woman was going to continue to nurture that bond even after moving out. He had no family besides Sarah. His maternal grandparents had disowned Sarah years before he was born, and his paternal grandparents hadn't been there for their own son, so they'd had no interest in his child, either.

"Mikey?" she called out again. "I have some snacks for you. Do you want me to put it out on the table on the deck?"

Was that where he'd gone after running inside? Outside again? That was usually what he did. He loved the swing set in the backyard. So did she.

She walked through the dining area of the big kitchen and pushed open the sliding door. But the chairs on the deck were empty, and the swings were completely still with not even a breeze to sway them.

"Mikey?" she called out again as she looked up at the window above the portico. "Mikey?"

The curtains didn't move this time like they had the night before. If he was in his room, he wasn't near the window. So maybe he couldn't hear her. She brought the plate back into the kitchen and set it on the white quartz counter. Then she headed upstairs.

A knock at his door went unanswered. She opened it and looked inside, but the bed was made like it had been that morning. He wasn't in it or on the chair in the corner near that window. He wasn't anywhere in the room.

"Mikey?" She turned and headed back out to check the bathroom. The door was open, the room empty. Her heart was beating harder and faster now. Where had he gone?

She hadn't heard the front door open except for when JJ left. Had Mikey slipped out with him? But JJ would have checked with her before letting her son leave with him. He had to be somewhere in the house yet since the fenced backyard had been empty.

"Mikey?"

The living room was empty as was the formal dining room. She ran back upstairs and checked all of the bedrooms up there again before returning to the main floor and the one room she hadn't checked.

The den.

It was where *he* slept. So she never went in there, not even to clean. On one of the few occasions he'd done more than nod when they'd crossed paths, Marsh had made it clear she didn't need to go in there. He hadn't done it in a rude way. In fact, he'd been very sweet. "You already have too much you're doing around here. You don't need to clean up after me," he'd said. "I take care of myself."

And while it had been sweet that he'd acknowledged how much she did and hadn't wanted her to put herself out on his behalf, it had also been sad somehow. That he was used to taking care of himself because nobody else had.

She could relate to that. She'd had to take care of herself and Mikey for so long on her own. Yet in moments like last night, when she'd thought she was alone on the deck, she could admit how alone she felt and that sometimes she yearned for more.

For someone to be there for her.

She lifted a shaky hand and knocked on that door, not that she thought Marsh was home. Even if she didn't see him, she could always sense when he was in the house, like she became more aware of everything around her, more alive.

It was weird. And another good reason to move out.

Nobody answered the knock, so she reached for the knob now. Was it locked? She wouldn't have even tried it if she hadn't knocked first to no answer. That meant Marsh wasn't in the den, but that didn't mean that Mikey wasn't.

He was clearly not acknowledging her calling out to him. And he had to be able to hear her, right? He had to be somewhere inside the house yet.

"Mikey?" She turned the knob and pushed open the door, but there was no sign of him. There was no sign that anyone was even staying in the room.

The brown leather couch, which was a pull-out bed, was neatly put back together. And the bedding and the clothes must have been stowed away in the built-in, dark wood cabinets that surrounded the TV.

Marsh wasn't wrong that he could take care of himself. Clearly he could because the room was probably the tidiest one in the house. And because it was so tidy, she doubted that a six-year-old boy could find anywhere to hide in here. While the built-ins had several doors and drawers, they would be a tight fit for a body to hide in, so they wouldn't be neatly closed with everything tucked away behind them.

But still, she thought about checking one of them. It felt like an invasion of privacy, though. Of the sheriff's privacy…

"Mikey?" she called out again, hoping against hope that this time he would answer her.

But nothing stirred inside the room except her bangs when she let out a shaky sigh. Then she turned and nearly collided with him. So much for always knowing when he was in the house.

She hadn't felt him or even heard his SUV or the front door, and she let out another squeak of surprise over his sudden appearance. Then she pressed one of her hands against her madly pounding heart.

"Sorry for startling you again," he said. "I know I promised I would stop doing that, but I didn't expect to find you in here."

Heat rushed to her face as he stared at her like he probably would a suspect across the table in an interrogation room. "I..."

"Were you looking for me?" he asked.

She shook her head. "No. I can't find Mikey, and..." She was starting to panic like she had that day of the fire. Not that anything was burning now, but she was worried.

"He's home from school?"

She nodded.

"When did you see him last?"

"About..." She glanced at her watch and gasped again at how much time had passed with her looking for him. "...forty-five minutes ago, getting off the school bus," she said. "And then he ran inside..."

"Rough first day?" he asked with sympathy in his deep voice.

She shook her head. "No. Just the opposite. He was so happy and then..."

"What happened?" Marsh asked.

She sighed. "He wanted to go to Hope's, and I didn't take him."

Marsh tensed a bit. "You don't want him hanging out with Hope?"

"I would love for him to hang out with Hope. I just don't want him picking out a kitten," she said.

"Oh…"

She sighed again, but it was shaky. "I really would love to let him have a pet, but I just can't make him any promises right now."

"I want to ask why," he said. "But let's focus right now on finding your son. Where have you looked?"

"Everywhere," she said. "In the backyard, every single room in the house…"

"Could he have gotten outside the house or yard?"

"The latch on the gate on the fence is too hard for him to open on his own, and the only time I heard a door open was when your dad left." She hadn't heard Marsh come inside, though, so it was possible that Mikey had left as quietly as Marsh had entered. And the thought of her little boy running around Willow Creek on his own had her knees going weak for a moment as she started to shake.

Marsh reached out like he had last night, closing his big hands around her arms as if to steady or comfort her. "I'll text Becca to see if he showed up there."

"He doesn't know where she lives."

But he released her to send that text. Then he shook his head. "He's not there."

"He has to be here," she said but that was because it was what she wanted to believe.

"Well, let's search everywhere again," he said. "Just to make sure that you didn't miss his hiding place."

"And if he isn't here?"

"We'll look *everywhere else* until we find him," he assured her. "We will find him."

She wanted to admonish him for making a promise he had no way of knowing if he could keep. Kids disappeared all the time, never to be seen again. Probably not in Willow Creek. But it happened in other places, so it could happen here. But as much as she didn't want another man making her empty promises, she wanted to believe him even more.

They had to find her son. She couldn't even consider the alternative, not without losing her mind and her heart.

MARSH HAD UNDERSTOOD why his dad had gone back into the burning house all those weeks ago. With there being a possibility that Mikey was inside, JJ had had to do everything he could to save him.

Marsh wasn't sure this was a life-and-death situation like that one could have been, had the boy been inside the house. But he still understood the urgency to find him, to make sure that he was okay. As much for Mikey's sake as for the boy's distraught mother.

Sarah's eyes were bright with the tears she kept blinking away. She was scared.

Marsh had to find her son. He had to keep that promise he'd made to her. Marsh wasn't one to make promises lightly, and he hadn't in this case. But he should have known there were things beyond his control, especially after living so much of his life with no control over his parents' health or their financial struggles.

Another sweep of the house and yard hadn't turned up the boy. Was he hiding?

Or was he just gone?

Marsh called Darlene, who was already on her way back to the house. She promised to help look. "The last time I was out at Ranch Haven, I played hide-and-seek with my grandsons. Kids that age are very good at hiding. You need to look everywhere," she advised.

Marsh had his cell on speaker so that Sarah could hear, too. "I think we did look everywhere," Marsh said. And his next call after Darlene was probably going to be to dispatch to send some deputies out looking for the boy.

"I didn't look for him like we're playing hide-and-seek," she said. "I probably should have checked in all the cabinets and the back of the closets…"

Marsh hadn't either, but he hadn't thought

that was necessary since they'd been calling for the kid. Even if he'd been intentionally hiding, wouldn't he have come out after a while and declared himself the winner?

Marsh and his brothers had never waited that long for whoever was "it" to find them when they were kids. They'd been too impatient to stay hidden, unless they'd fallen asleep. "Ooh…" he murmured as he clicked off his cell phone.

Remembering his childhood antics gave him a clue to where Mikey might be hiding, and he rushed back up to the kid's room. Sarah was right behind him. While she opened the closet door, Marsh dropped down to his knees to look under the bed. After lifting up the ruffle that hung down to the floor, he peered underneath and found a little blond-haired boy instead of dust bunnies. The kid was small enough that he'd managed to curl up in a ball under the box spring. And his chest moved slightly as he slept.

"Mikey," Marsh said, and his voice cracked a bit from the relief rushing through him. Thank God the kid was all right. "Mikey, wake up…"

The boy's blue eyes popped open wide, and he uttered a gasp as the color drained from his face. Marsh had startled him just like he kept startling the boy's mother. But Mikey had scared Sarah a lot more than Marsh had.

"You found him!" she exclaimed, and her voice cracked, too, with tears. And then she was on the floor next to Marsh, peering under the bed. "What are you doing under there?"

Mikey rubbed his eyes and blinked, trying to clear his vision—maybe because he didn't quite believe what he was seeing. Marsh and his mother, shoulder to shoulder, on the floor by his bed. "I must've fell asleep," he said.

"But why under the bed instead of on it?" she asked.

"It's dark under here," he said. "And quiet…" And he had obviously wanted to hide. From his mother? Or from Marsh? He kept shooting nervous glances at him. "Did you call the police on me, Mommy?" he asked.

"No, no," Marsh assured him. "She was scared, though, when she couldn't find you. Like that day at the ranch…"

Tears welled in the child's blue eyes now, and he murmured, "I'm sorry. So sorry…"

"It's okay," Sarah said. "You fell asleep. It was an accident."

And Marsh couldn't help but wonder if they were talking about today or that other day he'd gone missing, the day of the fire. Had that been an accident or a malfunction due to poor maintenance or…arson? He still couldn't believe it was arson; there was no motive for it, nothing to gain and only more to lose than they'd already lost.

"Come on," Sarah said. "Let's get you out of there. You must be hungry." She reached for him, taking his hands in hers to tug him out. But as she did, she flinched and jerked back. "Ouch. What's in your hand?"

"Are you okay?" Marsh asked them both, and then he reached under the bed and helped the little boy shimmy out without hitting his head on the box spring or the wooden side rail.

When the little boy lay between them on the floor, he opened his hand, and something shiny gleamed in the late afternoon sunshine pouring through his window. "I found this," he said. "I didn't take it."

He sounded a little defensive, and that might have been because of who Marsh was, a sheriff, or because of who the boy's father was. If the kid even knew...

"What is it?" Sarah asked.

"An earring," Marsh surmised. The post must have jabbed her when she'd closed her hand over her son's. "Is it yours?" There were hoops dangling from the post that were either purposely intertwined or had gotten tangled up together.

Sarah shook her head. "No. I don't wear jewelry." And she sounded a little defensive, like her son had.

And he had a pretty good idea why.

She stared at him, and her dark eyes widened like her son's had when he'd woken up to Marsh peering in at him. He hadn't done anything to startle her this time, but maybe he'd given something away with how he'd looked at her.

Like what he knew.

"Maybe it belongs to the lady that used to sleep here," Mikey said. "I found her charm bracelet in here, too."

"Livvy?" Marsh asked.

The little boy nodded. "Colton said she was really happy I found her bracelet. Her mom gave it to her."

Livvy's mom had passed away from breast cancer, just like Marsh and his brothers' mom had. "Yes, it's really special to her," Marsh said. "You did a good job finding that."

And he started to wonder what else the little boy might have found...

Like out at the Cassidy ranch.

HE'D DONE IT AGAIN. He'd scared his mom so much that he'd made her cry. Just like *that* day, that horrible, horrible day.

No wonder she wouldn't let him have a kitten. He was kind of surprised that she'd even let Miss Darlene take him back to the barn where she was going to live, especially since she hadn't let him go to Hope's ranch.

He wanted to see the kitties and mama kitty, but mostly, he wanted to see Hope. To see if she was still as nice as she'd been at school.

If she was really his friend.

If she was, maybe he could tell her about that day. That horrible day…

He knew he should tell Mom, especially since she kept asking him about it, but he didn't want to make her cry again. He'd already made her cry too much. And he felt really bad that he'd crawled under his bed to hide because he'd been so upset. And not just because Mom told him no about the kitten, but because he'd lied to her again.

"Hey, you okay?" Miss Darlene asked. "We don't have to do this today, if you're still tired."

He shook his head. "No. I'm not tired." But he was worried that he was something else, something that people always said his dad was: bad.

Miss Darlene pointed out the window. "You didn't even notice that we're here…at the veterinarian office."

He unbuckled the booster seat and scrambled out of the vehicle. But when he saw the barn, he stopped for a minute, remembering another barn. On the Cassidy ranch…

At least it hadn't burned down. At least something he'd tried to do had worked out right.

If only…

"Come on," Miss Darlene said. "Doc CC, who is Marsh's brother Cash, just brought a baby into the world a few days ago. A baby miniature horse." She took his hand and led him toward the open doors of the barn.

He rushed along beside her, eager to see this

mini animal. But the barn seemed dark after the brightness of the sunshine, and he held her hand a little tighter.

"Ah, now I see why I don't have a chance with you," a deep voice remarked. "You've already given your heart to another."

Darlene smiled. "Yes, I have, Dr. Miner. This is my special friend, Mikey Reynolds. He loves animals as much as we do."

A man with gray hair and dark eyes walked up to him. He had some lines around his eyes and mouth like he smiled a lot, like he was smiling now. "That's good news. I'm going to need another partner in this practice. Doc CC isn't pulling his weight anymore now that he's in love."

"Hey, I heard that," another man said.

Mikey recognized him because he'd been coming around the house lately; he was a new kid of Mr. JJ's. Really an old kid that hadn't been around for a long time.

"I'm not denying it," the man continued. "Just letting you know I heard you."

They all laughed. This looked like it would be a real fun place to work. "I want to be a vet, too," Mikey said.

"Ah, gunning for my job," Doc CC said. "Just like my soon-to-be daughter, Hope."

"Hope is your daughter?" he asked, awed. "You know Hope?"

"She's in my class," Mikey said. "She's really nice."

"Yes, she's pretty special," the man agreed.

Mikey felt a pang of regret that his mom didn't bring him over to her house to play and see the kittens. But the barn was full of animals that Darlene was showing him, like that mini-mini horse.

"She might be the cutest thing I've ever seen... next to you..." Darlene said, and her arms, which were holding him on the top rung of the stall fence, tightened around him in a hug.

She was so nice to him. Everyone here in Willow Creek was. But then, they didn't know the truth...

CHAPTER TEN

SARAH WAS STILL shaken over not being able to find her son. And she was even more shaken over what he'd said when they had found him, over how he'd apologized again. She wanted to be reassured that when he'd been so apologetic the day of the fire, it was just because he'd upset her like he had today. But she still couldn't be certain.

And she'd seen the way the sheriff had been watching him, like he had some suspicions of his own.

That was why she'd been so quick to let Darlene take him to her new job and living quarters. She hadn't wanted the sheriff to ask Mikey any more questions, not until she got the answers out of him herself. She needed to figure out how to do that, though, without having him shut down even more than he already had.

"I'm very sorry about that," Sarah said once she joined Marsh on the back deck, where he was already sitting in a chair. She'd had to take some time alone in the bathroom to pull herself together. She'd been so scared when she wasn't able to find Mikey. "You must think I'm a horrible mother, never knowing where her son is."

"I don't think that at all, Sarah," Marsh said. "In fact, I think you're a wonderful mother. You obviously love your son very much."

"With all my heart," she said. "He's the best thing that ever happened to me." He was the good that had come of all the bad.

"So, naturally, you would be concerned about him when you couldn't find him," he said. "You're a great mother."

Tears stung her eyes, and she squeezed them shut, trying to keep the tears from leaking out again. She'd just washed off the last ones she'd shed; she really didn't want to cry again. "I don't know about that," she said. "Half the time, I don't know if I'm doing the right thing or not." But she always tried to do the right thing. "No matter how much I try."

Marsh sighed. "Yeah, doing the right thing isn't as easy as it sounds."

She smiled at him sitting there in his white hat with the gold badge pinned to the pocket of his Western shirt. "Somehow, I don't think you have a problem knowing what the right thing to do is."

She usually didn't either. "I took him out of his last school and started homeschooling because he was being bullied."

"Then that was the right thing to do," he said as if it was that simple.

"But then he got even shyer than he used to be." And after the fire, he'd withdrawn even more.

"Why was he being bullied?" Marsh asked.

This was it: her opening to come clean about the past. Her knees shook a little with nerves, so she dropped onto the chair across from him. "Through no fault of his own," she said. "He was going to the same elementary school that I went to, the same one his father went to in my hometown."

"You met your ex-husband in elementary school?" he asked.

She tensed for a moment. "How do you know he's my ex-husband?"

He pointed across the table at her bare hand. "You don't wear a ring."

"That doesn't mean I ever did," she said, wondering how much of her history Marsh already knew. Had he checked her out?

He was a lawman, so he probably had.

She sighed. "But I did. We married out of high school, but not because we had to. We thought we were in love. We were just so young and naive." Her more so than he'd been. "I even put myself through college." With no help from her parents and, despite what some people had accused her of, with no help from her ex, either.

"Impressive," Marsh said.

She was pretty sure he'd done the same. JJ had obviously been in bad health for a while, and the ranch had been in disrepair, too.

She shrugged. "I thought my ex was working hard, too, but apparently he was stealing," she said. She sneaked a glance across the table at Marsh, but he didn't look surprised. "I swear I didn't know. And when he was arrested, I filed for divorce." Michael had been so upset about that, that she wouldn't stand by him. But how could she have trusted him again? He wasn't the man she'd thought he was. He wasn't even the boy she'd once known. "But people in small towns don't get over things like that."

"And they took it out on a little boy?" he asked, his voice gruff with emotion.

She nodded. "Yes, he was bullied over what his father did."

Marsh grimaced. "That's harsh. I have a feeling he's not the only one who suffered. You must have, too."

She nodded. "It was hard to find jobs. So I started doing the traveling nurse thing, trying to get away from where we grew up, where everything went so wrong." Heat rushed to her face, and she hastily added, "Except Mikey. He truly is the best thing that has happened to me. And I know he wouldn't be here without the bad." She sighed. "So it is what it is." She shrugged. "I just want to protect him from going through all that again. That's why I'm worried about applying for that job at the school. I'm worried about people finding out about Mikey's dad being in jail and calling him the horrible things that they used to." Emotion choked her as she remembered how upset he used to get at school. How he used to get off the bus crying, not like he had today, waving at the windows as it pulled away.

She wanted to stay here, wanted him to be happy and secure, but she wasn't sure how to make that happen. And like the night before, her frustration turned to tears again. Embarrassed, she buried her face in her hands.

MARSH FELT GUILTY all over again for running that check on her. He also felt guilty that she was crying again, like he'd brought on her tears with his questions. And maybe his suspicions.

He had a knack for getting suspects to talk. He'd honed the talent with his brothers, always making them confess to whatever dumb thing they'd done. Even recently, it had worked on his younger brother, making Colton confess to finding the lighter. And, usually, all it required was his silence and a look.

So he held himself responsible for her having to relive that pain and embarrassment she'd suffered. "I'm sorry, Sarah." He rose from his chair, came around the table to kneel in front of her and placed his hands on her shoulders. "I'm sorry."

"What...why?" she asked as she lifted her face from her hands.

"I keep upsetting you, and I'm sorry about that," he said.

"That's why Mikey apologized, too," she said with a tremulous smile. "He hates upsetting me."

"He's a good kid then. And he clearly loves you as much as you love him."

"Thank you," she said.

"It's the truth," he said.

She smiled. "No. Thank you again for helping me find him today and that day of the fire." Her smile slid away as if the mention of the fire upset her.

The lawman in him wanted to push, wanted to ask her more questions about it. But she'd had a long day, and he didn't want to upset her again. "I'm the one who should be thanking you," he said.

Her brow furrowed beneath her wispy bangs. "For what? I don't understand."

"For my dad, for taking such great care of him," Marsh said.

"He doesn't need me anymore," she said. "That's why I'm going to have to apply to that job at the school."

He could have told her that she didn't need to worry about the background check they might run on her. A routine employment one wouldn't turn up what he had. She had nothing on her record. But her ex-husband…

He was going to be in jail for a while. The detectives who'd caught him had investigated his wife as well but concluded that she'd had no idea what he'd been doing, just like she'd said. But the detective's notes were in records that the general public couldn't easily access.

Maybe they should be more easily accessible; then it could have been made clear in her old hometown that she and her son had had no knowledge of or involvement in her husband's crimes. Instead, she'd been denied work, and her son had been bullied.

But she'd found a way to support them and protect her son. "I'm sure you'll get the job," he said. He would make sure that she got a lot of letters of recommendation. "What I'm trying to thank you for is how you kept my dad alive and in good enough health that he made it until his heart transplant. Even though my brother couldn't treat Dad, Collin, the cardiologist, made it clear to me that you saved his life."

She shook her head. "No. I didn't do anything but follow his doctor's instructions for his care."

"You need to take credit for what you did," he insisted. "For how…amazing you are…"

Her eyes, still wet with tears, widened in surprise.

"Shoot, I did it again," he remarked. "I startled

you." He found it sad that a compliment would startle a woman like her, a woman who deserved a lot of compliments for her hard work and her compassion.

She smiled at him. "I just didn't expect you to..."

"Be nice?" he finished when she trailed off.

Her face flushed. "Not that. I know you're a nice man. You're so good to your dad and brothers and Darlene."

"But you didn't expect me to be nice to you," he concluded.

She shrugged. "I just... We haven't talked much..."

"Until last night when I found you out here."

She ran her hands over her face, brushing away her tears. "Doing what I'm doing now. You must think I'm an overly emotional wreck."

"I think you're a single mother with a lot of responsibility," he said.

"I think you know what that's like," she said as she met his gaze again.

He smiled slightly. "I'm not a single mother."

"I think you've always had a lot of responsibility," she clarified. "Because your parents were sick, I think you probably had to grow up really fast and learn to take care of yourself and your brothers."

Now he was the one who was surprised, his mouth dropping open a little with his shock that she saw him so clearly, that even though she hadn't been at the ranch then, she knew how he'd grown up. Fast.

For the first time in a long time, he felt seen as more than the sheriff or a son or a brother. He felt seen as a man. And the sensation was a little overwhelming.

He leaned closer to her then, so tempted to kiss her, with gratitude and with attraction. She was so beautiful and not just on the outside. She was beautiful on the inside, too.

But when he leaned forward, she jerked back. And he found himself saying, "I'm sorry. I'm so sorry—"

But she wasn't looking at him; she was looking over his shoulder, toward the patio door they'd left open. They weren't alone.

He turned around to find his grandmother standing behind him. And she was looking entirely too happy.

SADIE BARELY RESISTED the urge to slap her hands together with glee. Maybe this was going to be even easier than she'd thought because, clearly, she'd walked in on a special moment between her grandson and her son's nurse. If Sarah hadn't noticed her standing there, he might have kissed her.

"Grandma," he said. "This isn't what you think. Sarah and I were just talking." His face was flushed, though, and she wasn't sure if that was with embarrassment over getting caught nearly kissing the young woman, or if it was because he'd nearly kissed the young woman.

Sarah jumped up from her chair, and her face was flushed, too. "Mrs. Haven-Lemmon, I'm going to leave you two alone to talk."

"You don't have to rush off on my account," Sadie said as the young woman drew closer to where she stood in the doorway.

"I really need to get dinner started," Sarah said. "It's already past time that I should have, but Darlene took Mikey to check out the veterinarian practice. They should be back soon, and JJ...he should be here soon, too." She was clearly anxious, either to start dinner or to get away from them. When she stepped even closer, Sadie saw that her face wasn't just flushed, it was tear stained.

Not wanting to embarrass her any further, she moved aside and let the young woman pass her. But when Marsh started forward, as if he intended to follow, Sadie stepped in front of him, blocking him from entering the house. Then she joined him, pulling the door closed behind her. "What's going on between you two?" she asked.

"Like I said, it's not what you think," Marsh insisted.

But at the moment, she wasn't sure what she thought. "Why is she so upset?" Sadie asked. She loved her grandson, but she was very fond of Jessup's nurse as well.

"She had a little scare with Mikey earlier," Marsh said. "She couldn't find him."

"Oh…" She had to press her hand to her heart as pain jabbed it. She knew all too well how frightening and emotional it was not to know where your child was. For too many years, she hadn't known where Jessup was or even if he was still alive. "But she did find him. She said he's with Darlene."

Marsh nodded. "He's fine. He's safe."

There was something about the way he said it, with a fierceness and a protectiveness, that implied he intended to keep it that way. Sadie smiled. Things were going according to plan then—at least, her plan.

"What about you?" she asked. "Are you fine?" He might have been irritated with her for interrupting what might have been a kiss. Or maybe he was irritated with himself for almost kissing Sarah. Or maybe it was something else entirely…

But usually Marsh was the calm one, the unflappable one. Like his uncle that she'd lost much too soon.

"Dad knows what's going on with the ranch," Marsh replied. "He knows that the insurance company asked the fire inspector to reopen the investigation."

She sucked in a breath. "I guess we should have expected that."

Marsh sighed. "I'm surprised they let him know since they obviously consider him a suspect since he's the only one with something to gain."

Sadie had had a feeling she needed to check on Jessup even though she'd seen him that morning. Or maybe it was just that she'd gone so long without seeing him that she wanted to see him every chance she got now.

"I have to figure out what really happened, Grandma, or I'm afraid, like Dad is, that the insurance company is going to try to pin this on him." he said.

And now Sadie was frightened, too.

CHAPTER ELEVEN

SARAH WISHED SHE could rewind the entire day. No. She wished she could rewind even further, to the night before, so when Marsh joined her on the deck, she just got up and walked away from him.

Because now she felt exposed and vulnerable in a way that she hadn't since Michael got arrested. Since his whole secret life was exposed.

She hated secrets because people usually kept them to protect only themselves. But in rare cases, like the Cassidy family, people kept secrets to protect the ones they loved. Once the secrets had come out, JJ and Darlene had filled her in on the history despite her protests that it was none of her business. They'd been telling her for a while now they considered her family.

But she wasn't really. And she felt guilty for overhearing Marsh's conversation with his grand-mother. But they'd started talking the minute she'd stepped inside, and as she'd told them, she was making dinner, in the kitchen right next to where they were talking. While Sadie had closed the slider, a window was open, so she heard everything.

Now she understood why Marsh was asking questions about the fire. The insurance company must suspect arson. And his father?

Not JJ. While he was happy everyone had survived, he was upset he and his sons had lost the pictures and mementoes of his wife, their mother. He had also already accepted an offer on the property, the sale he needed to pay off all his medical debt. He hadn't needed to burn down the house for money.

And even if he had needed money, he wouldn't have committed arson. She knew he hadn't started that fire. But she wasn't sure that someone else hadn't.

"Mommy!" Mikey exclaimed as he ran into the kitchen and threw his arms around her waist. He hugged her tight before pulling back. "You should see the baby horse at Miss Darlene's work. It's so small. I never saw a horse that small before. Even the mama is small and she's old."

Sadie pushed open the slider and stepped into the kitchen with them. And Mikey's eyes went wide. "You know," she said, "my doctor tells me that when we get older, we start shrinking."

In her boots, the older woman had to be over six feet tall, nearly as tall as her grandson who stepped into the kitchen behind her.

Mikey stared up at her, and his mouth dropped

open with shock. "You used to be taller?" he asked.

She nodded. "At least an inch or so."

"Wow…" he murmured in awe.

Sadie smiled at him so warmly, and then she smiled at Sarah the same way. Instead of smiling back, Sarah had the urge to cry again at the guilt that rushed over her. But she really couldn't let herself think that Mikey had had anything to do with that fire, at least not intentionally. That wasn't why he'd apologized so emotionally that day. It wasn't.

But what if she was in denial? What if she was wrong? And now there was an investigation?

She glanced at the sheriff standing behind Sadie Haven. Apparently there were two investigations. The fire inspector's and his.

Was that why he'd been so nice to her? So interested in her and Mikey?

Heat rushed to her face again with the embarrassment over his grandmother catching them nearly kissing. Because if that was what he'd been about to do, Sarah would have welcomed his kiss. He was so good-looking. But more than that, he was a good man.

And no matter what his reasons, he had helped her find her son today. But now she didn't want the boy in the same room with him, at least not until she could talk to Mikey again and actually get answers out of him. "Hey, you better go wash up since you were playing with all those animals," Sarah said to him. And then she managed to smile for Sadie and Marsh. "Will you both be staying for dinner?"

"No," Sadie said. "I'm on my way out. I will catch up with my son another day."

"I'm leaving, too," Marsh said.

And something about his tone chilled her. Leaving to do what? Investigate her some more? Because she had a feeling that he hadn't been too surprised at what she'd told him. But he had been sweet about it.

"Is everybody leaving?" Darlene asked as she walked into the kitchen just as Sadie and Marsh were walking out.

"Yes, dear," Sadie said, but she paused to hug her. "We'll have to catch up another time."

Marsh just nodded at her as he followed his grandmother out.

Darlene tousled Mikey's hair. "Your turn to wash up," she told him.

Sarah smiled at her. Darlene was so kind and so nurturing and not just with Mikey. The little boy rushed off, probably more because Darlene had told him to wash up than because Sarah had. But she didn't care. She was beginning to realize she needed help with him.

"Are you going to stay for dinner?" she asked Darlene.

She nodded. "Yes, I promised Mikey that I would."

"He's going to miss you," Sarah said.

"Even though I moved out, I'll be over visiting a lot. I promise," Darlene said.

"Good, because I'm going to miss you, too," she said. "But I'm not sure how long I will be around." Especially if…

"You're not going to leave Willow Creek!"

"I don't want to," she admitted. "But I do need to find another job."

"JJ would love for you and Mikey to stay here," Darlene said.

Sarah would love that, too, but she already felt like she'd taken advantage of him. Then there was Marsh, and Sarah didn't trust herself around him for a few reasons now. She'd shared too much with him, and she felt vulnerable in a way that she hadn't in so long.

"JJ is very sweet," Sarah said. That was why she also had to make sure he didn't get blamed for something he didn't do. But she couldn't do that unless she learned what really happened. "How was Mikey?" she asked.

Darlene grinned. "So excited to be in a barn again. He loved all the animals."

Sarah felt another pang of guilt that she'd had to deny him a kitten. She really wanted him to have one. "I know how he feels about them," she said. "I just wish I knew how he felt about other things."

"What other things?" Darlene asked. "School? He seemed to enjoy it today. Sounds like he made friends with Hope."

Sarah gestured for Darlene to come closer, and she lowered her voice so that Mikey wouldn't overhear them like she'd overheard Marsh and his grandmother. "I know, and I'm happy that this situation might be better than our old one…"

"But what?" Darlene whispered back. "What's wrong, Sarah?"

"I don't know if I screwed up with the homeschooling and moving him around or if I should have done it sooner because of the bullying in his old school."

Darlene hugged her. "Take it from someone who royally screwed up as a mother: You're doing a great job with him. Stop beating yourself up."

Sarah held on to her for a moment before taking a deep breath and stepping back.

"If you want some of the answers to your questions, you could have him talk to someone," Darlene suggested. "My grandsons have a counselor who's been helping them deal with their grief over losing both their parents so suddenly."

Like everyone else living in Willow Creek, Sarah knew the tragic story of how Dale and Jenny Haven had died in a car crash. Their children had been in the vehicle with them, and fortunately, they'd survived. But the trauma they must have suffered…

She shuddered. "I'm so sorry that happened." Dale was Darlene's son, and she'd never even had the chance to meet his wife.

"Bad things happen," Darlene said fatalistically. "That's why we have to hang on extra hard to the good." She touched Sarah's chin when she said it, like she was saying that Sarah was the good.

Tears stung her eyes. The Cassidys and Havens had been so sweet and supportive of her, totally unlike her own family.

"Mrs. Lancaster works at the school," Darlene continued. "She's the school psychologist, so it would be easy for you to get her to speak with Mikey."

Sarah nodded. "I will keep that in mind. But with how shy he is with strangers, I'm not sure he would open up to her."

"He was talking very easily with Cash and Forrest…" Her face flushed a bit. "Dr. Miner. But then we were talking about animals, and that's his favorite subject."

It was. Sarah knew that about her son. She should know how to get him talking. "I think I'm going to try to get him to open up a bit more with me first, before I reach out to Mrs. Lancaster," she said.

Darlene nodded. "You'll know what's best. I'm the last one who should be giving parental advice. I'm very fortunate my kids are talking to me again."

She'd shared her history with Sarah. The tragic loss of her husband, for which she blamed herself and thought her children blamed her, too. Trying to find JJ to bring him back to his mother only to find him so close to death…

"The only advice I do feel confident giving is not to let things go too long," Darlene said. "Make sure you clear up any misunderstandings or confusion so that you don't have all the regrets that I have."

It was too late. There was already so much that Sarah regretted. And the most recent one was that almost kiss with Marsh. But she wasn't sure if she regretted that it almost happened or that it hadn't.

MARSH COULDN'T BELIEVE he'd almost kissed Sarah Reynolds and, unbeknownst to him, in front of his grandmother. He was losing his mind and maybe his perspective, too.

He needed distance to regroup and some counsel he could trust. While he loved his brothers, he was always the one who'd advised them.

And even though he'd already sought out his grandmother, he didn't entirely trust that she didn't have ulterior motives with all her advice. Obviously, she wanted him to get coupled up like all her other grandsons were.

The only one who'd effectively handled her, by turning her matchmaking on her, was Ben. Ben was more than his cousin; as the mayor of Willow Creek, he was essentially Marsh's boss as well.

He was also a lawyer.

Marsh regretted not going to him first. A quick text exchange let Marsh know where to find him, at his office at city hall. But when he walked into it, he found that Ben was not alone.

His fiancée and he were scrolling through something on a tablet she held.

"I'm sorry," he said. "I don't want to intrude."

Emily smiled at him. "You're not intruding. You're saving Ben from wedding planning stuff."

"Hey, I'm as into this wedding as you are," Ben said. "I just wish it would happen sooner."

They'd decided on a Christmas wedding. Marsh had already received a save the date. He couldn't help but wonder where he would be then. He couldn't continue to live with Dad, not at his age, and if he lost the election for sheriff, would he even stay in Willow Creek?

But no matter what he was doing or where he was living, he wouldn't miss his cousin's wedding. It was strange that, despite how short a time they'd known each other, Marsh felt so connected to all of his cousins, but especially to Ben.

"We agreed that it would be better to do it after the election, and so that we could honeymoon during my Christmas break from school," Emily said. She was an elementary teacher.

"And what if I don't win the election? Will you still want to marry me?" Ben asked.

She shrugged. "I don't know. But with Sadie campaigning for you, I don't think you can lose."

"If you'll still marry me, I'll win either way," Ben said.

She laughed. "I don't think you have to worry about losing."

"That makes one of us," Marsh said.

"Sadie will be campaigning for you, too," Ben said, "and so will I. You've really implemented some great things as sheriff."

"Like the retired deputy in the school," Emily said. "That makes us all feel safer."

"And you're enforcing the parking limits, which our downtown business owners appreciate very much," Ben said. "You won't have any issue winning an election. But I'm happy to help with your campaign."

"Thank you," Marsh said with great appreciation. "I could use your advice." He sighed, ready to get into the real reason for his visit. "And not just with the election."

Ben chuckled. "I figured as much. I overheard Lem and Sadie scheming earlier today. Is she already working the angle with you that she tried with me? That it would help my reelection campaign if I was married?"

"Married?" Marsh shuddered. "What does that have to do with politics?"

"A lot with small-town politics," Ben admitted.

"Is that why you're marrying me?" Emily asked, but she was smiling, so obviously she had no doubts about why he was marrying her.

Ben replied, "I'm marrying you because you asked me to, and I didn't want to turn you down and embarrass you in front of our audience."

She elbowed him, but it must have been lightly because Ben didn't even flinch.

He laughed instead, then he wrapped his arm around her and pulled her against his side. "And I am hopelessly besotted and in love with you," he added.

"That's how he's going to win the election," Emily said. "That ability for sweet-talking."

Marsh didn't have that ability or a wife. If that was what was necessary to win an election, though, he would rather lose. But as he saw how happy his brothers and cousins were, he couldn't help but feel a little like he'd already lost. Especially since he hadn't even gotten to kiss Sarah today.

"Two TRIPS OUT here in one day?"

Jessup glanced up at his mother's question. He was sitting in the formal living room that was rarely used, rocking a sleeping infant, when Sadie walked into the house at Ranch Haven.

Until just a short time ago, Juliet had been sitting in the chair next to his, rocking her grandson. Jessup held the little girl, and his great-niece was already wrapping him around her little finger.

"Yes," he said. "Am I wearing out my welcome?"

She snorted. "You know I would love for you to move in here. But I don't want you putting yourself at risk health wise."

"Health wise, I'm doing great," he said. It was everything else he was worried about, and if not for that, he might consider taking the risk of living farther from town. When once, as a rebellious teenager, he couldn't wait to leave his mother's house, now he couldn't stay away.

But that probably had less to do with the house than the people. He glanced down at his sleeping great-niece, but it wasn't just her who'd wrapped him around her little finger. He was quickly falling for someone else. But he had less to offer her now than he had before. So he probably should have stayed away.

His mom dropped into the rocking chair next to his. "Are you not doing great with other things?" she asked.

He sighed. "I wasn't going to tell you. I didn't want to worry you…" And he hadn't wanted to admit to his situation with Juliet, either. "But then I realized that nothing good came of all the secrets I'd kept, so I don't want to do that anymore. I don't want to hurt anyone I care about."

Sadie reached across and grasped his arm. "I talked to Marsh."

"Yes, this morning—"

"And again this afternoon at your house," she said.

"So you know?"

She nodded.

"Can you believe that they would think I would burn down my own house? My memories, like that?"

"I don't know what they believe," she said. "And neither do you, so you're the one who shouldn't be worrying."

"But I am worried," he admitted.

"Marsh was already on it," she said. "He will take care of it."

"I already rely too much on Marsh."

"Because he's strong," Sadie said, "and can handle it and so can I."

For so long, Jessup hadn't been strong. He'd been so weak physically and maybe emotionally as well. But his new heart had given him a strength he'd never had before. "I can, too," he said. "We'll be okay."

"We'll be better than okay," his mom said as she squeezed his arm again.

He looked up at Juliet as she descended the front stairwell into the foyer. Everything had to work out. He'd already lost one woman he'd loved. And even though the situation was completely different, he didn't want to lose another.

He didn't want to lose his son, either. And he wasn't sure how much of his burden he could keep expecting Marsh to carry for him. He needed to take care of himself now and make sure that Marsh had someone to take care of him for once.

Someone like Sarah.

CHAPTER TWELVE

SARAH WASN'T SURE if she should be relieved or upset that she hadn't seen much of Marsh since that day he'd nearly kissed her on the back deck. Of course, she'd been busy, too, over the past few days, polishing up her resume and getting letters of recommendation so that she could apply for that position at the school. An email had gone out to parents about the current nurse retiring, and then the job had been posted on the school website.

Sarah had filled out what she could online, and she'd been asked to stop by the office to pick up another document that needed to be completed before she would be interviewed. So she was driving Mikey to school.

He'd grumbled about wanting to take the bus instead, but she needed to be at the school before it opened, and she hadn't wanted to ask JJ to wait for the bus with him to make sure that he got safely on it.

So he rode in the back seat of her car, his lips

pursed in a slight pout. Now probably wasn't the time to try to talk to him, but she had tried a few other times during the past week, unfortunately at bedtime. So he'd closed his eyes and shaken his head as if he just wanted to block it out. Or maybe he wanted to block her out. Then he'd pretended to fall asleep.

"Mikey, I really want to talk to you about what happened at the ranch. You've been so quiet since then—"

"I'm always quiet."

That was too true.

"But if something's bothering you about it, I hope you know you can tell me what it is…" She glanced in the rearview mirror to see him shaking his head again, just like he had at bedtime.

So which was it? Nothing was bothering him? Or he didn't think he could talk to her about it? While she was in the office, picking up whatever paper the principal wanted her to complete with her application, maybe she would ask about Mrs. Lancaster. Even if Mikey didn't want to talk to the psychologist, Sarah could, and maybe a professional could help her figure out how to talk to her own child because she couldn't.

"I love you," she said, and she glanced in the rearview mirror again.

A smile replaced his pout, and in the mirror, he met her gaze. "I love you, too, Mommy."

She steered into a parking space in the school

lot and turned fully around in her seat to say, "I'm so proud of you. You're doing so well in school." The teacher had been sending her emails praising how well he was doing with the work, which made Sarah feel better about having home-schooled him the previous year.

"I like it here," he said as he reached for his belt to release himself from his booster seat.

"You're such a good kid," she added because she knew that he needed to hear that most of all.

But his hand stilled for a moment on the clasp he had yet to release, and his smile slipped away. Then he lowered his head and murmured, "But I make you cry..."

"Oh, honey, that's not your fault," she assured him. "There's just a lot going on right now. Mr. JJ is all better, which is a good thing, but it means that I need to find another job. That's why I'm here at the school, applying for the nurse job here. Is that okay with you?"

He shrugged. "If it means we'll stay in Willow Creek..."

"We will," she said.

Because if she didn't get this job, she would apply at the hospital and every doctor's office in Willow Creek. But Becca also had to find them a place to rent, and all she'd found so far were small apartments with no yards. Of course, JJ tried to convince her every day to just stay with him, that the house was too big for him and Marsh alone.

But because of Marsh, she couldn't stay. Since their almost kiss, she'd been spending most of her time in her room working on her resume and… avoiding Marsh.

Mikey stopped avoiding her gaze and met her eyes now, and his were hopeful. "We'll stay?"

She nodded.

And he unclasped his belt and pushed open the back door. When she stepped out to join him, he threw his arms around her and tightly hugged her.

So happy to see him happy, she leaned over and kissed his forehead. "And maybe you'll even be able to get a kitten, if Hope's mom can convince a landlord to let us have a pet." Given how badly Becca wanted to get rid of those kittens, she would probably try very hard to find an accommodating landlord for them. But even though the apartments allowed them, Sarah knew Mikey needed a yard, so hopefully Becca could find them a small house or condo with one.

His blue eyes lit up with that hopefulness she hadn't seen in him in so long. Maybe he was okay. Maybe she was worried about nothing.

Having to wait until the bell rang before he could go inside, he ran out to the playground to wait for the other students to arrive. He waved at her as she walked toward the front door. She had to wait, too, after she buzzed for the door to be opened. "I'm Sarah Reynolds," she said as she walked into the office. "I have to drop off some paperwork and pick up something."

"This is what the school district requires all applicants to have done before they are even interviewed," the receptionist said as she passed a paper across her desk to Sarah.

Sarah glanced down and saw what it was: a request to be fingerprinted.

"You can have it done right at the sheriff's office," the receptionist said, as if being helpful.

But that wasn't helpful to Sarah because it undid everything she'd been working so hard to do all week: avoid seeing Marsh.

MARSH SHOULD HAVE been happy that he hadn't run into Sarah the past few days. But he wasn't happy. Maybe that was because of everything else going on with the fire investigation, with not knowing what the Moss Valley Sheriff's Office might find.

But Sarah was on his mind more than anything else. And it wasn't because he thought she had any more secrets. It was because he hadn't had the chance to kiss her, and now he was stuck wondering what it might have been like.

But she might have pulled back even if Sadie hadn't appeared. She probably wasn't interested in him. As she'd pointed out, she had a lot of responsibilities.

And so did he.

He sighed as he leaned back in his desk chair. He needed to talk to his old boss and the fire inspector and see if they had found any reason to change their original finding of poor maintenance to arson. For some reason, the insurance company, probably to get out of paying the claim, was pushing that agenda. But if there was no evidence of arson, he and his brothers and now his dad could be worried about nothing.

At least, concerning the fire.

Marsh was worried about Sarah, though, and why he couldn't get her out of his mind. Even now, through his open door, he imagined he could hear someone saying her name.

"Sarah Reynolds?"

"Yes."

That was definitely her voice answering Mrs. Little. The sound of it jolted his body out of his chair, and he rushed out to the reception desk. A window of glass and a door separated Mrs. Little from the public reception area. Sarah stood on the other side of that glass.

Her hair was down today and curled around her heart-shaped face. Instead of scrubs, she wore a pastel-patterned dress that wrapped around and tied at her waist. She looked so beautiful that, for a moment, he lost his breath.

"Uh, what's she doing here?" he asked Mrs. Little.

The older woman glanced at him over her

shoulder. "The elementary school requested that she be fingerprinted and have a background check run on her."

He'd already run the in-depth background check that the school needed, but he hadn't fingerprinted her yet, which they would also require, like many other companies, for the safety and security of their other employees and students. "I can take care of that," he offered.

Mrs. Little lowered her eyebrows and stared at him. "It's not a problem for me—"

"I know Sarah," he interrupted. "She works for my dad."

A smile spread across Mrs. Little's lips. "Ah... Sadie strikes again?"

Heat flushed his face, and he shook his head. "It's not like that."

Sadie had had nothing to do with Sarah's hiring. She hadn't even known that her son was still alive at that point. He opened the door. "Sarah, come on back. I can help you."

She hesitated for a moment before walking through the door he held open for her. He could see how stiffly she held herself, as if making sure that she didn't even accidentally touch him. He'd already suspected she'd been avoiding him the past few days, and the way she was acting now pretty much confirmed that suspicion.

"I have a fingerprint scanner in my office," he said. And he escorted her down the hall and through the open door. Not wanting Mrs. Little to eavesdrop, he closed that door.

And Sarah tensed.

"I'm sorry," he said. "I should have already apologized before now. Obviously, I'm making you uncomfortable, and I don't want you to feel that way in your home or here." He reached for the knob to open the door again, but before he could turn it, her hand covered his.

"What are you talking about?" she asked.

"I think you've been avoiding me the past few days, and I am pretty sure that I know why," he said, and his face felt even hotter than it had in the reception area. "And I owe you an apology for making you feel uneasy. I'm really sorry that I almost kissed you—"

"Why?" she asked.

He tensed. "Why am I sorry? Or why did I almost kiss you?"

Her lips curved into a slight smile. "Both."

"I don't want you to feel unsafe in your home—"

"It's not my home."

"It's not mine, either, and I can leave if that would put you more at ease—"

"I'm not uneasy," she said.

He pushed back his hat and arched an eyebrow to show his skepticism.

And she smiled. "Well, maybe a little."

"About the kiss?" he asked. Or his questions...

"What kiss?" she asked. "Nothing happened."

"And it wouldn't have without your consent," he assured her. "And if just the fact that I wanted to kiss you makes you uncomfortable—"

She moved her hand to his face, and she pressed her fingers across his lips. "Stop," she said. "Stop apologizing for something that didn't happen."

But he wished that it had and spent entirely too much time imagining what it would have been like.

"But if it makes you uneasy, we need to clear the air about this," he said.

"Then tell me why you wanted to kiss me," she said. "Was it out of pity?"

He snorted. "Pity? Why would I pity you? For being strong and resilient? For being compassionate and beautiful?"

Her lips parted on a soft gasp.

And he wanted to kiss her again. So badly. But she'd avoided him for days after his last clumsy attempt, so he wasn't about to risk it again.

Then she wrapped her hand around the nape of his neck and pulled his head down while she rose up on tiptoe and pressed her mouth to his. The shock of her silky lips brushing across his caught him off guard, and he tensed instead of doing what he really wanted to do: wrap his arms around her and kiss her back.

She jerked away before he could react, though. Then she pressed her hand over her mouth and murmured, "Oh, no. I'm so sorry…"

"Please, don't be," he said. "I'm not." But he was unsettled. Just that slight brush of her mouth across his had affected him. "I've been wondering what it would be like…"

Her face was so flushed, but her eyes widened in surprise, as if she'd been wondering the same thing.

But knowing just made him want to kiss her again, which was crazy. He had no time for anything but his family and the election. But he wanted to make time for her and found himself asking, "Would you go out with me?"

And her dark eyes widened even more.

"It doesn't have to be a date," he said. He hadn't been on one in so long, he wasn't even sure what a date was anymore. "It can just be a thank-you for all you've done for my dad. And Mikey can come along."

While it wasn't his motivation for asking her, it occurred to him now that maybe outside of the house, in a relaxed environment, they could talk more freely about the day of the fire. Maybe one of them would remember something that could help prove it was the poor maintenance the fire inspector had concluded was the cause. At least, that was the excuse he gave himself for asking and for pressing when he could see her hesitation. "We can take him for ice cream or something. Just a thank-you, Sarah, for taking care of my dad all these months. For keeping him alive."

She shook her head. "That's a big overstate-ment of what I did."

"He's alive," Marsh said. "And I think you're a large part of the reason for that. And that's not my opinion alone. That's Collin's, too, and he's a cardiologist."

"It's not necessary," she said.

"It's just ice cream, Sarah."

She nodded then.

For some reason, he felt like she'd agreed to be his date for prom—he felt like a teenager again. But this wasn't a real date, and he would have to remind himself of that. It was just ice cream. And they would have a six-year-old chaperone along, so there would be no more kisses.

As happy as he was to spend some time with her and her son, he felt a pang of regret that there wouldn't be another kiss. But he should have been relieved. As he kept telling everyone else, he had no time for romance.

DESPITE NOT GETTING to ride the bus that morning, Mikey was having a good day. And his favorite part of the day was recess, when he got to play with not just his class but with kids from other classes and grades, like Miller, Ian and Caleb.

"Do you want to play cops and robbers?" Caleb asked. They'd just been playing rodeo riders on the spring animals on the playground. Caleb wanted to be a rodeo rider like his uncle Dusty Chaps.

Mikey thought Hope was the better rider, though. She didn't even slip in her "saddle," no matter how much her "horse" was bucking.

But Caleb's question made Mikey nervous, and he slid off the spring animal to walk over near the fence. But the others followed him.

"We can play over here," Caleb said. "We just gotta figure out who's the cops and who's the robbers. But you probably know who you wanna be, Mikey."

Did they already know? Had kids from his old school talked? He couldn't even look at them, so he stared down at the asphalt and asked, "Why do you say that?"

"You know why," Ian replied for his best friend. He and Caleb were more than cousins; they were super close.

Mikey felt sick, his stomach bucking up and down like the horses Dusty Chaps used to ride in the rodeo. "No. I don't. Why?" he asked again.

Bailey Ann sighed then and said, like he should have known, "Because the sheriff is going to marry your mom."

"What…" he murmured. He knew they'd talked a few times, but he hadn't even seen the sheriff over the past few days.

"Ew…" Caleb said with a grimace. "No more lovey-dovey talk for me. I'm heading over to the monkey bars. Come over if you wanna play." He headed off across the playground with Ian right behind him, while Hope, Bailey Ann and Miller stuck around the fence with Mikey.

Maybe they knew he felt funny all of sudden, kind of dizzy like they'd been spinning on an old merry-go-round instead of riding the spring animals. "The sheriff and my mom?" he asked. "Getting married?"

"They're the only ones left," Hope said. "All Uncle Marsh's brothers and cousins are either married or getting married like Cash is going to marry my mom soon."

"And Daddy already married Mommy," Bailey Ann added in with a big smile. "Uncle Marsh is gonna be next, and your mommy is the only one close to his age." Her forehead scrunched up. "At least, I think they're close in age."

"Yeah, they are," Miller Haven chimed in. "Marsh is cousins with my dad and uncles."

"So if your mom marries Uncle Marsh, we'll all be cousins," Bailey Ann said.

"The family will be even bigger," Hope said, and she was smiling so big that Mikey found himself smiling back a little. Then her smile fell away, and she suddenly looked really sad.

And Hope never looked sad, so Mikey quickly asked, "Are you okay?"

She nodded. "Yeah, it's just that…for so many years, it was just me and my mom. Uncle Cash

was around, but he was just Uncle Cash then…
and now I have all kinds of family…" She blinked
and smiled again. "And friends…"

Family and friends. That was something Mikey
had never had. Just like Hope, for so many years,
for all his life, it had just been him and his mom.
But then they'd moved into the Cassidy ranch
and had Miss Darlene and Mr. JJ and the others.

"So do you want to play cops and robbers, so
you can be the sheriff?" Miller asked.

He shook his head. "I like to play vet and fix
animals."

"They're no animals here," Bailey Ann said.

"Yes, there are." Hope giggled and pointed to
Caleb and Ian, who were hanging off the monkey bars making monkey noises.

Miller snorted but laughed, too.

And a strange noise slipped out of Mikey: a
giggle of his own. He was happy, and the thought
of being part of a family, of having cousins and
uncles and aunts and a…dad…filled him with
warmth.

But then that warmth reminded him of the fire
and how it had burned down the one place he'd
felt safe and happy.

And he doubted that he would ever have any
family or even any friends if the truth came out…

CHAPTER THIRTEEN

FROM THE OTHER side of the fence separating the playground from the parking lot, Sarah heard her son's giggle. A sound she hadn't heard in so long, and tears rushed to her eyes.

He was doing well. He was going to be okay.

She just wished that she knew if she would be okay. Or had she lost all her common sense along with her self-control? That was the only explanation for why she'd kissed the sheriff. But he'd been saying such sweet, sincere-sounding things to her.

And it had been so long since someone had looked at her the way that he did, like he really believed she was beautiful, and he made her believe it, too. He made her believe a lot of things were possible that just weren't.

Now she wished she hadn't accepted his invitation. But it was just ice cream, and Mikey would be along with them. It wasn't anything romantic.

Because she didn't have time for romance.

She might actually have a job, though. The

principal had already called her for an interview, and she wasn't even sure that he would have received the results of her background check yet.

So, once again, she found herself buzzing to be let in the door, and then she was in the principal's office. He seemed like a very kind, older man. "I didn't expect to hear from you so soon," she admitted.

He smiled. "Well, our current nurse would really like to retire as soon as possible. She and one of our parents are really not comfortable with the level of care one of the students needs."

Bailey Ann. But the principal probably couldn't release the child's name or medical condition.

Then he continued, "And you have so much experience with someone with those needs. You also come highly recommended from several of our Willow Creek citizens."

She'd dropped off some letters of recommendation, but those had been from doctors and patients she'd worked with in other areas. "From Willow Creek?" she asked.

"Yes, one of our teachers and several of our parents recommended you, as well as Sadie Haven herself."

Sarah bit her lip, uncertain if she should protest or not. She wanted this position, but she wanted it on her own merits. "I didn't ask any of them to do that," she said. "I want to get this job because

I deserve it, not because someone asked you to give it to me."

He grinned. "They didn't ask, but there was some mention of how foolish I would be if I didn't hire you immediately."

Sarah's face flushed like it had after she'd kissed Marsh Cassidy.

"But I already determined that myself from the glowing letters of recommendation from every patient you've ever had and from every doctor you've ever worked with. They also share in those letters that you're not just a great nurse, but you're also a great mother."

"To be totally honest with you, I am a good nurse," she said. She knew that; she knew how to treat patients and doctors. "But I'm not always so sure about how great a mother I am," she admitted. "I was actually going to ask to speak to Mrs. Lancaster."

"That's what makes you a great mother," he said. "Knowing when to ask for help."

She'd never had anyone she could ask before, not until she'd started working at the Cassidy ranch. Then Darlene and JJ had stepped in like surrogate grandparents to her son. And the rest of the family was amazing, too.

But instead of thinking of all of them, she thought of only one, of a cowboy lawman in a white hat.

MARSH COULD NOT remember the last time he'd been on a date. Not that this was really a date.

It was just ice cream with his father's nurse and her kid, as a thank-you for how well she'd cared for him. "Pretty lame thank-you," he muttered to himself as he sat in his truck at the curb outside the house.

He should have taken her to dinner and a movie or something even fancier. Maybe to Sheridan to a fancy restaurant and a show or something.

But that would definitely be a date and one that they couldn't include Mikey on. So Sarah probably would have refused to go out with him then. And he wanted to talk to the boy, not just about the ranch, but about school and his interest in animals. He wanted Mikey to feel comfortable around him, but that was probably asking a lot when kids were never comfortable around him.

He really had no business trying to date a woman with a child, especially given how busy he was. Not that it was a date. It didn't sound like Sarah would have accepted if she'd thought it was anything more than ice cream.

But she had kissed him. His lips still tingled from that all-too-brief contact. After she'd done that, he'd asked her out. So it felt like a date to him.

He felt as nervous as if it was one. He wasn't even sure if he should just walk into the house or if he should ring the doorbell for her to answer.

And that was ridiculous, acting like a teenager showing up for the first time at his girlfriend's house, afraid to meet her father. After all, the man in this house was *his* father, who was probably going to be pretty confused if Marsh rang the doorbell.

He was probably going to be pretty confused by Marsh taking out his nurse and her son anyway. And he was probably going to be pretty pleased, too.

JJ would definitely get the wrong idea, just like Sadie had the other night when she'd interrupted their almost kiss. But she hadn't been there to stop Sarah that afternoon.

Why had she kissed him? She'd apologized, but she hadn't explained why she'd actually done it. Though he was really glad that she had.

Staring at the house as he was, he noticed curtains moving in the living room. Was she in there, watching him and wondering if he'd changed his mind?

If he'd chickened out?

He faced danger a lot in his job, and he never hesitated to rush in, to rush to the rescue. But Sarah didn't need anyone to rescue her. She was the one who took care of everyone else, her patients, her son.

Maybe it was Mikey looking out the window. Hopefully, the kid was eager to go out for ice cream with him. Hopefully, Marsh didn't intimidate him too much as he tended to do to other kids. He got out of his truck and headed up to the front door, and he hesitated for a moment, uncertain again if he should knock before letting himself in. But he shook his head at the silliness of that and opened the door to step inside.

Then he glanced through the foyer into the living room. But it wasn't Mikey and Sarah who'd been watching him through the window; his dad stood there.

"What's wrong?" JJ asked. "You were sitting in your truck for a long time."

"I was…" He couldn't admit that he was scared, not to his dad, who always relied on him to be strong. "I was finishing up some emails on my phone." Now he was the one lying.

His dad snorted. "You were staring at the house the whole time."

"I…just have a lot on my mind," he admitted.

"I'm sorry," JJ said. "I know I dump all my troubles on you—"

"Dad," Marsh interrupted him. "I wasn't thinking about you."

Heels clicked against the hardwood floor, and they both turned to where Sarah was walking in from the kitchen. She was still wearing that pretty dress with sandals that she'd been wearing earlier.

She blushed when he met her gaze. "I can change," she said.

"No!" he said a little too forcefully. "I mean…
you look…" Beautiful.

"It's just ice cream," she said.

"Ice cream?" JJ asked, and he was watching
them with a smile on his face and twinkling in
his dark eyes.

"Yeah, I'm taking Sarah and Mikey out for ice
cream," Marsh said.

"To celebrate her new job?" JJ asked.

Marsh turned back to Sarah. "You got it?"

She smiled, and her whole face glowed with
happiness. And something shifted inside Marsh,
making his breath catch for a moment in his ach-
ing chest.

She was so beautiful.

"That's great," he said. "Congratulations."

"So you didn't know before you invited her
and Mikey for ice cream," JJ said, musing aloud.

"I'm taking Sarah out to thank her for taking
care of my ornery old father all these months,"
Marsh remarked. "How she ever managed to put
up with the curmudgeon, I'll never understand."

JJ laughed, and so did Sarah. And that bright,
happy laugh affected Marsh even more than her
smile but not as much as her kiss.

Mikey must have heard the laughter because
he appeared on the stairs. But he didn't run down
them like the Haven children did; they always
sounded like a herd of stampeding mustangs
when they came downstairs. Mikey was quiet,

as he always was, but he was smiling as he stared at his mother. "What's funny, Mom?" he asked.

"Mr. Marsh was teasing his dad," she said.

Mikey glanced at him then quickly looked away again.

"Ready for some ice cream?" Marsh asked.

Mikey hesitated. And Marsh didn't know if it was because he was shy or if he just didn't like him.

"Or he can stay here with me if he'd like," JJ offered.

Marsh shot his meddling father a glance. Was his dad offering that for Mikey's sake or for another reason, like matchmaking? "Are you Sadie?"

"That's why you ate all your vegetables, so you could have a hot fudge sundae," Sarah said, as if to remind her son that he had agreed to this. She also sounded a bit desperate, like she really wanted him to come, or maybe she just didn't want to be alone with Marsh.

"Hot fudge," Marsh said. "My favorite. I'd sure like to eat one with you, Mikey. Will you come along with us?"

Finally, the little boy nodded, making his blond curls bounce on his head, and he offered Marsh a shy smile.

And like when Sarah smiled or laughed, it affected Marsh, making him smile, too. He was glad the little boy was coming along with them and not because he wanted to ask him questions, but because he genuinely wanted to spend time with him.

"Are we going to walk to the ice cream place?" Sarah asked. "Because I should probably change my shoes." Her sandals were heels, though they weren't very high. "And my dress…"

"I can drive," Marsh offered because he really didn't want her to change. She looked so pretty.

"But they're having that movie in the park thing," Sarah said. "So it might be hard to find a place to park. I don't mind changing so we can walk."

"You look nice, Mom," Mikey said. "That dress is prettier than your work clothes."

Marsh liked the dress, too. With her out of her work clothes, he didn't feel quite as weird about taking out his father's nurse. Not that JJ needed her anymore. And now she had a job.

Sarah sighed, but she did it with a smile. "Okay, I'll leave the dress on and just slip into some flats." She had a pair by the door, and once they were on, she reached for the door handle.

But Marsh was also reaching for it, and their hands touched. He felt a jolt pass through him. And he was doubly glad that Mikey was coming along with them. Or he might want another kiss.

And this wasn't supposed to be a real date. It was just a thank-you and now a celebration of her getting the job at the school.

Marsh had also considered asking them more about the ranch, but he felt guilty even thinking about it for some reason. Like he was betraying them both—and maybe even himself—by not focusing only on them. But maybe that was the betrayal, to start something he really didn't have time for.

JESSUP WANTED TO tell himself that he kept going out to the ranch just because he'd missed it all the years he'd been away. But it was more than that.

It was Juliet.

It was also his mother. And all the other people around the ranch. It felt like it was in his blood more now than it had been even when he was a kid. Maybe that was his new heart. The heart he suspected had belonged to his nephew who'd died earlier that year.

Dale had loved the farm so much that he'd been the ranch foreman with his older brother Jake as the overall manager. Jessup didn't want to step into either of those roles. He hadn't managed the Cassidy ranch well enough to keep it going. Of course, his health had limited his capabilities then. Ranch Haven was so big now, so much bigger than when he'd grown up on it, that they had a big staff. They probably didn't need help, but he would love to pitch in where he could.

At the moment, he enjoyed helping with the babies. He enjoyed helping Juliet, seeing her, talking to her.

Like Marsh with Sarah today.

The look on his face when she'd laughed…

It was probably the same look on his when Juliet smiled at him when he walked into the kitchen at Ranch Haven a short while after Marsh, Sarah and Mikey had left for ice cream. She was at the sink, cleaning up the dishes from the dinner they must have just finished. It looked like everyone else was already gone but for his mother and stepfather, who sat yet at the long table.

"Hey there, stranger," Juliet greeted him.

This was his first visit to the ranch today. Had she missed him like he'd missed her?

Sadie, sitting at the end of the long table, snorted. "Stranger? He's been hanging around here every day lately. You might as well move in," she said, and that twinkle was in her dark eyes.

Lem, sitting next to her, chuckled around a bite of cobbler he'd just spooned into his mouth. "You'd love that," he said, and he squeezed her hand.

It had been strange at first not just to see his mother with another man besides his father but that that man was Lem Lemmon, her old archrival. But they made such sense that he couldn't help but smile at them.

"Lem, I really do feel like your son's house is

too big for me now," he admitted. "What with first Collin and now Darlene moving out…"

"And Sarah got the job at the school," Sadie said, "so I'm sure she and Mikey will get a place of their own."

He chuckled. "How do you know that she got the job? Or should I even ask?"

"You already know the answer," Lem said with a conspiratorial wink.

No doubt she knew it because, like most things, she had probably made it happen, just as she'd gotten Colton moved from the Moss Valley Fire Department to the Willow Creek one. And how Marsh somehow wound up taking the interim job of sheriff after the previous one suddenly retired.

It was good that she knew about the issue with the fire at the ranch. He had no doubt that she would probably somehow take care of that as well. After some sleepless nights, he'd figured out that there was nothing he could do. And since he knew he'd done nothing wrong, he wasn't going to worry about it.

That was money and property, and he'd learned a long time ago that people were what mattered most.

The people you loved.

Maybe he should move into the ranch. While Collin had wanted him closer to town in case there were issues with the transplant, Jessup wasn't as concerned about that as he had been.

And Baker, who'd taken his brother Dale's place as ranch foreman, was a paramedic. He'd saved Sadie's life when her heart had stopped, ironically the same day as the fire, probably because she'd heard about it and she'd worried she'd lost him all over again.

But he was here. And he wanted to make up for all the years they'd missed being together.

"You should have brought Mikey and Sarah along with you today so we could celebrate her new job," Sadie said.

Jessup grinned at her. "Actually, she has a date."

Sadie's dark eyes went wide. "A date?" The twinkle was back. "With Marsh?"

"They're both determined not to call it a date," Jessup warned her. "And they insisted on bringing Mikey along with them. Maybe as a buffer, so that they won't fall for each other."

Sadie laughed. "Having kids around doesn't prevent love. In fact, I think our little guys at Ranch Haven have been the reason some have fallen in love. Bailey Ann, too."

Jessup chuckled at that and over the look he'd seen on his son's face, and not just when he'd looked at Sarah but when he'd looked at Mikey, too. "Marsh doesn't stand a chance."

CHAPTER FOURTEEN

SARAH WASN'T SURE what she expected since this wasn't supposed to be a date. Marsh claimed it was just his way of thanking her for what she'd done for his dad. She wanted to say it was the same as she'd done for every other patient she'd had, but JJ wasn't just a patient to her. He was family. And tears stung her eyes at the thought of moving out and away from him.

JJ would be fine without her. She wasn't sure that she would be fine without him, though.

"Hey, this is supposed to be a celebration," Marsh said softly as he leaned closer to her where they sat on one side of the outdoor picnic table at the ice cream parlor. Mikey sat on the other side, shoveling his sundae into his mouth.

Of course Marsh wouldn't have missed the hint of tears in her eyes. She doubted he missed much being as observant as he was. He was probably a very good lawman.

"Are you okay?" he asked.

She nodded. "Yes. I am going to miss your dad, though."

"He's sincere about you staying with him," Marsh said. "He will really miss you and Mikey, too."

She doubted that Marsh would miss them, though. Until this week, he hadn't ever paid them that much attention. And she couldn't help but wonder why he seemed so interested in them now. Or was it the fire that he was interested in?

When she'd overheard Sadie and Marsh talking about it, Marsh had already known about the insurance company asking the fire inspector to reopen their investigation.

"We really need a place of our own," she said. For her and Mikey. She wanted to give him a home and roots, a sense of security that neither of them had had for a long time.

"And can we get a kitty for our new place?" Mikey asked hopefully.

"Miss Becca, Hope's mom, is going to try to find a landlord that will let us have a pet," Sarah said.

So far, Becca hadn't found anything, but she was stepping up the search for houses, warning that the rent and deposits would be higher. Now that Sarah had the job at the school, she was willing to pay more so that Mikey could have a yard and a kitten.

"There's Miss Becca now," Mikey said, his

voice rising with excitement. "And Hope and Doc CC!" He jumped up from the bench and ran across the grass to meet them.

Marsh emitted a low groan and grimaced slightly. Obviously, he wasn't thrilled about running into his brother. Was he ashamed of being caught on an outing with Sarah and her son?

Maybe he should be concerned about that, though. A single mother whose ex-husband was in prison wasn't the best company for a sheriff up for election to be keeping.

"It's okay," she said. "We can tell them we just ran into each other."

"What?"

"You don't have to tell them that you asked us to come here with you," she said. "You can say you just ran into us."

He sighed. "It's not that I don't want to be seen with you and Mikey," he said as if he'd read her mind. "It's just that my family all have match-making on their minds right now, and they think everybody they know needs to couple up."

"And you're the last man standing," she said. She'd heard JJ and his brothers teasing him about that.

He nodded. "That's why they are all so determined to meddle in my life," he said. "But I don't have time for that, not right now."

Because he had so many other things to deal with. Like the fire...

Sarah wondered if that was why he asked them out for ice cream, to interrogate them over sundaes. But he hadn't asked about it yet, and with his brother, Becca and Hope walking up to them now, hopefully he would not have the chance.

Because she didn't want him talking to Mikey about it until she had the chance to find out what really happened.

"WELL, WELL, WELL…" Cash murmured as he walked up to the picnic table where Marsh sat yet with Sarah.

Marsh swallowed the groan burning the back of his throat, not wanting to offend her again like he seemed to have with his first one. Like she thought he was ashamed to be seen with her or something. Maybe that was because of how people had treated her after her ex-husband's arrest, like she was a criminal, too. The only thing she'd done was trust someone she loved.

Maybe that was why Marsh was so opposed to marriage, because he wasn't sure he would be able to trust someone like that. And it wasn't just because of his job but because of all the secrets their dad had kept from them.

Like Cash's paternity. His brother, with his blond hair, most of which was under his brown cowboy hat, and his blue eyes, looked more like little Mikey than he did Marsh or Colton or Collin.

"Well, well, well," Marsh replied back to his brother. "What brings you here?"

"Family outing," Cash said. "Becca and Hope and I are going to watch the movie in the park." He glanced at his watch. "But we have a little time to kill before it starts and decided to get some ice cream. Seems like you had the same idea…"

Family outing. That was probably what people thought of him, Sarah and Mikey all getting ice cream together. That they were a family.

He waited for the panic he usually felt when he thought of having a family of his own. But it didn't come. Maybe because he didn't have time with Mikey and Hope running up to join them. Then the little girl said to her new friend, "See, I told you that Uncle Marsh is going to marry your mom."

Sarah gasped before he could, even though he felt like he'd been sucker punched. "What?" Sarah asked, her face flushed a bright red. "Where did you get that idea?"

"Hope," Becca said, and the slight sharpness of her tone was an admonishment of its own. "You are not scheming with Grandma Sadie again, are you?"

Hope shook her head. "No. Bailey Ann said it first, that Uncle Marsh and Miss Sarah are the only ones left that aren't married or engaged yet. So they have to get together." She clapped her hands. "And here they are." She bumped her shoulder against Mikey's. "Told ya."

Mikey's face flushed, too, as if he was embarrassed.

"We're just here for ice cream to celebrate Miss Sarah getting a job at the school," Marsh said. That was easier to explain to the kids than that it was a thank-you for taking care of his dad.

But he wondered if maybe he should have gone with that when his older brother pushed back his brown cowboy hat and arched an eyebrow at him.

Becca cheered. "That's wonderful, Sarah. Congratulations! I'm sure Collin will be so happy that you'll be there to take as good care of Bailey Ann as you did JJ. That is cause for celebration for all of us. And maybe a kitten for you guys."

"I should wait," Sarah said, "until you find us a place to rent that allows pets."

"Of course," Becca said. "I actually might have a lead on the kind of place you need, with the yard and…" She glanced from Sarah to Marsh. "But I'm not sure yet if it will pan out."

Did Becca also think he was going to wind up with Sarah? Why? Just because they were the last singles their age in their group of acquaintances? He was sure there were plenty of other singles their age in Willow Creek. Probably teachers at the school. Would Sarah meet one of them now that she was working there?

That would be a safer bet for a spouse for her, someone with the same schedule and interests.

Marsh really had nothing to offer her but very limited time. And yet, he didn't want the night to end, even though they had all finished their ice cream.

"Are you going to watch the movie, too?" Hope asked Mikey. "It's supposed to be scary."

"A scary movie for family movie night?" Marsh teased his brother.

"It's *Fantasia*," Becca said. "The 1940 animated version."

"What's that?" Mikey asked.

"Mickey Mouse," Marsh answered him. "We watched that when we were kids. When my dad or mom was sick and it was too late for me and my brothers to go outside, we would watch movies with the volume really low."

Cash's eyes glistened for a minute. "I remember that, too. Watch it with us."

"We didn't bring chairs or anything," Marsh said.

"We have extra blankets, and we can all sit on those," Becca said.

"We really couldn't impose," Sarah said.

And he wasn't sure who she was worried about imposing on, Becca and Cash or him, because she glanced nervously at him.

"Please, Mom," Mikey asked. "Can we watch it?"

"I'm sure the sheriff is busy—"

"No, I'd like to watch it again," he said. Especially with the brother who'd been missing from his life for so long. "Unless you need to get back to the house, Sarah."

"Your dad left just as we did," Sarah said. "So I don't think he'll need me tonight."

"He's probably heading out to the ranch again," Cash said. "I definitely think he has a crush on Melanie's mom."

So even his father was coupling up. Then Marsh would definitely be the last man standing. But he had to stay that way; he had too many responsibilities already to take on a wife and a child, too. He wouldn't be able to give them the time or the attention they deserved.

He didn't mind taking the time for ice cream and now for this movie. Once they made it to the park and found an area big enough for them all to sit together, the movie started to roll across the screen of the amphitheater in the center of the park.

Somehow, Marsh wound up sitting between Mikey and Sarah. At first, the kid leaned away from him, closer to Hope, who sat on his other side. Like his mother leaned away, too, as if unwilling to touch Marsh.

But then as the movie continued to play out with all its animated drama, Mikey edged closer and closer to him. And so did Sarah.

At one point, when the evil monster appeared

on the screen, the little boy gasped and reached for Marsh's hand. And instead of taking just his hand, Marsh slid his arm around the little boy's slightly shaking shoulders. "I've got you," he said. "You're safe."

That was what he used to tell Collin and Colton when they'd get scared during that part. But he hadn't been able to keep them safe. Their mother had died, and they'd nearly lost their dad so many times. This little boy had suffered, too. In a sense, he'd lost his dad, and he'd been bullied because of what his father had done. Marsh didn't want him to suffer anymore.

Sarah leaned closer to him, her hand sliding over his, and she whispered in his ear. "Thank you."

He wasn't sure what she was thanking him for...

He was the one who was supposed to be thanking her. Now he wished he'd done that with something other than ice cream. He wished he'd done it with a kiss.

Or that this was a real date because then he could look forward to maybe kissing her at the end of it. But it wasn't a date. Like he'd had to keep reminding his family.

And himself...

"So," Lem said when he closed the door to their suite. "What part did you play in *all* of this?"

All of this was Jessup agreeing to spend the night instead of driving back so late. It was Sarah getting that job at the school. And it was Sarah and Marsh…

Sadie smiled at her husband, who knew her so well. "Actually, not as much as you might think…"

But she was so pleased with how everything was going, and with a big smile, she took a seat in the rocker recliner in the sitting area of their suite.

Once Lem settled into the easy chair next to hers, Feisty jumped up and claimed her seat on his lap. That little dog loved him.

Everybody did. No one more than Sadie herself.

She couldn't believe that herself sometimes. But it had worked out that way, entirely unlike what she would have chosen for herself, and maybe that was what was happening with Marsh right now.

Despite how determined he was to stay single, he'd taken Sarah and her son out for something. No matter that they both claimed it wasn't a date, it sure looked and sounded like one.

She glanced down at the screen of her cell phone now to look at the picture Cash had texted to her a short while ago. Marsh sat in the middle of a blanket on the grass with Mikey pressed up against him on one side and Sarah on the other, while the light of the screen played across their rapt faces.

But they weren't staring at the screen; they were looking at each other. Marsh at Sarah and Mikey at Marsh and Sarah at them both. And they looked like a family...and as she could tell her stubborn grandson, family was *everything*. It was more important than anything else.

And because they were family, they would figure out the rest of it like the fire...

CHAPTER FIFTEEN

SARAH WAS SCARED and not because of the animated film they'd watched that was probably going to give Mikey a nightmare tonight. She was scared because of how sweet Marsh had been with him, how he'd comforted and protected him.

Even now, he was carrying him home. What had started out like a piggyback ride was now Mikey asleep on Marsh's shoulder, his arms draped around his neck from behind him. Every time she looked at them, she smiled and her heart ached with a yearning sense that this was what she wanted for her son.

A strong male role model. Someone who would love and protect him and never ever hurt him. And while Marsh looked like he fit the part now, she knew it wasn't a role he wanted. He'd said several times now that he was too busy, had too much on his plate, and now another burden weighed on his shoulders: her child.

"I can carry him the rest of the way," she offered. Again. But like the times she'd offered before, he shook his head.

"I've got him," he said. "And look…"

They were nearly in front of the house. The porch light illuminated the front of the traditional brick two-story house. It even had a white picket fence around it. This was what Sarah wanted, too.

"Did JJ leave the light on for us?" she asked. She didn't see his vehicle in the driveway, though.

"I left it on," Marsh said.

Because, as a lawman, he would think of things like that, like security. Which was what she wanted more than anything else for her son. But she was going to have to be the one who provided it for him. She couldn't count on anyone else. Not even Marsh Cassidy.

"I'll get the door," she said as she rushed ahead of him to punch in the code for the digital lock. Because so many people had been staying at the house, it had been smarter to install this than make copies of keys for everyone.

But while the house had once seemed full of people, now it was eerily empty. Collin was gone. Darlene had moved out, too, and tonight, even JJ was gone.

"I wonder where your father is," she murmured with concern.

"He's at Ranch Haven," Marsh replied, his voice a low whisper. "Cash got a text from Sadie while the movie was playing. It got late, and he didn't want to make the drive in the dark."

Or he wanted to give them some time alone like he'd tried to do when he'd offered to watch Mikey for them. Part of her wished that JJ had watched the little boy.

She didn't want her son to believe what Bailey Ann and Hope were saying, that she and Marsh would wind up getting married. That wasn't going to happen.

Marsh had the election to think of and that fire. While she was attracted to him—or she wouldn't have foolishly kissed him like she had—she wasn't the right choice to be the wife of a public official. She'd seen too many campaigns where opponents went after the spouses and family of the candidate more than the candidate themselves, and she was not about to put her son through a nightmare like that.

It would be worse than the one he was probably going to have tonight after that movie. But at least the nightmare he had tonight he would be able to wake up from.

A vicious campaign would ruin more than one night for them. It would ruin the life they were building in Willow Creek. He had friends. And she had a new job.

And hopefully, they would have a place of their own soon. But it wasn't soon enough now, with the prospect of her being alone in the house with

Marsh. Because she was worried that she would be tempted to kiss him again.

"Don't worry," he said. "If you're nervous about him not being here, I'll sleep at the office tonight. I have some things I need to take care of anyways."

Of course he would notice her uneasiness. He didn't miss anything.

But Sarah couldn't help but wonder if she had missed something at the ranch that day of the fire, when Mikey had gone missing…

She reached out for her son. "I can bring him upstairs and tuck him in."

"I've got him," Marsh said, and he started up the stairs with her son dangling off his back.

She followed them up, sticking close in case Mikey slipped. But Marsh had one hand behind his back, holding him securely. Keeping him safe from a fall.

But who was going to protect her from one? Because she could feel herself starting to fall for this man with his white hat and white-knight manner of taking care of everyone around him, like he'd probably been doing since he was a boy himself.

Once in Mikey's room, she helped him remove the little boy from his back and settle him into his bed. She probably should have woken him up, but he was so limp with exhaustion that she didn't have the heart. He hadn't been sleeping well for

weeks now; he needed his rest. She pulled the
blankets up to his chin and stepped back from
the bed and brushed up against Marsh, who stood
behind her.

She tensed with nerves and awareness.

"We should go out in the hall," Marsh whispered close to her ear, and his warm breath made
her shiver a little. "So we don't wake him up."
He stepped back then, the floorboards creaking
beneath his weight as he moved into the hall.

Sarah followed him, but just so she wouldn't
wake up Mikey. She pulled the door partially
closed behind them, so that Mikey wouldn't hear
them.

"You don't have to leave tonight," she said. She
didn't want to make him leave his own home.
"I'm going to stay in Mikey's room, in case he
has a nightmare."

"I'm sorry," Marsh said. "I should have thought
of that. That movie used to scare the twins when
they were even older than Mikey is."

"Not you?"

He shook his head.

He was so tall and broad, so muscular and
strong, not just physically but emotionally, too.
While his brothers had had their bouts of getting upset over their dad's health or with their
dad for the secrets he'd kept, Marsh had always
been calm and patient.

"Does anything scare you?" she wondered aloud.

Marsh stepped a little closer to her and stared intently down into her face. So intently that Sarah couldn't breathe for a moment; she couldn't swallow. She could only stand there. And she kind of wished she'd kept her heels on so she wouldn't feel so small and vulnerable in front of him. And maybe so that she could reach him again like she had in his office, so that she could kiss him.

But then she didn't have to because he leaned down. Their lips met, both of them coming together. The kiss was a jolt that went through her, that made her feel alive in a way she hadn't for a long time.

If ever...

But before she could wrap her arms around him, he pulled back, and his gruff voice finally answered her question. "You, Sarah. You scare me."

MARSH WAS SURPRISED he hadn't fallen down the steps when he walked away from Sarah. But he'd had to leave so that they wouldn't be alone in the house. He didn't want Sarah to feel at all threatened or intimidated.

Like he felt.

He'd once stared down the barrel of a carjacker's gun at what he'd thought was a routine traffic stop and hadn't felt as scared as he had in the hallway with Sarah, kissing her. That was why he'd gotten out of there as fast as he could.

He hadn't run away from the carjacker, though. He'd actually managed to talk the guy into giving him the gun. But he couldn't talk to Sarah, not without wanting to kiss her. And that was why he was definitely safer back at the sheriff's office. So he wouldn't do something stupid, like start falling for her.

Sarah deserved more. She was so compassionate and caring, and she'd already handled so much on her own that she deserved to have someone who could dote on her and Mikey, who could give them all their time and attention and who would never put them through any more pain and loss. Because what if the next carjacker couldn't be talked out of using his weapon?

Marsh had a dangerous job where he couldn't be distracted. And he'd already let his interest in Sarah distract him too much, from the upcoming election and from the fire at the ranch.

When he got back to the office, he found a note dispatch had left on his desk. The Moss Valley sheriff had returned his call requesting the meeting, and his old boss's reply was that they needed to talk as soon as possible. He had some vital information for him but was going out of town for the weekend, for a fishing trip where there was no cell reception. They would have to wait until Monday to meet up.

Marsh would have to wait until Monday to find out what this vital information regarding the fire was. Had the fire inspector changed their initial determination? If so, maybe Colton could find out since he'd worked for the Moss Valley FD before getting transferred to Willow Creek.

Marsh had to find out if the fire was going to be ruled arson. But he couldn't imagine anyone intentionally wanting to burn down that decrepit old farmhouse. It had to have just been an accident.

A horrible accident like how he was messing up with Sarah. He had to be sending her mixed signals, saying one minute that he was too busy to get involved with anyone, but kissing her the next.

And while he hadn't intended this evening to be a date, it definitely felt like one to him. It must have to her, too. So his only excuse for the mixed signals was that he was mixed up himself. While he kept saying that he had no time for anything but family and his job, he wanted to make time for Sarah and Mikey. But Marsh was used to putting other people first, like his mom and his dad and his brothers. And putting Sarah and Mikey first meant understanding they deserved more than he could give them.

MIKEY HADN'T BEEN sleeping like they thought he'd been. Because as tired as he was, he was also really excited. Not the nervous stomach excited like the night before school, but like the night before Christmas excited.

Hope was right. The sheriff taking his mom and him out had to have been a date. Hope insisted that because they'd eaten and watched a movie, it was. And once Mom and the sheriff dated for a little bit, then they would get married.

Or maybe they would just get married like Bailey Ann's parents did. They weren't exactly sure how it worked when people were older like Mom and the sheriff. Hope just knew that once they started kissing, they got married.

And tonight, through the crack in his door, Mikey was pretty sure he saw them kissing. But he hadn't wanted them to hear him, so he'd been super careful to move really quietly and not get too close.

It was weird seeing his mom with anyone. Mikey didn't even remember his dad; he'd been in jail so long. Mom offered to take him there to see him if he wanted, but Mikey didn't want to go to jail.

He really didn't want to wind up there like his dad, like the kids at his old school said he would. And he'd been so careful…had tried so hard to be good…

Like tonight. He'd worked hard to be good so that the sheriff wouldn't get upset with him. He'd tried to be big, but that movie had been so full of loud music and creepy cartoon monsters…

And Mikey had gotten scared.

But not about the sheriff. He wasn't as scary as Mikey had thought he was. He was actually really nice and really strong. And Mikey felt safe with him…until he thought about the fire.

Then he got scared again because he knew it was just a matter of time before the sheriff or someone else figured out that it was all his fault.

CHAPTER SIXTEEN

SARAH HAD SPENT a restless night in Mikey's room, sleeping on an air mattress next to his bed. He hadn't had a nightmare, but she had. In her dream, Marsh was slapping cuffs around her son's thin wrists, and Mikey was crying and screaming for her to stop him.

To save him…

She awoke with tears running down her face and Mikey patting her hair. "Mommy, it's just a dream. It's just a dream. You're okay."

But she wasn't.

Thankfully, Darlene had shown up that Saturday morning with a "job" for Mikey to help her at the vet barn. Otherwise, Sarah might have smothered him with hugs and kisses and freaked him out with her overprotectiveness.

It was just a dream. It wasn't going to happen. Her son had done nothing wrong. But then why had he apologized that day?

She knew she needed to find out. But she also needed to get out of the house where Marsh lived.

With Darlene gone and JJ spending more time out at Ranch Haven than with them, it would look to others like she and Marsh were living together.

And while it wasn't like that, it would probably start rumors that could affect his election. Mostly, it just unsettled Sarah too much for her to stay.

So once Mikey left with Darlene, she left for Becca's office. The realtor had mentioned, while they were at the movie the night before, that she would be at her office in the morning.

And now Sarah was there, too, pushing open the door to the empty reception area. Phyllis Calder wasn't at the desk. "Hello?" Sarah called out.

"I'm in my office," Becca called back.

Sarah walked through the open door to join her. Becca was at her desk, studying the screen of her computer. But she wasn't dressed in her usual business suit work attire. Instead, she wore jeans and a button-down shirt, and her usually perfect dark hair was mussed.

"Don't mind me," Becca said. "I mucked out the stalls this morning before popping in here to go over some documents for a closing next week. I figured what was the point in changing since I'm going to head right back to the barn after this."

Sarah smiled. "Makes sense. And I have a feeling that you like ranching more than real estate."

Becca shook her head. "No. I really enjoy

both," she said. "I've always loved animals, but I also love helping people find their homes."

"You found me one?" Sarah asked hopefully. "You mentioned last night that you had a lead?" Because she really, really needed more space from Marsh, or she had no doubt that she would fall for him, especially when he was so sweet and affectionate with her son.

She couldn't risk Mikey getting attached to him any more than she could risk herself getting attached to him. And she was getting worried that it might be a little too late for her.

"Is that why you're here?" Becca asked. "Or is it about my daughter putting ideas in your son's head? I'm really sorry about her talking about you getting married. I'd blame Sadie for putting the ideas in *her* head, but I think she would have come up with them on her own. Cash and I are pretty sure she's a mini-Sadie."

"She looks like a mini-you," Sarah said.

"Acts like me a lot, too, according to Cash," Becca said. "But I would be the last one to meddle in anyone else's love life. I didn't do so well with my own."

"But you and Cash are engaged," Sarah said. "Isn't that what you want?"

"Yes," she said. "I wanted it for twenty years, and I wish I'd told him earlier how I felt about him. But I was afraid that I would lose him and his friendship if he knew how I felt."

"Sometimes we outgrow those childhood crushes, though," Sarah said. "So maybe it's best not to act on them until we're older and wiser."

"Speaking from experience?"

Sarah nodded. "Unfortunately, yes. But I got Mikey out of it, and he's the best thing that ever happened to me."

"Same with Hope," Becca said. "I chose to have her on my own because I wanted so badly to be a mother. There's nothing better than having a child."

"Or scarier," Sarah said. She was so worried that she was doing the wrong thing with Mikey and that she was going to mess up his life and lose him.

"Love is pretty scary, too," Becca said.

Sarah stepped closer. "Are you sure you and Cash are okay?"

Becca smiled. "Definitely. But it was really scary letting him know how I felt about him, letting him know the mistakes I made over the years in not being totally honest with him. Cash has a thing about secrets. He hates them. But he forgave me for keeping some big ones from him. I was so afraid that he wouldn't."

Secrets.

Sarah had kept her share, but she'd told Marsh about her past. She just hadn't told him about her suspicions about the fire.

"But," Becca continued. "He understood that sometimes we keep secrets to protect the people we love."

Like Mikey.

That was what Sarah needed to do more than anything else. Protect him. "So about that place you might have found for me?" she asked. "How soon will it be ready? Today?"

Becca chuckled. "I can't believe JJ is kicking you and Mikey out."

"No, of course not." JJ was too sweet to do that. "He would like us to stay, but I told him that we needed to find our own place." Like Darlene and Collin had found places of their own already.

"Any reason you're so eager to leave?" Becca asked.

"It just doesn't feel right to take advantage of JJ's hospitality," Sarah said.

Becca narrowed her dark eyes and studied Sarah's face with obvious skepticism. "Is this about not taking advantage of JJ or is this because of JJ's son who still lives in that house?" she asked.

Sarah sucked in a breath, surprised at how astute the real estate agent was.

"You and Marsh seemed to be getting along last night," Becca said.

"I thought you didn't put those ideas in Hope's head," Sarah teased.

Becca held up her hands. "I swear. No meddling. I just haven't seen Marsh out with anyone in a long time."

So had he really asked them out for ice cream

just as a thank-you, or had he intended to interrogate them? She couldn't imagine, with him as busy as he kept saying he was, that he was actually interested in dating her.

"I wondered if he actually took us out to ask about the fire again," Sarah admitted.

"Fire? At the Cassidy ranch?"

Sarah nodded. "Mikey and I were there that day."

"Of course you would have been," Becca said. "That must have been so scary."

"It was," she said. "I couldn't find Mikey for a while. That's how JJ and Marsh and Collin all got hurt, going back inside to look for him." She shuddered as she relived those horrifying moments.

Becca jumped up from her desk and came around to hug her. "I'm so sorry." She pulled back. "About the fire and about Marsh asking those questions." She shuddered now. "He interrogated me once about that fire."

"Why?" Sarah asked in surprise.

Becca sighed. "Apparently, after it was out, Colton found Cash's lighter in the cellar. I guess, because Cash was gone so long, his brothers were worried that he might have started the fire out of spite. Marsh was asking me if I let Cash onto the property, in the house."

"Darlene and JJ filled me in on what happened

with Cash, why he was estranged from his family for so long."

"He was never estranged from me," Becca said. "And so Marsh thought I would know what happened. Cash stayed away more out of guilt than anger. He would never have risked hurting his family any more than he felt he already had."

"But the lighter…"

Becca shrugged. "I don't think it had anything to do with it. But it is a mystery how it got into the house since Cash never set foot inside. He suspects he lost it in the barn when he was checking out Darlene's mare a couple weeks before the fire."

The barn. A lighter. The house.

The words swirled through Sarah's mind like that nightmare she'd had. She shuddered again. "I—I should let you get back to your paperwork," she said, and she took a step back. "And I should go check on Mikey. He's with Darlene at Willow Creek Veterinarian."

"Hope is there with Cash today," Becca said. "They're going to have so much fun."

Sarah didn't want to take Mikey away from that, away from his friend. She would have to wait to ask him the questions she needed to ask him. But she needed answers. Soon. So she knew what and whom she had to protect him from.

The outer door creaked open, and a deep voice called out, "Hello?"

Her heart seemed to jump in her chest, and her pulse quickened. And Sarah wondered who was going to protect *her* from *him*.

MARSH HADN'T EXPECTED to find Sarah in Becca's office. And, clearly, she hadn't expected to see him, either. All the color left her face, making her eyes look even darker and bigger and more unfathomable.

"I—I was just on my way out," she said, almost defensively.

As if she expected him to argue with her. Then she turned sideways and tried to squeeze through the doorway without touching him. But her body brushed against his, and he sucked in a breath at the jolt of attraction that rushed through him.

And he heard her breath catch as well. Maybe that was why she was so eager to get away from him; this attraction between them unsettled her as much as it did him.

"I'll let you know when I hear back from the landlord," Becca called after her.

But the outer door was already closing behind Sarah, who'd gone back to being as skittish around him as that bronco Dusty had already moved out to the Cassidy ranch because nobody trusted it around the kids at Ranch Haven.

Marsh had no doubt that Sarah could be trusted around kids, or he wouldn't have offered his own letter of recommendation for the school to hire her. But he wasn't sure that he could trust her around him.

Or, at least, around his heart. He was determined to protect that, to not trust it to anyone, but he was afraid that if he wasn't careful, she might just steal it from him.

"What'd you do last night?" Becca asked him.

Heat rushed to his face. "What do you mean?"

"Well, she couldn't get out of here fast enough," she said, pointing toward the door that had just closed behind her.

"Maybe that was your fault," Marsh said defensively. "Maybe your daughter got those ideas about marriage from you, not Sadie."

Instead of being offended or defensive, Becca laughed. That was what he'd always liked about her, how straightforward she'd always been. Except, apparently, with Cash. Marsh hadn't realized how she'd really loved her best friend all these years. Maybe he wasn't as observant as he'd prided himself on being.

"Are you here to interrogate me about meddling?" Becca asked. "Or do you have another reason for this visit?"

"I heard you say last night that you were coming in this morning," he said.

"Yeah, that's *how* you knew *I* would be here," she said. "But that doesn't explain *why you're* here."

That was the other thing he really liked about

her; she was smart. He chuckled. "I'm here for you to find me a place," he said. "I think it's about time." He couldn't spend another night in his office.

"Yeah, it is about time," Becca agreed. "Your dad texted me last night, and he's going to tell you this today. He wants me to find someone else to sublease the house he's renting from Bob Lemmon."

Marsh sucked in a breath. "I know he was saying that it was too big, but he also offered to let Sarah and Mikey stay as long as they want."

"Yeah, and that could be the end game for them to stay in the house, unless you want to sublease it. Your dad is going to ask you first."

Of course he would. But Marsh shook his head. "It's too big for me." It was really too big for Sarah and Mikey, too...unless she found someone. She was young and beautiful; surely she would get married again and maybe grow her family. He should have been happy for her and her possible future happiness, but instead, he felt sick.

"I'm not sure Sarah will want it, either. She wants something right away. And you're still living there—"

"I can crash with Colton for a while at his place until you find me something," he said.

Becca nodded. "That could work," she said. "Then when he and Livvy get married, and he moves into her grandpa Lem's old place with her, you can take over Colton's lease."

Marsh nodded. "Yeah, that sounds good." It also sounded really lonely for some reason.

"Unless…" Becca murmured.

"Unless what?"

"Unless you plan on getting married soon yourself."

Marsh laughed, but he had to force it, and it echoed almost hollowly in her office. "You're listening to your daughter's schoolyard tales, too?"

She smiled and shrugged. "I don't know…you and Sarah are the last ones…"

"That's hardly a good reason to get together," he pointed out.

"No, but you were out with her and Mikey last night," she said. "Why?"

And now she looked at him like she was the one interrogating him. He backed out of her office.

"I'll leave you to get back to work," he said. "Sounds like I don't need your help at all." He doubted Colton would turn down his request to crash at his place for a while. As a paramedic and firefighter, the guy spent a lot of time at the firehouse.

Becca laughed and clucked her tongue, making chicken noises at him. "You probably have more help than you even realize yet."

Sadie. She was warning him or mocking him

about Sadie and her matchmaking. But her meddling wasn't going to work this time.

Not with him.

ONCE JESSUP HADN'T been able to get away from the ranch and his mother fast enough, now he couldn't wait to get back.

But not just to her...

Not that he was going to be staying in the house. He was going to use the foreman's cottage that nobody was using anymore because the kids loved everybody being in the big house together. After they'd lost their parents, making Miller, Ian and Little Jake feel secure and happy was the priority. As it should be.

But having not been around any kids except Mikey for a while, Jessup figured he needed to get used to the constant commotion in the big house. And maybe he needed a place to rest away from it. Not every kid was as sweet and quiet as Mikey was. In fact, he was worried about the boy, which was why he'd rather leave the house and have Sarah and Mikey stay in it. Permanently.

He hesitated for a moment as he threw clothes into a duffel bag on his bed. Maybe he shouldn't leave Mikey and Sarah yet, not until he was sure they were all right, that Sarah would be able to afford to rent on her own. Not that Bob Lemmon was charging much, but it was probably a special offer to Jessup since they were stepsiblings now with their parents married.

"Where are you going?" a deep voice asked.

Jessup looked up to find Marsh standing in his open doorway.

"Becca just told me you were giving up the lease, but I didn't realize you were going to take off right away," Marsh said. "Where are you going?"

"I'm sorry," Jessup said. "It was a sudden decision. But I intended to tell you and Sarah and Mikey."

Marsh shrugged. "It's fine. I understand that the house is a lot for you. Where are you going, though?"

"The ranch."

"But Collin said that will be too far away if something happens..."

"If my new heart rejects me?" Jessup assumed that was what his son meant and couldn't bring himself to say, like voicing his worst fear aloud would superstitiously make it come true.

"I'm not worried about this heart rejecting me," he assured his son.

He was worried about someone else's heart rejecting him, though. Juliet had been treated so badly by her ex-husband that she probably wouldn't be willing to risk her heart again on anyone, least of all someone with his health issues and his penchant for secrecy. But he was leaving that all behind him now.

"Baker might have given up his paramedic job, but he knows what he's doing," Jessup said. "He saved Sadie before, and he constantly monitors her. I'll be safe out there."

"But why move out right away? Is this about the insurance money?" Marsh asked.

Jessup shook his head. "I really don't need the insurance money. Dusty insists on buying the ranch, and the insurance company can't indefinitely hold up the sale when it doesn't affect them. Sadie already has Ben and Genevieve working on that."

Marsh grinned. "Of course she does." His grin slipped away. "But you once planned on buying this place when the ranch sale went through. Why did you change your mind? Are you afraid something's going to happen?"

"No." He was hopeful that Juliet might take a chance on him, but he didn't want to share with Marsh that he was probably about to really be the last bachelor in the Haven/Cassidy family. "Are *you* afraid of something happening?"

Marsh shook his head. "No. I'm sure everything is going to be all right. The fire investigator would have to have some evidence to change their determination from accidental to arson."

Jessup had just about forgotten about the fire. But if that wasn't what Marsh was afraid of, was his real fear of something happening between him and Sarah?

CHAPTER SEVENTEEN

AFTER A LONG weekend spent avoiding the house and Marsh, Sarah was happy with how fast her first week on the job at the school was going. Bailey Ann wasn't the only child who needed to take medication throughout the day, nor the only one Sarah needed to monitor to make sure she was doing okay. Despite the health issues and behavioral issues some were being treated for, the kids were well-adjusted and happy. Maybe happier because of the treatments, because the parents made sure their children got the help they needed.

Which made Sarah feel even more like she'd failed her own child. So she'd made an appointment with Mrs. Lancaster for herself first. She settled onto one of the small chairs around the table in the brightly painted office of the school counselor. The other chairs around that table were occupied by stuffed animals and dolls, making Sarah feel like Alice in Wonderland.

But Mrs. Lancaster wasn't the Mad Hatter. She was an older woman with gray hair and warm blue eyes. "Call me Beth, please, Sarah," she said. "I'm so happy you've joined us on staff at the school."

"Thank you," Sarah said. "Everyone's been so kind and welcoming." But she wondered if that would have been the case if they'd known about her ex-husband. For the older woman to help her son, though, she would have to tell her the truth. And she couldn't help but worry that the rumors would start to spread then.

"You're already doing a great job," Mrs. Lancaster said. "You haven't called me once this week to help you with any of the students."

Sarah furrowed her brow with confusion. "What? Help me with what?"

"Some of the children need to be convinced to take their medications," she said.

Sarah shook her head. "No. They were great. And I checked to make sure that they really swallowed them."

Mrs. Lancaster smiled. "Yes, hiding them under their tongues is unfortunately something children do all too often."

"Not just children," Sarah said. "I've had my share of adult patients who have done the same."

"But I have a feeling you're not here to talk about the patients," Beth said.

"No," Sarah said. "I want to talk to you about my son. I'm concerned about him."

Mrs. Lancaster's brow furrowed now. "His

teachers haven't shared any concerns. And from the times I've seen him around the school, he seems to be settling in well."

Sarah's anxiety eased some.

But then Mrs. Lancaster added, "He just seems to be quite shy."

"I have concerns about that," she said. And about the fire. "After homeschooling him, I was worried he would have trouble with socialization."

"He has friends," Mrs. Lancaster assured her. "I've seen him on the playground with all the Haven and Cassidy children and, of course, Hope Calder."

Would they still be his friends if they knew the truth? Marsh knew it, but maybe he hadn't shared it with anyone yet.

"I need to tell you some things that I'm concerned might make that situation change," Sarah said. For both of them.

"Whatever you say to me is confidential," Mrs. Lancaster assured her.

So Sarah shared her history with the older woman, who responded much the same way Marsh had, with little surprise and more sympathy and respect.

"I can understand why you have concerns about him," Mrs. Lancaster said. "But he seems to be doing so well."

"Will you talk to him?" Sarah asked. "Just to

make sure? I've tried to get him to talk, but he just shuts down every time."

The older woman's blue eyes narrowed. "Is there something you specifically want to know?"

Sarah nodded. "Yes, he's been even more quiet and withdrawn than usual since the fire at the Cassidy ranch. I want to know why."

"It must have been quite frightening for him," Mrs. Lancaster said.

"For me, too," Sarah admitted. "And maybe I just freaked him out. Or…"

"Or what?"

"Or maybe he had something to do with it starting," Sarah admitted, dread gripping her. But ever since Becca had told her about the lighter—about the shiny lighter—Sarah's suspicions had increased. "I need to know…" So that she could help him, so that she could protect him.

MARSH'S MEETING WITH his old boss gave him more questions than answers. So he sought out his new roommate for his opinion. But, as he'd predicted, Colton was rarely at the apartment they shared now, so he had to track him down at the Willow Creek Fire Department.

"Man, you keep turning up everywhere I am," Colton joked when Marsh walked through the open garage door of the bay housing a shiny red firetruck. "I might have to report to the sheriff that I have a stalker."

Marsh snorted. "Yeah, right. I have to track you down here because I haven't seen you since I moved in. You sure you live there?"

"Sometimes it feels like I live here," Colton said. "Or at the hospital. But that's not such a bad thing." Because he got to see his fiancée at the hospital. Livvy was an ER doctor.

"Well, I'm glad you have so many places to live," Marsh remarked.

"I'll give you my place as soon as I can get my beautiful fiancée to the altar," Colton promised. "But I don't want to rush her."

Livvy's former fiancé had been a controlling narcissist, so it was good that Colton was giving her time. His brother was a smart man and a good judge of character.

"So why'd you track me down?" Colton asked.

"I had a meeting with my old boss today," Marsh said. "Did you get a chance to talk to yours?" After the message from Sheriff Poelman, Marsh had called Colton to get him to reach out to his former fire captain.

Colton groaned. "Stupid insurance adjuster is putting pressure on the inspector to take another look at the scene. But there were no signs of arson."

"But you found that lighter," Marsh reminded him.

"I wish I'd never seen it," Colton admitted.

"Even if you hadn't, this wouldn't be over,"

Marsh said. "That insurance adjuster is also push-ing the Moss Valley sheriff to pull some people in for questioning."

Colton groaned again. "Dad?"

Marsh nodded.

"Is he going to do it?"

"No," Marsh said. "Sheriff Poelman isn't going to question anyone about poor maintenance, or he'd have to question himself." Marsh chuckled like his boss had during their meeting when he'd shared this *vital* information with him. "But if the inspector changes his report..."

"He'll have to bring Dad in," Colton finished for him, and now he released a shaky sigh.

"And Darlene and Sarah and Mikey." That scared him even more than his dad being ques-tioned. Mikey was such a shy little boy, and Sarah was so worried about them being judged because of what her ex-husband had done. After the bully-ing they'd both suffered, she had reason to worry.

Someone might judge them because of that.

Marsh would hope that his former boss wouldn't, but from working with the man, he knew that the Moss Valley sheriff was a pretty cynical guy from all his years in law enforcement. And he did tend to rush to judgement. Like if one member of a person's family had committed a crime, he tended to believe the whole family were criminals. That had been the case with some of the families in Moss Valley.

But it wasn't the case everywhere else. He hadn't been able to convince his boss of that, though. That was another reason he was so happy to have his job in Willow Creek. He was definitely in a more positive environment, and he was the one who set the example for his deputies to be open-minded and fair.

Unlike his former boss.

Marsh didn't want him talking to Sarah and Mikey; he didn't want him judging them unfairly. And he most certainly didn't want them getting hurt.

They'd already been through too much. They deserved happiness and security. Hopefully, even though he couldn't offer that to her, Sarah would find that in Willow Creek. But the thought of her finding that with anyone else made him feel sick again.

"You okay?" Colton asked with concern. "You look a little pale."

Marsh nodded. "Yeah, I'm fine."

"I'm not sure I am," Colton admitted. "It doesn't sound like the issues with the fire are going away."

"Not until we prove what really happened," Marsh said.

What had really happened?

"IT WAS MY FAULT," Mikey said. And when he said it, he felt like a balloon that someone had popped

with a very sharp pin. Like all the air left him…
and he was just deflated and a little relieved, too.

Mrs. Lancaster didn't look shocked and upset
with him like he was sure his mom would. She
smiled at him across the table, where he sat like
he was having a tea party with all her stuffed
animals.

He wasn't sure why an old lady like her had
all the toys. He didn't even like toys that much,
especially not stuffed ones. He'd rather have real
animals than pretend ones.

Like that cat in the barn and Miss Darlene's
horse. And he'd just been trying to keep them
safe.

"I don't understand," Mrs. Lancaster said.

And he felt even more deflated.

She'd promised that they could talk about anything and everything and that she would help him
understand stuff. And he'd been so hopeful that
things would get better. That it would all make
sense.

But if she didn't know what happened, how
could he explain it?

He wasn't even sure now what had happened.
It had all gone so wrong so fast.

"What do you think is your fault, Mikey?"
Mrs. Lancaster asked.

"The fire," he said. "It's all my fault…"

CHAPTER EIGHTEEN

MIKEY'S FIRST MEETING with Mrs. Lancaster was right after school on Friday. Sarah didn't get the chance to ask either of them what they'd talked about, though. When she opened her mouth to ask the school psychologist, Mrs. Lancaster just shook her head then explained, "Mikey will fill you in when he's ready."

Then Sarah noticed how despondent Mikey looked. His head was down, and he wouldn't even meet her gaze when she called his name. Her stomach knotted with dread. But Mrs. Lancaster reached out for her hand and gave it a reassuring squeeze.

"It's not going to be as bad as either of you think," Mrs. Lancaster said. "We're all going to be fine."

And the pressure on Sarah's chest eased a bit, but Mikey didn't look up and his shoulders stayed bowed, as if he was carrying some weight on them. She wanted to cheer him up, and thanks to the voicemail Becca had left her a short while ago, Sarah might be able to do that.

So once they were safely buckled up in her car, she started up the engine and headed away from the school. But she didn't turn toward town.

"We know for sure that we can have a pet at our new place," Sarah told her son.

Ironically, she didn't know for sure yet where that new place was. Becca's voicemail had reminded her that she didn't care as long as it was safe and Mikey could have an animal. But she promised her more details soon and invited them to come out to the ranch to pick out a kitten before they were all gone.

She glanced into the rearview mirror, but Mikey was still looking down, physically and figuratively. "Did you hear me?" she asked.

"What?"

"We can go pick out a kitty," she said.

He didn't say anything.

"Don't you want one?"

"I… I do…but…"

"But what?" she asked.

"If I can't take care of it, will you?"

"You took good care of the mother cat at the Cassidy ranch, and you helped Miss Darlene take care of her mare," she reminded him. "You'll be great with your new furry friend."

"Mommy?" he asked, and there was some urgency in his voice. And this time, he met her gaze in the mirror. "Will you?"

"Of course I'll help you," she said. "I will always do everything in my power to help you, my sweet boy."

He let out a breath, like he'd been holding it, and he finally seemed to relax a bit.

She really needed to talk to Mrs. Lancaster, or maybe she just needed to talk to her son. Really talk to him…about everything. But Mrs. Lancaster's words seemed to caution Sarah against pushing him; she'd said he would tell her when he was ready.

Becca's ranch wasn't far, so Sarah didn't have the chance to get anything else out of him. She was glad that she hadn't tried and upset him when she saw all the other vehicles in Becca's driveway. A truck with Willow Creek Veterinarian Services was parked behind Becca's SUV. A truck with a light on the roof was parked behind that; it must belong to the firefighter, Colton. And then the sheriff's SUV was parked behind that.

The only Cassidy brother not present was the doctor, unless he'd ridden with one of the others. Sarah thought about backing up and turning around to drive off, but before she could shift her car, Hope was running up to the vehicle. So she turned off the ignition and unlocked the door that Hope then opened for Mikey.

"You came!" she exclaimed. And she sounded so happy to see him even though they'd been together just a short while ago at school. "I want to show you my horse and Mama's horse, and

Cash has one here now, too, that's really big. Do you like big horses like Caleb likes that rodeo bronco?"

Sarah held her breath while she waited to see if Mikey would answer his friend or if he'd entirely shut down.

"I like Miss Darlene's mare," he said. "But I don't like it when animals are too wild."

Hope chuckled. "My horse is really calm. But some of the kitties are pretty wild. They were climbing all the curtains, so Mom made me move them out to the barn. The mama kitty is out here, too." She took Mikey's hand in hers. "It's right this way."

"He probably could have figured that out for himself," Becca said as she appeared beside Sarah.

Sarah knew Becca wasn't the only one who'd walked up to her. She could feel Marsh there, too, because her skin was tingling slightly. And there were several shadows on the asphalt around her vehicle. But she was focused on watching the kids run off toward the barn which wasn't that far from the house.

"She's like you were with me when we were that age," Cash said. "Bossy."

"You better run out there with them," she told him.

And he laughed. "Some things never change." He started after the kids, but she ran up and kissed him. And he laughed again. "And some things do."

"You're whipped," Colton, the firefighter, teased his brother as he followed Cash toward the barn.

"And you're not?" Cash teased.

Colton shrugged. "I'm not saying it's a bad thing. I'm not like Marsh, who swears he's staying single. But you know, I do remember saying that myself...until I met Livvy. Love changes everything." He turned back and stared at someone standing behind Sarah.

"Some things never change," Marsh said pointedly. "Becca's still bossy, and you're still a pain in the butt, little brother."

"If I'm so bossy, what are you doing standing here instead of going out to the barn with your brothers?" Becca asked.

"I didn't hear you tell me to," he said.

She jerked her thumb in the direction of the other Cassidys. "Sarah and I have some business to discuss. And as you pointed out, you didn't need me to find you a place to live."

"You found another place to live?" Sarah asked him. That explained why she hadn't seen him the past several days. She figured he'd just been avoiding her like she'd been avoiding him after that last kiss.

He nodded. "I'm crashing with Colton for now, until he gets married. Then I'll take over his place."

"His bachelor pad," Becca said. "I wonder why that sounds so sad…"

Marsh grunted. "Because Sadie has brainwashed you."

"Nothing wrong with thinking like Sadie Haven. She knows how to fix things and get things done," Becca defended her future grandmother-in-law. "She's brilliant. I wish I thought like her."

Sarah did, too. Maybe she could figure out how to protect her child while still doing the right thing.

MARSH WAS UNCOMFORTABLE leaving Sarah alone with Becca, especially since it seemed that his future sister-in-law was all in with Sadie's matchmaking. Even her daughter was all about marrying off whoever was still single.

But he had to agree with Becca, that bachelor pad now sounded sad to him, too. Lonely.

And Colton's place, with him gone so much for work or with Livvy, was a lonely place without Sarah fussing over everyone and Mikey quietly playing. He missed them more than he missed his dad.

"There he is again," Colton said when Marsh joined him and Cash in the barn. "He's following me all around. It's kind of sad…"

There was that word again. The word that had never been applied to Marsh before. Now,

Mikey—that little boy looked sad way too often.
Except now.

Now, he and Hope played with the kittens that
Becca had confined to one of the empty horse
stalls. Or, at least, she'd tried to. They climbed
up the door, their nails sinking into the wood.
Hope giggled while Mikey kept catching them
before they went over the top. His little forehead
was furrowed with concern as he worked hard
to make sure that none of them fell.

"You followed me," Marsh reminded him. He
was the one who'd wanted to talk to Cash again
about the lighter.

"But I beat you here," Colton pointed out.

"And I should give you a ticket for speeding,"
Marsh said. "You were driving too fast."

"Occupational hazard," Colton said.

"You are a hazard."

Cash laughed. "I would say I missed this,
but…" His grin slipped away. "No, I did miss
this. A lot. I really missed you guys."

Marsh's throat filled with emotion that he had
to swallow down. He'd missed his older brother
so much. The twins had always had each other;
he'd felt the closest to Cash. Then he was gone
not long after Mom passed away.

That pain and loss echoed inside his heart,
making it feel hollow and empty. But it was safer
to leave it like that than to give it to someone,

someone that he might lose like he lost Mom and Cash and nearly Dad so many times.

He couldn't lose him over this, over a fire that wasn't his fault. That was probably nobody's fault, or so Marsh hoped. He guided Cash a bit farther from the kids, out of their earshot. They were busy with the kittens in the stall, so they were safe.

Marsh wanted to keep them that way. "Hey, I wanted to ask you about your lighter again."

Cash groaned. "I've already told you I don't know how many times. I wasn't in the house. I don't know how it even got there."

"You still carried that thing with you always?" Marsh asked with some surprise.

Cash nodded. "Yeah, since I'm not a smoker, I just carried it as a good luck charm."

"Like a rabbit's foot," Marsh remarked.

"Yeah, but my luck actually got better after I lost it," Cash said. "That was when I finally realized I was in love with Becca, probably my whole life."

"Maybe you should lose the thing, too," Colton suggested. "Maybe your luck would improve, too, Marsh."

Marsh wished he could lose it. But it was potentially evidence, so he couldn't, in all good conscience, destroy it. But he worried that if he didn't, he might wind up destroying someone's life.

SADIE'S CELL BUZZED, vibrating on the table next to her easy chair. She glanced down at the screen, but she didn't recognize the number.

"Are you going to answer that?" Lem asked. His eyes were closed; she'd thought he'd fallen asleep watching his news. But he hadn't, and he hadn't lost his hearing yet, either.

She wasn't sure who it was, but with everything going on in their lives, she didn't dare miss a call. So she swiped to accept. "Hello?"

"Mrs. Haven-Lemmon?"

"Yes, who is this?" she asked. Hopefully not a telemarketer.

"Uh, this is Sarah. Sarah Reynolds, Mrs. Lemmon."

"Sarah!" Sadie exclaimed. "I'm so happy that you called." She hadn't even realized the young woman had her number, but she was so glad that she did.

"I… I…"

Alarm shot through Sadie, and she sat up straighter in her chair. Attuned to her, Lem sat up straighter, too, and Feisty growled in protest of his movement. "Is everything all right, Sarah?" she asked with concern.

"I'm… I'm not sure."

"Jessup is here," Sadie said. "He seems fine…"

"He is," Sarah said.

"So this isn't about Jessup?"

"No," Sarah said. "I just need some advice. And you…"

"I would be happy to help you," Sadie said.

Lem chuckled. "Try thrilled," he muttered.

"Please, come out tomorrow. It's Saturday, so we can make a day of it." A party even.

"I just need a few minutes of your time—"

"I have all the time in the world for you," Sadie said. "And bring Mikey with you. Two o'clock."

"Thank you," Sarah said.

"You're welcome," Sadie said. "I can't wait to see you both." And she disconnected the call before the young woman could reconsider her request or realize what Sadie was up to.

But Lem knew. "Is she walking right into your web, my dear?"

"Did you just call me a spider?"

"It's better than the things you used to call me," he reminded her.

Better and probably pretty apt. She was weaving a web, but she wasn't trying to catch Sarah Reynolds for herself. She was trying to catch her for Marsh.

But she suspected Sarah's call for advice had nothing to do with Sadie's grandson. And suddenly, her blood chilled and she shivered.

Lem immediately lifted her blanket from her lap to her shoulders, making sure she was warm. Taking care of her.

He really was the sweetest man. But he couldn't

chase away this chill. Because Sadie had a bad feeling that things weren't going to go exactly as she planned.

All she could hope for now was that nobody got hurt.

CHAPTER NINETEEN

SINCE SHE'D MOVED to Willow Creek, Sarah had heard all about Sadie Haven. The woman was a legend for how she protected her ranch and her family and had even used a crowbar to rescue a dog from a hot car. She didn't hesitate to step up and do the right thing.

That was what Sarah needed to do. So she'd taken Becca's advice and reached out to ask Sadie for advice. She was less fearful about talking to this fearsome woman than she was her own son.

The trip to Becca's ranch had cheered up Mikey yesterday, so Sarah hadn't wanted to bring him back down by asking him about his meeting with the school counselor the previous day. She waited until the drive out to the ranch the next day before she asked, "What did you and Mrs. Lancaster talk about?"

Silence was his reply. She glanced into the rearview mirror to see if he'd fallen asleep. Even though his eyes were closed, his small body was stiff with tension. He wasn't sleeping. He was avoiding her question, like he'd avoided having a real conversation with her since the fire.

"I can pull over, and we can talk," she offered.

"No," he said.

She swallowed a groan. How had Mrs. Lancaster gotten him to spill to her during one session and Sarah couldn't get him to talk to her at all?

"Mikey, you've been shutting me out since the fire," she said. "And I want to know why."

"I don't want you to hate me," he said.

And now she knew what she'd suspected for a while. "Mikey, I could never, ever hate you," she vowed. "I love you so very much."

His breath caught. "No matter what I do?"

"No matter what," she assured him. And it was true. He was her son. Her heart. And she knew him so well that she knew whatever he'd done hadn't been on purpose; it hadn't been malicious, which was why she'd made this appointment with Sadie. She wanted the older woman's advice on how to protect her family like Sadie always protected hers. "I love you so much, Mikey."

"But it was all my fault," he said, sobs making his voice shake like Sarah was starting to shake.

She tightened her hands around the steering wheel. "What, Mikey? What are you talking about?"

"The fire…" he murmured, his voice choked now as the sobs overwhelmed him.

"You apologized to me that day," she said. "But

that was because I didn't know where you were, because you were in the barn…" She glanced in the rearview again, and he was shaking his head.

"I think I started it…"

"What?"

"I didn't mean to," he said.

"I know that. Of course you wouldn't mean to…"

"I found this old lighter in the barn," he said.

The lighter that Cash had lost. Of course Mikey would have found it; he always found things, especially if they were shiny, like Livvy Lemmon's charm bracelet and that earring.

The little boy continued, "And I didn't want it to start a fire out there with all the hay and Miss Darlene's horse and the cat…"

He would have been concerned about the animals because they had been his only friends out there.

"So you brought it into the house?" she asked when he trailed off. And she saw him nod in the mirror. "What happened then?"

"I dunno…" he murmured. "There was smoke."

"Where did the smoke come from?" she asked.

"I dunno," he said. "I didn't see the fire, but it must have started it. I touched it, Mommy. I touched the lighter. I must've started it."

She wanted to pull over now; she ached to hold him, to comfort him. "Whatever happened, it was an accident, Mikey," she said. "It wasn't your fault."

"The sheriff won't arrest me?"

"No," she said. She would make certain Marsh understood it was an accident.

"Will he still marry you?" he asked. "Will he be my daddy even though I'm bad like my daddy?"

"Mikey!" she exclaimed, and now she had to defend her son from himself. "You are a good kid. You are such a good kid. You are so sweet to every living thing in this world. You would never intentionally hurt anyone." But people had intentionally and unintentionally hurt him.

"I didn't mean it," he said. "I didn't mean for anybody to get hurt."

"I know," she assured him. She pulled her gaze from his in the rearview mirror and peered through the windshield at the sign for Ranch Haven. She was here. For a second, she considered turning around and going home, packing up and leaving. But that wouldn't protect her son.

And that was what she had to do above anything else. She had to make sure that Mikey was safe and that he could forgive himself for what happened. She was pretty sure that everyone else would.

As she neared the house at the end of the long drive, she noticed all the other vehicles parked near it. There were even more here than there had been at Becca's house. All the Havens and the Cassidys were here.

So she was probably about to find out if she was right, if they would really forgive them for the fire.

SADIE HAD SUMMONED everyone to the ranch this Saturday. Marsh figured it was to celebrate her oldest son finally moving back home. But then he saw Sarah's vehicle pull into the driveway, and he wondered.

Sure, Sarah was close to his dad; she could have been invited to the celebration. But was that his grandmother's real reason for inviting her, or was she playing matchmaker again? And why didn't that possibility annoy him like it once would have?

He still didn't have time for her games. He probably had less time than he had before. With the fire investigation, with the election coming up. But he was thinking less about them lately than he was about Sarah and her son.

So he stepped out of his SUV and headed toward her vehicle. She jumped out of the driver's door and jerked open the back door, and then Mikey was in her arms. The way they were clinging to each other had alarm shooting through Marsh.

He ran toward them. "What's wrong? Did something happen?"

Mikey wriggled loose from his mother, and he stared up at him with wide blue eyes full of fear.

"What's wrong?" he asked again.

"Nothing," Sarah said. "Nothing that you need to be concerned about…"

But he was concerned, very concerned. "I… care about you two," he admitted. "I want to make sure that you're okay…"

She nodded. "We're fine." She squeezed her son's shoulders. "Everything's going to be fine." But she sounded as if she was trying to convince herself of that as much as she was her son or Marsh.

"You're here!" Hope yelled as she ran toward them. Bailey Ann was close behind her, and then the rest of the boys followed, their white cowboy hats bobbing on their heads. "We were just going to go for a ride around the ranch. This place is so much bigger than ours. Come with us."

Mikey turned back toward his mother, and that fearful look was back on his tense face. "Can I?"

"Of course," she said. "As long as there's enough supervision."

"There will be," Baker said as he walked up behind the kids. His oldest brother, Big Jake, was right behind him. Baker turned toward Marsh. "You still know how to ride, Sheriff?"

Marsh grinned. "I might be a little rusty, but I still know how."

"Want to help keep these little cowboys and cowgirls in line?" Baker asked.

"They might be better at keeping me in line," Marsh said. "But yeah, I'll go." He wanted to keep an eye on Mikey, make sure that he was really okay. But before he could follow the others off toward the barn, Sarah grabbed his arm.

"Can I... Can I ask you something?" she asked.

He nodded. "Of course. What?"

"Did... Did a lighter start the fire in the house?"

He tensed with dread because now he had a pretty good idea why she and Mikey had been so upset. "I'm not sure what started it," he replied honestly.

"You asked Becca about Cash's lighter," she said.

"Yes, because it was found in the house." And he suspected she knew how it had gotten there. "But the Moss Valley fire inspector originally ruled that poor maintenance caused it."

"But they reopened the investigation," she said. "I heard you and Sadie talking about that."

He nodded. "But that—"

"Sheriff!" Baker yelled out. "You coming?"

"Sarah—"

"Go," she said. "I would appreciate you looking out for Mikey."

"Of course," he said. "I will. I'll make sure that nothing bad happens to him." And not just during the ride around the ranch.

Tears glistened in her eyes as she stared up at him. "Thank you, Marsh."

He wanted to kiss her then, so badly, to comfort her. But he'd already made her a promise that he might not be able to keep.

JESSUP STUDIED JULIET'S FACE, which was flushed either from running around after the kids or from the oven she'd just closed. She was working in the kitchen with Taye.

Miller, his seven-year-old great-nephew had been cooking with them until Caleb had pleaded for everyone to go for a ride around the ranch. Big Jake, named for his grandfather, Jessup's father, had caved in first to his stepson's plea, and Baker had been right behind him with the nephews he and Taye were going to legally adopt. Then the girls, Hope and Bailey Ann, had wanted to go, too. Baker and Jake claimed they could handle all the kids, but Colton and Cash said they were going, too. Since Collin, Genevieve, Becca and Livvy had been busy in town, Cash and Colton were responsible for taking care of both girls.

But now, they stepped back into the kitchen. "What?" he asked his sons. "You guys forget how to ride?"

They both chuckled. "No, we're going to see if Marsh did, though."

"What? Marsh is here?"

"He just drove up, or maybe he was just sitting in his SUV until Sarah got here."

"Sarah's here, too?" Sadie asked the question from where she sipped a cup of coffee near the hearth.

"Like you didn't know, Grandma," Cash scoffed.

Jessup's heart warmed hearing him call her that. He glanced at Juliet, who was smiling, too. Cash could have been a living example to her of her husband's infidelity, but she was so forgiving and kind that she looked at him as family. Period. And so did Sadie.

Jessup was so fortunate to have so many strong and loving women in his life, like his late wife. She'd felt so bad when she'd found out that Cash's father was married; she'd had no idea. But Jessup felt now that she was at peace knowing that her family was reunited and that Juliet wasn't bitter and resentful.

"Did you get a chance to meet Sarah the last time she was here?" he asked Juliet.

She nodded. "We didn't talk much, though. She was very quiet. Her son, too. But having all the Havens in one place can be a bit overwhelming for people who aren't used to all of you at once."

"You're a Haven now, too," Sadie said.

She wasn't yet, but Jessup wondered if she would consider becoming one.

Then Sadie added, "I think Sarah and Mikey had a situation much like you and Melanie had with Shep." Melanie and Dusty were upstairs with their newborns.

Juliet sighed. "Where the man she married wasn't who she thought he was..."

"You know?" Sarah asked. She'd slipped into the kitchen behind Colton and Cash, and since they were so big, they'd blocked her from everyone's sight. "You all know about my ex-husband?"

"Know what?" Colton asked.

"Sarah," Jessup said, and he didn't want to hurt her feelings or offend her, but he probably should have already told her this. "One of the nurses in the cardiologist's office told me and Darlene about your ex-husband before we hired you."

She grimaced. "Told you or warned you?"

He shrugged. "Maybe she thought she was warning us. I think she was just jealous because you're so much better at your job. Darlene and I knew, but we didn't tell anyone." He glanced at his mother. "I'm not sure how she knows."

"How she knows everything..." Lem remarked. He was at her side as usual, but he was bouncing Little Jake on his lap. With that long, snowy white beard and his bright blue eyes, he looked so much like Santa Claus that it was no wonder the toddler was so drawn to him.

Sadie had always been drawn to him, too, even when she'd thought she hated him. And probably the only reason she'd thought she hated him was because he knew her so well; he'd seen her in a way that nobody else had.

And that made a person feel vulnerable, like Sarah clearly felt vulnerable now.

"So you were keeping more secrets," Cash remarked.

Jessup tensed, worried that his son was going to be angry with him again.

But Cash smiled. "To protect someone…"

"But Sarah doesn't need protection from that," Sadie said, and she stared at the younger woman, her dark eyes intense. "Nobody should judge you because of what your ex-husband did."

"Nobody should, but they do," Sarah said. "And Cash is right about not keeping secrets. I should have told everybody already about my ex-husband. He is in jail for robbery. Apparently, he'd been robbing places for years. I thought he was working construction out of town. I had no idea."

"Of course not," Sadie said.

"Does Marsh know?" Cash asked. "Have you told him?"

Sarah nodded quickly, but her face flushed. "I think, like his grandmother, he already knew, though." Then she focused on Sadie. "I didn't realize that everybody would be here."

And, clearly, she felt ambushed and was starting to back up into the hall. "We can talk another time…"

Sadie jumped up from the table, and despite her age, she moved quickly, pushing through her grandsons to take the young woman's hands in hers. "I'm sorry, Sarah. We can go into my suite and talk privately."

Jessup considered stepping in to save Sarah from his mother. But he wondered now which of them had instigated this meeting. Before he could intervene, Sadie had whisked Sarah down the hall toward her private rooms.

Cash and Colton stared after them as if they wondered if they should rescue the young woman, too. "Poor Sarah..." Cash murmured.

"Because of her ex or because she's now alone with Grandma?" Colton asked with a chuckle.

Cash laughed, too. "Both. Maybe we should go catch up with the others on their ride." And his sons walked away, leaving Jessup, Lem and Juliet alone in the kitchen. The other Havens who were home were probably upstairs helping with the twins, who he could hear almost half-heartedly crying.

"I think Sadie is going to have her work cut out for her getting Sarah and Marsh together," Juliet mused quietly.

"Why?" Jessup asked and then bristled slightly. "He won't judge her for what her ex-husband did."

"He doesn't have to," Juliet said. "She's the one judging herself. And after being married to a man who turned out to be bad, she might not be willing to take that chance, to risk her heart, again."

"Even on a good man?" Jessup asked. And he wondered if Juliet was talking about Marsh and Sarah or about them. Not that he had always been a good man. But Marsh certainly was. He definitely wouldn't judge Sarah for her ex; he would respect her even more for how she was raising her son alone.

Jessup didn't want her to be alone any longer, though. And he realized he didn't want to be alone any longer, either.

CHAPTER TWENTY

So MANY EMOTIONS pummeled Sarah. Shock and fear over what Mikey had confessed to her. And then Marsh...

He'd been so sweet, so protective, so much the white knight rushing to her rescue. But that was just who he was; she couldn't take it personally. And once he knew the truth, he would have to follow the law no matter what promises he'd made her. She didn't expect him to keep them.

She'd also felt disappointment and humiliation walking into the kitchen and hearing them talking about her and about her mistakes. And she'd just made another one. Instead of following Sadie into her private suite, she should have run out of the house. But she couldn't leave without her son. And she had no idea where he was riding on the ranch with the others. But she did know that Marsh would make sure he didn't get physically hurt. That promise he would keep.

But the others...

"This was a mistake," she said aloud.

"I'm the one who made the mistake," Sadie said. "I shouldn't have invited everybody else out. I just thought this was a great opportunity—"

"To meddle." She should have been furious, but it was somewhat heartening to realize that Sadie knew about her past but still wanted to match her up with her lawman grandson.

Sadie gestured toward the chair next to hers. "Please, Sarah, sit down. Let's talk."

She shook her head and stayed near the closed door, ready to make her escape. But to where? To sit and wait in her car until Mikey returned from the ride?

"Sarah, I am very sorry," Mrs. Haven-Lemmon said. "I did take advantage of your request to talk to me to set up this little get-together in the hopes of bringing you and Marsh together as well."

"You wasted your time," Sarah said. "Your grandson will never want a relationship with me. Not once he knows..."

"You said that he knows about your ex-husband."

She nodded. "I told him that, though, like you and JJ, I think he already knew." She shouldn't have been surprised that Dr. Stanley's nurse would have "warned" them about her. Glenda was a gossip.

"Then what could he learn that would make him not want to date you?" his grandmother asked.

Sarah shook her head. "I can't tell you. This was a mistake." When she'd asked Mrs. Haven-

Lemmon for her advice, she'd only had a suspicion, but now she knew.

"We all make mistakes, Sarah," Mrs. Haven-Lemmon said. "I made a big one today with you, by inviting the others to come out, too. And I am very sorry that I did that and didn't warn you."

Sadie had apologized many times, so Sarah found herself softening. "I appreciate that," she murmured. "And I should be flattered that you want to set me up with your grandson even though you know about my past."

"It's not your past," Mrs. Haven-Lemmon said. "It's your ex-husband's past. None of that was your fault, Sarah. And Marsh knows that."

"Voters might not," Sarah pointed out. "You shouldn't want me for Marsh. I would only hurt him. While you and your family don't judge me, other people do, like the nurse at the cardiologist's office. And the parents of the kids at Mikey's old school. Being involved with me in any way could hurt Marsh's chances of getting elected." And she didn't want him sacrificing a career he obviously loved.

"Sarah, that's—"

"It's the truth," she interrupted to insist. "But it doesn't matter. I don't have time for anything but my son. I have to figure out how to protect him. And that's why I came to you for advice, because you try so hard to protect the people you love."

Mrs. Haven-Lemmon smiled. "They don't always appreciate that," she said. "And it doesn't always work."

"But you try."

The older woman nodded. "So try me, Sarah. Ask me whatever you want."

Sarah bit her bottom lip. Once it was out, she wouldn't be able to take it back. "This might be one of those secrets that need to be kept." That was probably the best way to protect her son.

"You took care of my son when I couldn't," Mrs. Haven-Lemmon said, and her deep voice was even gruffer with emotion while tears glistened in her dark eyes. "You helped him survive until his transplant, and you took care of him when he was recovering from the transplant. You gave him back to me, and after everything and everyone I've lost, it was the greatest gift anyone could have given me."

She glanced down at her hand and the tattoo on her finger. "Well, besides finding the love of my life right under my nose. But Jessup coming back into my life was a miracle that I never expected. You gave me that miracle, Sarah."

Sarah shook her head. "No, doctors and surgeons and probably JJ's nephew's heart were responsible for that miracle," she said.

The tears in Sadie's dark eyes spilled over and slipped down her face. "None of that would have mattered if he hadn't made it, if he hadn't been healthy enough for the transplant. You are part of the miracle, too, Sarah. And the least I can do after everything you've done for my son and my family is give you my loyalty, Sarah. You have it. You can trust me and know that I will always be here for you. I will always give you my support and protection."

The sincerity in the older woman's voice and on her face overwhelmed Sarah. And tears rushed to her eyes. "When I married my high school sweetheart, my parents disowned me...even before I had Mikey. So I didn't dare go to them after his father's arrest. I know they would have just said that they'd told me so. And they had..."

"So you had no one," Sadie said.

Sarah nodded. "It was always just me and Mikey." That was why she was so afraid that she was going to screw up and screw him up. Had she? "Having support means so much to me."

Despite her age, Sadie easily jumped up from her chair then and pulled Sarah into a tight hug. And her big body shook slightly in Sarah's embrace.

"What's wrong?" she asked, worried about the older woman's health. Mrs. Haven-Lemmon had her own heart issues.

"You just..." She pulled back and stared at Sarah. "The way you look, your sweetness and now your situation with your family...you remind me so much of Jenny."

"Who?"

"Jenny is…was…my first granddaughter-in-law," Sadie explained. "She died in the crash with her husband, Dale."

Sarah sucked in a breath. Poor Jenny. She'd lost more than her life; she'd lost the chance to mother her sons. "Leaving those three boys orphaned…"

"Orphaned but not alone," Mrs. Haven-Lemmon said. "And you're not alone now, either, Sarah. Whatever you need, I will help you."

"I'm not sure how you can help," Sarah admitted. "I don't know what I expect you to do except maybe just listen and not…"

"Judge," Sadie finished for her. "I hate how alone you've been for so long, Sarah."

"I wasn't alone," she said. "I have Mikey. And I can't lose him."

"You won't," Sadie promised. "We'll figure this out. We'll make everything all right."

Just like her grandson had, this woman was making Sarah promises she probably wouldn't be able to keep. But she was so desperate that she wanted to believe them. And she really didn't have any other options.

So she told Sadie the truth and hoped that she wasn't making a terrible mistake.

MARSH HAD MADE a terrible mistake. He should have kissed Sarah when he had the chance, every chance he'd had. But that wasn't the only mistake he'd made.

He should have spent more time with Mikey while the boy and his mom had lived at the Cassidy ranch. The kid loved horses, but he didn't have any idea how to ride. So Marsh helped him on the horse and taught him the basics before they started off on their ride.

Then, on the return trip toward the big red barn they could see in the distance, when the sun beat down on Mikey's blond hair, Marsh took off his hat and put it on the little boy's head, but it slid down over his whole face.

The other boys laughed at him.

"You have a white hat like ours now," Caleb said.

"But it's too big," Miller said. "Here, use mine." He threw his hat like a Frisbee toward Mikey. But there was no way the kid could see it coming; he couldn't see anything with Marsh's hat covering his entire head.

But he instinctively took one hand off his reins and reached out for it, nearly sliding out of the saddle. Marsh was riding close enough that he was able to grab him and steady him.

"That looks fun!" Caleb said, and he threw his hat, too. Ian, of course, followed suit. The hats landed near Miller's in the mud along the trail.

It was good that they were heading back to the barn now because Mikey was probably going to be sore and maybe a little sunburned from the ride. Marsh hadn't done a good job taking care of him like he'd promised his mom he would. Marsh stopped both their horses and dismounted to pick up the hats.

Jake and Baker were in front of him, trying to keep up with Hope and Bailey Ann. Bailey Ann rode on the same saddle with Hope, her arms around her while the little girl galloped toward the barn. Hope rode like her mom, like she was born in the saddle. Caleb, hatless, put his horse into a gallop to try to catch up with the girls.

"Hey," Jake said. "You need to get your hat." He sighed. "I'll catch up with them." And he urged his horse, a tan quarter horse, to a gallop, too.

Marsh was trying to pick up all of the hats while holding his horse and Mikey's steady. Then Baker, who'd turned back to help, came up beside the horses to steady them.

"Maybe white wasn't the best color to pick for them," Marsh mused as he hit each hat against his leg and tried to get the mud off them.

"Jake got the boys those hats for his and Katie's wedding," Baker said. "But now they wear them every chance they get, not just for weddings, although we've had quite a few of those, too." Baker reached out and tried to raise Marsh's hat above Mikey's face. "This guy could use the same milliner we had fit the boys."

Marsh would buy Mikey a hat the first chance he got; the boy should have one of his own, especially if he kept hanging out with Hope. And Marsh had a feeling that he would. She'd already promised to teach him to ride. But Bailey Ann had insisted on being taught first, so she'd ridden with Hope instead of Mikey.

Mikey should have a lot of things, like a dad he could count on, one who would be there for him like Marsh wished he could. But with his job and his family, he wouldn't be able to give Mikey the time and attention the little boy deserved.

That the boy's mother deserved.

He plucked his hat from Mikey's head and put it back on his own, then he put Miller's on Mikey. The little boy smiled shyly at him, and something shifted in Marsh's heart, making him gasp at the intensity of it. This kid deserved so much, but he didn't expect it, and whatever attention he got, he seemed to appreciate so much.

"You're doing great," Marsh told him. "You're a natural rider."

"Really?" he asked. "Like Hope?"

The fact that he recognized how good Hope was proved he would be good, too.

Marsh nodded. "Yup, you'll be riding right with her in no time."

Instead of being pleased, the little boy's smile slipped away, and Marsh had that feeling he'd had when he'd first approached Sarah and Mikey by her car. Something had happened. Something emotionally traumatic for them both. He wanted to help, but he wasn't sure that she would let him.

That she would let anyone help her. She was so fiercely independent and protective of her son. And with good reason: they'd both been hurt.

Mikey followed the rules that Marsh had taught him, hanging on with his legs while tugging gently on the reins, and he rode along to the barn.

Baker took Caleb's and Ian's hats from Marsh so that he could climb back onto his horse. "Your brothers were wrong about you."

"What?" Marsh asked. "Did they think I forgot how to ride?" It had been too long, though. He missed it.

"They thought you might not be able to handle all the kids," Baker said. "But you're a natural."

Marsh chuckled and shook his head. "No. They were right about that. I've never been good with kids."

"I used to be uncomfortable around them, too," his cousin confessed, which was ironic since he was adopting his three orphaned nephews, and they clearly all already looked at him as a father figure rather than just an uncle now.

"I was the one who made them uncomfortable," Marsh admitted.

"Mikey's a shy kid," Baker said. "But he looks pretty comfortable with you."

"That's new," Marsh said. But that was because

he was making an effort, one that he should have made sooner. But Sarah had made him uncomfortable, Sarah and all the feelings she'd inspired in him—the ones Marsh had been trying so hard to ignore. The attraction, the fascination…the warm fluttering in his stomach and his heart.

"Something's weighing on the kid," Baker said.

Marsh shouldn't have been surprised that Baker had noticed; Mikey's shoulders sagged as if the weight was almost literal.

"I saw that same weight on Miller after Dale and Jenny died," Baker said. "He blamed himself for his parents' accident."

Marsh sucked in a breath. "That's horrible."

"Yeah, guilt is a horrible weight to bear," Baker said.

And Marsh suspected his youngest cousin had carried that weight himself. Baker had been the first on the scene of that horrific accident.

"I can't imagine…"

Baker stared at him for a long moment. His eyes were a lighter brown than his brothers' or cousins', like topaz. "I think you can…"

Marsh had felt guilty that he hadn't done more for his parents, for his brothers, that he hadn't been able to do more, to help more with their medical issues and the ranch.

"That's too much weight for a kid to bear," Baker said.

Mikey needed help. And Marsh really wanted

to be the one to help him. But he wasn't sure how he could or if he would just make it worse.

By the time he and Baker got back to the barn, Mikey was gone. Marsh rushed out of the barn to see Sarah driving away with her son, as if she'd just been waiting for him so she could leave.

And he had a moment's panic that they might not just be leaving Ranch Haven. They might be leaving town, and he wouldn't get the chance to see either of them again. A sense of loss rushed over him, overwhelming in its intensity, reminding him of how he'd felt when his mom died and when Cash left, reminding him of why he was so determined to stay single, so that nobody could hurt him again.

But he had a horrible feeling that it was too late this time. Sarah and her son had gotten to him.

SADIE HAD HAD Cash and Colton watching for their brother. And the moment he got back from the ride, they took him to her suite.

"Grandma, I don't have time for this," he protested.

"You told me you took the morning off work," she reminded him.

"It's not work," he said.

"It's Sarah," she surmised.

His face flushed, but he shrugged. "It's a lot of things."

"The fire," she said. "I know you're worried

about that, about what the fire inspector is going to rule. I can tell you what it was."

He tensed. "What?"

"Arson," she said.

He sucked in a breath. "You think someone purposely burned down the ranch?" Because clearly he didn't think that was the case. He knew it was an accident.

So did she. But she had promised her protection. So she said, "Yes, I know it."

"Grandma…"

"And I know who did it."

He groaned and closed his eyes. "I don't think I want to know…"

She had a pretty good idea that was because he suspected, and probably had for a while, who was responsible.

She sucked in a breath, bracing herself before revealing, "It was me."

"What?" he asked, his dark eyes open and full of disbelief.

"It was me," she insisted almost defiantly. Lem was probably going to divorce her over this. But she'd made a promise. "I burned down the ranch."

CHAPTER TWENTY-ONE

SARAH AND MIKEY came home to a little bundle in a basket inside the door. Someone must have given Becca the code to the digital lock. And now Sarah knew why the real estate agent hadn't been at Ranch Haven with Cash and Hope. She'd been out making deliveries.

Sarah was glad Becca had when she saw how happy Mikey was when they opened the door to the kitten chewing on the basket. "I forgot which one you picked that day," she said. Marsh had been there, so she'd been distracted.

"She picked me," Mikey said as he dropped down onto the floor next to the kitty. It had the tiger markings of its gray tabby mother, but its hair was longer and fluffier. "Hope and I sat on the floor, and she came over to me first and climbed right up." As if on cue, the kitty did it again, climbing up his chest to settle onto his shoulder like a parrot. It rubbed its face against his. And Sarah could hear it purring.

"She loves you already," she said as she eased down onto the floor next to them.

Mikey reached up to hold the kitten against his face. "I love her."

"And I love you so very much," Sarah said.

"Still?"

"Always," she promised.

"No matter what?" he asked.

"Definitely," she said. "But you know what happened…"

"The fire," he said, and there was the catch of tears in his voice. One slid down his cheek, and the kitten chased it with her paw.

"It wasn't your fault."

"It was."

"It was an accident," she said. "You didn't do it on purpose. You won't get in trouble for an accident."

He turned toward her. "I won't?"

With Sadie vowing her support and protection, she didn't think anything would happen to a six-year-old who'd accidentally started a fire. But remembering the destruction and the injuries because of it, Sarah felt sick. "We should tell the truth, though," she said.

Mikey released a shaky sigh and nodded. "I felt better just telling Mrs. Lancaster."

And she mentally kicked herself for not getting him help earlier.

"She said it was an accident, too," he said.

"And it really was, Mommy. I just didn't want that lighter in the barn with the animals…and I brought it in the house to give it to you. But you and Mr. JJ and Miss Darlene weren't inside. And then there was the smoke, and I didn't know what to do."

He'd said the same thing in the car, but Sarah wasn't driving now and could focus more on what he was saying. "I think the sheriff has the lighter now," Sarah said.

"Good. He'll make sure it doesn't start any more fires." Mikey shuddered, and the kitten cuddled closer to him.

"We should tell him, too, about what happened," she said.

Mikey tensed. "He'll arrest me…like my daddy."

"Marsh didn't arrest your daddy," she said. "And your daddy did the things he did on purpose. What you did was an accident. You're a good kid, Mikey. The sheriff won't arrest you." She wasn't exactly sure what he would do to him.

How much trouble could a six-year-old get in for an accident?

Sarah drew in a deep breath, acknowledging that it was time to find out.

"Bailey Ann says her family has a rule," Mikey said.

"What kind of rule?"

"That they always have to be open and honest," he said. "No secrets. No lies."

Sarah sighed. "That's a good rule."

"Yes," he agreed. "We can go tell the sheriff what happened."

She had a feeling that he already knew.

SADIE HAD TRIED to talk Marsh into taking her into the office, where she could write out her confession. He'd told her she was full of it and that he wasn't taking a false confession. He didn't bother pointing out that the fire wasn't even in his jurisdiction because he hadn't wanted her to confess to his old boss, who might have taken it. And she'd told him he would be hearing from her lawyer. He figured it was Ben. But a couple of hours later, it was the deputy mayor who walked into his office, not the mayor.

He hadn't intended to work this Saturday, but it had been pretty obvious that his grandmother wasn't going to let this rest. "What are you doing here?" Marsh asked his step-grandfather after the receptionist escorted him back.

Lem held out his hands over Marsh's cluttered desk. "Arrest me."

"For what?" Marsh asked. "Did you strangle your stubborn bride out of frustration? The woman is infuriating." And wonderful, too.

Lem shook his head. "No. I'm here to confess that I was the one who started the fire, not my wife."

"Of course," Marsh said. The old man loved

his wife so much that he would probably take a bullet for her, and apparently even a prison sentence for arson.

Lem wiggled his hands. "So, are you going to slap the cuffs on me?"

"No."

"What about your grandmother?"

"I'm not going to slap them on her, either," Marsh assured him. "I don't believe either of you started the fire."

"You don't?"

"Why would you?" Marsh asked the question that his grandmother hadn't been able to answer, either. "What would the two of you gain by starting that fire?"

"Uh…maybe to get Jessup to move home?"

"He could have died going into that burning house," Marsh said. "There is no way she would have risked that. Grandma nearly died when she heard about the fire. She was at Ranch Haven in front of witnesses." As he'd pointed out to her.

"But *I* still could have done it," Lem persisted.

"But you didn't," Marsh said. "I don't know why you two are spontaneously confessing." But he had a pretty good idea. "I am not arresting either of you or letting you make any more false confessions. The only thing I will do is walk you out." He stood up and escorted Lem to the door between the back and the public reception area.

"There are other people here to see you, Sheriff," the receptionist said.

And he groaned, imagining that his entire family was standing in the public reception area. But when he opened the door, he didn't see any Havens or Cassidys. He saw Reynoldses: Sarah and Mikey. This wasn't a confession he wanted to take, either, but this might be the only honest one.

"Sarah," Lem said. "Sadie told you that she would take care of this. You shouldn't be here."

So Lem knew and Sadie knew. It was time that Marsh knew, too.

"Thank her," Sarah said. "But Mikey and I have talked about this, and he wants to tell the sheriff everything."

Marsh knelt down in front of the little boy, who was staring at the floor. "I appreciate this, Mikey. You are very brave and very honest."

The boy's chin quivered a little, but he nodded.

Then Marsh looked up at Lem. "Tell Grandma everything will be fine." There was no way he was letting a six-year-old carry any weight of guilt. Just like Baker had said, it was too much for him to bear.

He reached out to take Mikey's hand in his. "Everything will be fine," he assured the child, and he gently squeezed his small hand. It was so small.

Then he looked up at the boy's mother, and he was glad he was on his knees or his legs might have given out. The look on her beautiful face, the mix of gratitude and fear and fierce love for her child...

She'd never been more beautiful or more vulnerable. And Marsh had never been as affected by anyone...ever...

He managed to get to his feet and guide her and Mikey down the hall to his office. Then he shut the door behind them, and he went around his desk to fall into his chair before his legs actually gave out. "Sarah, if this is about what I think it is, I want to remind you that it's not my jurisdiction, but I will still have certain legal obligations to share what I learn."

She nodded. "We understand. But it was an accident. And maybe you can help us explain that to the right people."

He nodded now. "I will do everything within my power..." But he didn't have as much power as she or his grandmother thought.

She held his gaze for a moment, as if trying to determine if he was telling the truth. Then she nodded. "Okay, Mikey, you can tell Sheriff Cassidy what you told me and Mrs. Lancaster."

"Mrs. Lancaster?"

"She works at the school, and she's been helping Miller, Ian and Little Jake, too."

"Good," he said. If Mikey was going to tell him what he thought, the little boy was going to need some counseling. "Okay, Mikey, you can tell me."

"You won't put me in jail?"

"Of course not," Marsh said. "And whatever happened, I believe your mom, that it was just an accident."

Mikey nodded, sucked in a breath and then released it and a long, run-on sentence of an explanation of what had happened. He'd talked so fast that Marsh had to rewind the conversation in his head, and then he started asking questions to clarify what had happened.

"So you found the lighter in the barn?"

Mikey nodded.

"And you didn't want it starting the barn on fire?"

"I didn't want the kitty or Miss Darlene's horse to get hurt," he said.

"So you brought it in the house?" Marsh asked.

Mikey nodded.

"He was going to give it to me or JJ or Darlene," Sarah rushed in to explain, "but we were already outside then."

"You didn't see them going out to the barn to see Miss Darlene's horse?" he asked.

"I always ran around to the back of the house because I didn't want to wake up Mr. JJ if he was sleeping in the front room."

Marsh's heart warmed with the boy's consideration for others. He really was a sweet kid.

"We must have just missed each other," Sarah said. "He must have been going in the back when we were coming out the front. The front was easier for your dad when going down to the barn."

None of the steps had been in very good condition. The house had gotten really run down.

"Then what happened?" Marsh asked.

"I started the house on fire," Mikey said, and tears pooled in his blue eyes.

"How?" Marsh asked.

"With the lighter, in the kitchen."

Colton had found the lighter in the cellar because the kitchen floor had collapsed into it. Most of the house had collapsed into the cellar because it had been so structurally unstable even before the fire.

Marsh opened his middle drawer and lifted out the bag with the lighter inside it. Ever since he'd talked to Cash, a thought had been niggling at him. "How?" Marsh asked. And he came around his desk, opened the bag and handed the lighter to the little boy. "Show me."

"Marsh!" Sarah exclaimed.

"Show me how it works," Marsh said.

The little boy stared at it. "I dunno…"

"How did you even know it was a lighter? Did you see a flame come out of it?"

He shook his head. "Mr. JJ showed me a picture of it once. Doc CC was holding it, but he looked a lot younger than he does now."

So Dad had still had a picture of Cash despite Marsh trying to hide them all after his brother had run away. He smiled. "So you don't even know how it works?"

"No, Mr. JJ told me that they're really dangerous, though, and to give them to an adult."

"You didn't try to use it?"

The little boy's face flushed. "I tried, but it hurt me, and I started coughing. There was so much smoke."

"Try to use it now," Marsh said. He pointed toward the wheel. "You push that down with your thumb."

Mikey bit his bottom lip and pressed on the wheel, but then he jerked and dropped it onto the floor next to Marsh. "Watch for the smoke now."

"There's no smoke," Marsh said. "And there's no fire." He picked it up and tried to spin the igniter with his thumb. A metal burr jabbed him. "Ouch," he said with a grunt. But he kept the pressure on it, trying to turn it. It was frozen in place. Cash had carried it like a rabbit's foot, but he hadn't actually used it. So nobody had realized it didn't even work.

"No way," Marsh murmured. And then, thinking of all the weeks he and his brothers had obsessed over this stupid lighter, he started laughing.

MIKEY TENSED. He'd been so scared coming here. Sure, Mom said that the sheriff wouldn't arrest him, but he hadn't really believed her. He'd started a house on fire, so of course he would go to jail.

He was bad.

But the sheriff wasn't arresting him. He was laughing at him.

"What is it?" Sarah asked. "Why are you laughing?"

Mikey was glad she'd asked because he wanted to know but was too afraid to ask.

The sheriff was actually crying now, or at least, wiping away a tear. "The lighter doesn't work."

"What?" Sarah asked.

He tried to push his thumb down that little wheel thing and grimaced.

Mikey knew why; it had hurt his thumb, too. "It's like it bites."

"Yeah, it is," the sheriff agreed. "I'm so sorry, Mikey, that you thought you started it this whole time."

"I did."

"But you couldn't have started it with the lighter," he said. "It doesn't work."

"Oh…" Confusion pounded at his head. "But there was smoke…"

"Are you sure it was after the lighter, or was there smoke when you walked into the house?"

He shrugged.

"Try to remember."

He'd tried so hard to forget that day, to forget what happened. But because the sheriff told him to, he thought hard about it. "It smelled funny when I walked in the house. The back door opens into the kitchen, though, and sometimes Miss Darlene burns stuff."

Marsh chuckled. "Yes, sometimes she does."

"She had made lunch that day," his mom said, "because I was doing the laundry."

"A stove left on or a dryer," Marsh said. "I'm pretty sure one of those things started it, not any of the people who confessed."

"Who else confessed?" his mom asked.

"My grandmother, Sadie, confessed earlier today, and the deputy mayor just confessed, too," Marsh said. "That's what he was doing here when you two came in."

"The guy who looks like Santa Claus?" Mikey asked. "He burned down the ranch?"

"No. He didn't, and neither did my grandma and neither did you," Marsh said. "I am really sorry that you thought all this time that you did."

"It was bad," Mikey said. "I felt so bad."

"You should have told somebody," Marsh said.

"Open and honest," Mikey repeated. Bailey Ann was even smarter than he thought.

"Why weren't you?" Marsh asked, and he glanced at Mikey's mom, like maybe he thought that she told him not to.

"I didn't tell nobody," Mikey said. "Because I didn't want to get in trouble. I didn't want everybody to think I'm bad like they did at my old school."

"Those people were wrong," the sheriff said. "And they shouldn't have called you that. You are a very good kid. Your only mistake was in not telling somebody, at least your mom, about what happened. What will you do if something like this happens again?"

"I'll do the right thing," Mikey replied. "That's why we're here, that's what Mommy says we have to do."

"Your mommy is very smart," Marsh said with a smile. "And very pretty."

Mikey felt little butterflies in his stomach, happy ones, though, that made him feel excited, not scared. Maybe Hope was right. Maybe the sheriff would marry his mommy, and then they would all be family. A big family.

"Your father is here," a woman said as she opened the door to Marsh's office. "Sorry," she said, "but he insisted on seeing you right away."

Marsh started laughing again as he turned to look at Mr. JJ standing in the doorway. "Let me guess—you're here to confess, too."

"Yeah, it was me," Mr. JJ said. "Don't listen to what Mikey is telling you."

"Mikey is the only one telling me the truth," Marsh said. "And because of that, we figured out that nobody started the fire, especially not with a lighter that doesn't even work."

"It doesn't work?" Mr. JJ asked.

Marsh nodded.

And then Mr. JJ started laughing until tears ran down his face like they had the sheriff's a little while ago.

Mikey wasn't sure what was so funny. Mom wasn't laughing, either. But there were tears running down her face. He wanted to reach for her, but then Marsh turned back to Mikey and held out his hand.

Mikey didn't know what he wanted, but then Marsh took Mikey's hand and shook it. "Thank you, sir," he said to Mikey. "You helped me figure out a big mystery. You were so helpful. I should probably make you a deputy."

"Probably," Mikey agreed.

Then the sheriff pulled him into a hug. And Mikey linked his arms around his neck and held on. He liked the sheriff's hugs. Mom's were nice, too; she was soft and warm.

But the sheriff was so big, and that made Mikey feel safe like he hadn't felt in a long time. But then, over the sheriff's wide shoulder, he saw his mom's face.

And there was such a funny look on it, like she was the one who was afraid now. Did she think he was still in trouble? Or did she think she was in trouble?

CHAPTER TWENTY-TWO

SARAH SHOULD HAVE been relieved. And part of her was. But another part of her was angry with herself for not questioning Mikey earlier and for not questioning his confession like Marsh had.

Poor Mikey had spent all these weeks blaming himself and feeling guilty. And Sarah felt guilty about that. But, in addition to the relief and the anger and the guilt, she felt something else.

Something she had no business feeling. But when Marsh was so sweet with her son and enfolded him in that bear hug, she fell for him. Hard.

Still, part of her couldn't help thinking that this was all he had really wanted from them: the truth about the fire. And that was fine, but suddenly Sarah wanted more from him.

But that wouldn't be right or fair. Not when she knew how a relationship with her might hurt him. Or, at least, his chances in the upcoming election. She closed her eyes, shutting out the image of Marsh holding her son, comforting him in a way that she hadn't been able to no matter how much she'd tried.

Because she hadn't been able to prove to him that he'd done nothing wrong. And that was what mattered most to Mikey, that he wasn't bad, that he did the right thing.

Now Sarah had to do the right thing. "Uh, Mikey, we should let the sheriff get back to work," she said. "And we should get back to your new kitty."

"You have a new kitty?" Marsh asked.

"Yes, Becca dropped it off while we were at Ranch Haven," Sarah said. "I hope that's okay," she added to JJ.

He grinned. "Of course. I know she worked it all out with Bob Lemmon."

"Good," Sarah said. "But we should get going…" If she could pry Mikey away from the sheriff.

"Dad, can you take Mikey out to the reception area? I know Mrs. Little keeps some candy in the bottom drawer of her desk that she shares with really good kids."

"And we have a really, really good kid here," JJ said, and he reached for Mikey, swinging him up in his arms.

The nurse in her worried for a second that lifting the boy wasn't good for her heart transplant patient, but Mikey was light, and JJ was so much stronger than he'd been for probably a very long time. She wished she was as strong as he was…

emotionally. She had to get away from Marsh. "I'll walk out with you both," she said, but when she started forward, the sheriff encircled her wrist with his hand.

"Please, talk to me for a minute," Marsh said.

She wanted to do more than talk; she wanted to hug him like he'd hugged her son. But it wouldn't be fair to either of them if she acted on her feelings.

"We really should get back to that kitten." She'd put her in the laundry room with food and water and a litter box. But she still didn't want to leave her alone for long.

Marsh's hand on her wrist held her long enough for Mikey and JJ to slip out of the office and close the door behind them. But the minute the door shut, he released her. "I just want to apologize, Sarah."

"Then I was right..." she muttered more to herself than to him since sobs were rushing up the back of her throat.

"Right?"

"You were just being nice to me and Mikey because you thought he had something to do with the fire," she said, and she was still whispering because she didn't want her son to hear that.

Marsh didn't immediately deny it, which she actually appreciated. Instead, his face flushed a bit. "I never thought he started it on purpose or that anyone did," he insisted. "The fire wasn't the reason I wanted to spend time with the two of you…"

She narrowed her eyes even as her pulse quickened. She wasn't sure she believed him, but she wanted to. Then, reminding herself and him, she said, "It doesn't matter, Marsh. It doesn't matter." Because it didn't change anything; she was still not good for him, not when he had an election coming up.

"Sarah—"

"Thank you," she interrupted him. "Thank you for helping him figure out that it wasn't his fault at all. He was carrying that guilt way too long." Her heart broke over that, over letting her son suffer. "I'm glad you got what you wanted, Marsh."

Then she stepped around him, opened the door and rushed out. And she couldn't help but feel like she was leaving behind what she wanted.

MARSH CALLED A meeting in Moss Valley with his old boss and with the fire inspector. They met in the sheriff's office in Moss Valley. Marsh dropped the bag with the lighter in it onto his desk. "This was found in the cellar of what was left of the house."

"So it was arson," the sheriff said.

"No," the fire inspector and Marsh said at the same time.

Marsh unsealed the bag and dropped the lighter

onto the surface of the desk. "Try it," he said. "It doesn't work."

"Then why did you bring it to me?" the sheriff asked. "And why didn't you already turn this in?"

"While this was found in the house, it didn't start the fire," he said. "The fire was not intentionally set. Two witnesses there that day confirmed to me that an oven was used earlier that day and the dryer was on."

"That tracks with my first report," the inspector said. "The fire was caused by poor maintenance. Either the dryer vent had never been cleaned out or maybe the wind jammed it open and birds or mice made a nest in it, but I am certain the fire started there. The damage to the dryer indicated from the beginning that the fire originated there."

"Why doesn't the insurance company believe that?" the sheriff asked.

"Because that adjuster is notorious for pushing for arson charges so that he can deny claims," the inspector said. "He gets a bonus for every claim he denies or a percentage or something."

"So he's the one you should be investigating," Marsh told his old boss. "I know if he tries this in my jurisdiction that I will make sure it gets handled correctly, so that people who've already suffered a loss don't have to suffer more."

Suffering made him think of Sarah and Mikey, of the suffering they'd endured. The bullying, the judgement...and the way she'd turned on him in his office earlier this afternoon had him feeling like a judgmental bully himself.

He wasn't sure how he could make that up to her, to them, but telling her that the police investigation was closed was a start. And with the sheriff and the fire inspector closing the official investigation, the insurance company wouldn't be able to keep it open, either.

JESSUP COULDN'T BELIEVE the turn his day had taken. When he'd left Ranch Haven, he'd intended to turn himself in for something he hadn't done. He was pretty sure that Marsh wouldn't have actually arrested him, but Juliet hadn't been as confident. And when he'd left the house, she'd sent him off with a kiss and the promise to bake him a cake with a file in it.

He smiled just thinking about her, about that kiss, about how alive he felt. But he'd refrained from rushing back to her because he was concerned about Sarah. Even though she had proof that her son had done nothing wrong, she was still upset. And Jessup was worried that maybe *his* son had done something wrong.

He followed Sarah and Mikey back to the house to retrieve the kitty, and they'd all gone to Willow Creek Veterinarian Services to fill Darlene in on what happened and to have Dr. Miner check out the kitten.

Not that Cash hadn't probably already done that. But Mikey was nervous about making sure that she was big enough to be away from her mommy.

Dr. Miner took the little boy to his office to evaluate the feline while he and Sarah talked to Darlene. Her hazel eyes filled with tears. "That poor little boy," she said, "thinking he'd caused it…"

Sarah's breath hitched as she nodded, her eyes filled with tears, too. "I was worried that he had something to do with it with the way he kept apologizing when we found him in the loft. He was so sorry."

Darlene nodded. "I know. I wondered about that, too."

Jessup had been in an ambulance at that time, so he hadn't seen Mikey's reaction to the fire. But he'd been so quiet after it. The boy was always quiet, though, so Jessup hadn't been too concerned about him. "I really just thought it was poor maintenance or, like Marsh pointed out, that the oven or the dryer caused it."

Darlene's face paled. "The oven. I was baking something before we went outside. Did I leave the oven on?"

"I was drying clothes," Sarah said. "It might have been that…"

Jessup winced as he tried to remember the last time he'd cleaned out the vent. He would have had to get out a ladder to do it, so he doubted that he had. And he'd always forgotten to ask the boys to do it when they'd come for a visit.

"No matter what caused the fire," he said, "it was an accident. No one is at fault."

Sarah nodded.

"Why aren't you happier?" he asked.

She shrugged. "I just feel so bad for doubting my son…"

"What about my son?" Jessup asked.

She tensed. "What about him?"

"You seem upset with him," Jessup said.

She shrugged. "I appreciate how he handled the situation with Mikey."

"What about you?" Jessup asked.

She shrugged again. "That's it. The sheriff got what he wanted. The truth. That's all he wanted."

"Are you sure?" Darlene asked the question now.

Sarah nodded.

"I'm not sure that's the case," Jessup said. He saw the way Marsh was with Sarah and Mikey. "I think he's really interested in you."

She shook her head. "He was just interested in how the fire started. He's told me many times that he's too busy to date, and he has the election coming up. Being involved with me wouldn't help him win that."

"Sarah," Darlene began, "I hope you know how beautiful you are, how deserving of love you are. Marsh would be lucky to have you in his life."

Sarah blinked several times as if trying to clear away tears.

"She's right," Jessup said.

Sarah smiled. "My son loves me, and I love him. It's more than enough." And she walked away from them, heading toward where Dr. Miner had taken Mikey and the kitten.

"Oh, Sarah…" Darlene sighed. "I wish she would realize how amazing she is."

"Ditto," Jessup said.

"What?"

"You," he said. "You have no idea how amazing you are, Darlene."

She blinked like Sarah had, like she was fighting tears. He didn't want to make her cry. Darlene had cried too many tears over the years. She'd lost too much.

He noticed Dr. Miner walking out with Sarah and Mikey, the kitten cuddled against him. The way the veterinarian was watching them brought a smile to Jessup's lips. Someone had realized how amazing Darlene was even though she hadn't. Apparently, he considered Jessup a threat, which was funny. Darlene was his sister, his best friend, his savior for years.

"Hey, little man," Dr. Miner said to Mikey. "Your kitty is in great health. So, do you still want to be a vet?"

Mikey tensed and turned toward the older man. "I…uh… I might have changed my mind."

"Really?" Dr. Miner asked. "What do you want to be now?"

"Maybe a sheriff."

Jessup laughed and so did Darlene, but Sarah was curiously quiet. Jessup loved that the little boy was idolizing Marsh. Marsh deserved it. He deserved Sarah, and she deserved him. But they weren't the only ones who deserved some happiness.

Dr. Miner sighed. "So I've lost another one," he said. He turned toward Darlene. "I hope *you* still love me."

Her face flushed, and her eyes glittered. "I tolerate you," she said.

Jessup laughed because he knew she more than tolerated him. She wouldn't have taken this job— wouldn't have moved into the barn—if she wasn't excited about her future.

Like he was excited about his.

His only concern was Marsh and Sarah. He wanted them to find their happiness, too.

CHAPTER TWENTY-THREE

SARAH WAS LIVING out of boxes, waiting for Becca to set her up in her new place, which Becca had promised would be ready soon and that she would love. And even though both JJ and Mr. Lemmon had assured her it was fine, she felt strange staying in the house that JJ had rented.

Sure, he and Darlene had been as sweet as they could be, so supportive and kind. But she knew now that they wanted her to wind up with Marsh. But that was for her sake, not for his. They didn't consider what was best for him. So she had to.

She knew that *she* was not what was best for him.

And that was what she told him when she opened the door a few days after that eventful Saturday. "You shouldn't be here," she told him, but she stepped back and let him walk past her into the house.

Maybe he'd forgotten something when he'd moved in with his brother.

Everybody was gone but her and Mikey. And

they would be gone soon, too, once Becca told her where they were moving. She should have pressed the realtor for more information, but she'd been busy with her new job and with her happy son and his new kitten. She'd started packing up some of their stuff so they would be ready to move as soon as the new place was ready.

She wondered now, as Marsh walked into the house, if she should have moved away from Willow Creek just so she could get away from the sheriff and the feelings she had for him. But Mikey was happy here. He loved the school and even the bus and most especially his friends. He loved this house with its big backyard, so she wasn't in a hurry to move him out of it.

"Why shouldn't I be here?" Marsh asked.

"People shouldn't see you hanging out with me," she warned him. Too many people knew about her ex-husband for the gossip not to have started, not that anyone had started treating her any differently. Yet.

"What people and why not?" Marsh asked.

"Voters shouldn't see us together," she clarified. "If they think I'm as big a thief as my ex was, they'll never trust you, either."

"Sarah…"

"What?"

"Is that why you've been avoiding me?" he asked. "For my benefit?"

"I haven't had to avoid you much since you got

what you wanted," she pointed out with a pang of hurt striking her chest.

"What did I want?"

"To find out what happened with the fire, and now that you know that Mikey had nothing do with it, you've been leaving us alone." It hadn't been that long since she'd seen him, but it felt like it had been.

"I know that Mikey had nothing to do with it," Marsh said. "But you don't know what caused it."

Her stomach tensed because she knew that he knew. "What was it?"

"The dryer."

"So it was my fault." Horror washed over her. JJ, Marsh and Collin had gotten hurt because of her.

"No, it was the fault of me and my brothers, who didn't keep up on maintenance at the ranch," he said. "We didn't clean out the vent. Or maybe it was the fault of the birds or the mice who put a nest in it. It was not your fault, Sarah."

She loved him for saying that. And just plain loved him. She knew that now without a doubt. He was such a sweet man. Such a champion for everyone he cared about. He took responsibility for everyone else, whereas her ex-husband refused to even take responsibility for himself.

"Marsh…" she murmured.

"Sarah," he murmured back. "I missed you."

"It's only been a few days since I've seen you,"

she reminded him. But it had felt like forever. It had felt like so much longer than it had actually been.

He stepped closer, and her mouth dried out as attraction overwhelmed her. "Why are you here, Sheriff?" she asked.

"To tell you what happened and that the insurance company has to settle. It's over, Sarah."

"Yes, Marsh, it's over," she agreed.

"Are you mad at me?" he asked.

She wished she was mad at him. It would make it easier for her to resist him, to ignore her feelings for him. But it was because she loved him that she had to resist him.

"I don't think you were completely honest with us, even though you wanted us to be honest with you," she pointed out. "I think you only started paying attention to us because of the fire."

"I honestly think that Mikey is an amazing kid. He's sweet and considerate and empathetic. He's such a good boy. And you…"

She didn't want to ask, but she didn't stop him, either.

He continued, "And you're amazing. You're beautiful and smart and compassionate. You're a loving mother and life-saving nurse."

"Marsh…" She wanted to tell him how amazing he was, too. He was righteous and kind.

"Go out with me again, Sarah," he said. "Just you and me, a real date."

She shook her head.

"Why not?" he asked.

"For your sake, I can't," she said. "You shouldn't be seen with me."

"Why not?" he repeated.

"I just explained to you that I could hurt your campaign for sheriff," she said. "Even your own family had questions about me."

"Who?" he asked.

She shook her head. "It doesn't matter." She cared about him too much to allow him to risk his future for them. "Go, Marsh. You've said a million times that you don't have time for a relationship, that you can't give anyone outside your career the time and the attention they deserve."

He opened his mouth, but he didn't say anything. Obviously, he couldn't argue with her. But she didn't give him the chance. She left him standing in the foyer and ran upstairs, desperate to get away from him before she did something stupid and selfish.

Before she told him that she loved him.

MARSH WATCHED HER run away from him, and he didn't know what to do. He didn't want to run after her and put pressure on her to give him a chance. He wanted her to be with him because it was what she wanted, not because it was what he wanted.

He wanted a relationship with her and Mikey

so very much, though. But he stood helplessly at the bottom of the stairs, staring after her.

"Hey…" a little voice murmured.

And he turned to find Mikey walking in the front door behind him.

"Did you just get home from school?"

Mikey nodded. "Mom lets me ride the bus now."

"Of course, she would," Marsh said. "You're very responsible." He'd brought a gift for Mikey. Sarah hadn't noticed the box, but Mikey did, his eyes wide. "This is for you."

Mikey stared at the box Marsh handed him.

"Open it," he urged him.

Mikey glanced around as if waiting for his mom to stop him or give him approval to open it. But then the temptation must have overwhelmed him because he took the top off the box and pulled out the white cowboy hat Marsh had had made. "For me?" he asked, and his voice quavered a bit.

"Yes," he said. "See if it fits."

And Mikey put it on his head. It fit perfectly, like Miller's hat had.

"It's white like yours," Mikey said.

"Yes. Do you like it?"

"I love it," Mikey said. Then he threw his arms around Marsh's waist and hugged him. "I love you, too."

"And I love you, Mikey," Marsh said. He loved the boy's mother as well.

But he didn't know how to make her believe it. And, even more, he didn't know how to get her to give him a chance, to love him back.

WHEN MARSH WALKED into her suite, Sadie held out her wrists. "Are you here to arrest me, Sheriff?" she asked. She knew that he wasn't here for that, but she did wonder why he was here.

He chuckled. "No," he said. "I'm not here to arrest you. Didn't you already figure out what caused the fire?"

"Me," she said. She would much rather take the rap than have a child be put through any more trauma than he'd already endured.

"Are you a stuffed-up dryer vent?" Marsh asked. "Because that's what the fire investigator determined right after the fire happened and again after the insurance company urged him to take a second look."

"Really?" Sadie asked with surprise. "It was a dryer vent that caused it?"

"Yes, it hadn't been cleaned out for a while or a bird or mice made a nest in it. Either way, the vent was clogged, and it caused the dryer to catch on fire," he said.

"Then why hasn't the claim been settled yet?" she asked with quiet fury.

"Because the insurance adjuster gets bonuses for every claim he denies."

"We'll see about that," Sadie said. She had to make certain that didn't happen again.

"I suspect he might not have a job after you're done with him," Marsh said.

"I don't want him putting any other family through this," Sadie said, justifying what she was about to do, what she had to do, so that her grandson didn't think she was just being vindictive, no matter how much that would have been justified as well. The adjuster had put a recent heart transplant patient through an unnecessary investigation. "I want to make sure that nobody else has been hurt because of his greed. And I want to make sure that he doesn't hurt anyone else."

"That's why I love you," Marsh said.

A smile twitched her lips even as warmth flooded her heart. "Why do you love me?"

"Because you use your powers for good," he said, and his lips were twitching, too, as if he was trying not to laugh.

She smiled and then sighed. "That's what I've been telling you." That was really all she wanted for her family. She just wanted them all to be as happy as she and Lem were now.

"That's why I'm here," Marsh said.

"It's not to arrest me?"

"Or Lem," he said.

"Lem?"

"He confessed, too, and Dad tried as well."

She smiled, so impressed with the men she loved. "But that's not why you're here," she said. "Why are you?"

"Because I need your help, Grandma."

CHAPTER TWENTY-FOUR

THIS WAS THE day that Sarah would finally get to check out where she and Mikey were going to be living. So she should have been excited, but she felt listless instead. Mikey was excited, but he'd begged off going with her to check it out so that he could stay at Becca's ranch with Hope. Cash was going to supervise Hope teaching him to ride. She stared through the windshield at them as Becca backed her SUV, in which Sarah was a passenger, out of her driveway.

Mikey was all ready for the outing with that adorable white hat on his head. He looked like a little cowboy with that and the boots she'd bought him. Her eyes misted with how fast he was growing up.

And now he was happy and bubbly. He loved school, and he loved all his friends, though he'd admitted to Sarah on the way to Becca's that he wished they could be family, too.

He wanted more than just her and him and their new kitty. But she couldn't give it to him, at least not with Marsh. She couldn't risk affecting his career. Yet, she wasn't interested in dating anyone else, not even the nice male teacher who'd asked her out for coffee. She wasn't interested in dating anyone who wasn't Marsh.

"You're quiet," Becca said, and she glanced over the console of her SUV at Sarah. "Don't worry about Mikey. Cash and Hope will both make sure he doesn't get hurt."

"I'm not worried about Mikey," she said. And that was a strange new sensation, to not be worried that she was going to screw him up, that she was failing as a parent.

"And don't worry about your new place," Becca said. "You're going to love it."

Sarah nodded. She wasn't sure about that. "Aren't you driving away from town? I thought it was still in town?"

"It is," Becca said. "I have to take a bit of a detour. Road construction or something. You know..."

There was always some project going on in Willow Creek. It was being revitalized and re-energized. Sarah hoped the same would happen to her. Maybe the new place would help. But she loved where she lived right now. She loved that deck off the big kitchen and the fenced backyard with the swing set for Mikey and for her, where they had their nightly competition to see who could swing higher, high enough to touch the stars.

She loved that place. Maybe that was why she hadn't packed up much of their stuff yet. Not that they had much. They'd been nomads for so long. "Maybe I should buy..." she muttered.

"This place has an option to do that," Becca said. "I have a feeling when you see it, you'll want to stay."

Sarah didn't feel like they were ever going to get there, though. Becca seemed to drive around the entire perimeter of the town before she finally turned and started heading through it. Then she turned onto a familiar street. And Sarah leaned forward in the passenger's seat. "It's right in the same neighborhood?"

"I know you and Mikey are happy here." And then she pulled into the driveway of the house that JJ had been renting from Bob Lemmon, the house where she'd been living since the fire.

"I can't afford this, though," Sarah protested.

"The rent is on the low end of what you said you could afford. And as for purchasing, you have enough for a down payment as well. The payments wouldn't be much higher than the rent," Becca said. "You could handle this on your own. But you don't have to be alone anymore."

"What do you mean?" Sarah asked. "I can't take money from anyone." But she could pick up shifts at the hospital; Sue had already reached

324   A MATCH FOR THE SHERIFF

out to ask her to help out when they were short-staffed. She had always made certain to have a sizeable emergency savings fund, just in case something happened and she had trouble getting another job. That fund had accumulated quite a bit. She could do this, and Mikey would be so happy. She turned toward Becca and narrowed her eyes. "Does Mikey already know?"

"My daughter has a big mouth."

"She must get that from her mother. Because how else would Hope have heard?" Sarah asked, but she was smiling.

Instead of being offended, Becca laughed. "I'm tired of keeping secrets. It's better to be open and honest, but I did want to surprise you."

"I am surprised."

"Come on," Becca said, as she reached for her door handle. "Get out. Let's check out your new place."

"I just left here..." Longer ago than she'd realized when she glanced at her watch. "I know what it looks like."

"But then it wasn't yours," Becca said. "It's yours now. And somehow I don't think the house is the only thing that's yours."

"What are you talking about?"

But Becca had already hopped out of the vehicle and shut her door. So Sarah got out, too. Becca was fast; she'd already rushed into the house. Sarah followed slowly, hesitantly, as if she needed to be cautious. She felt a little like she was being ambushed again, like she'd felt at Ranch Haven a week ago.

But the house was as empty as she'd left it when she and Mikey had headed to Becca's ranch. Even Becca was nowhere to be seen.

She called for the realtor. "Where are you?" She glanced up the stairwell, but she didn't hear any footsteps overhead.

"Out here," Becca said. "What a gorgeous backyard."

It really was. JJ had liked it so much, too, that Sarah was surprised he'd left it. But he was home now, where he'd grown up, from where he'd run away. Where he belonged.

And maybe this was where Sarah and Mikey belonged. In Willow Creek. In this house.

But then other images flashed through her mind, of Marsh holding her son, comforting and protecting him. Of Marsh holding her, comforting and protecting her, and then the kisses they'd shared.

She released a shaky breath before walking through the kitchen and then through the patio door Becca had left open. She stepped out onto the deck to a profusion of flowers and balloons and even more twinkling lights than had already dangled off the pergola over the deck.

"Surprise!" a chorus of voices rang out.

One of those was her son's, and Mikey ran up

to her, his white hat bobbing on his head. The other boys were there with their white hats. And he really did look like one of them, like he was a Haven. But that wasn't possible.

"Mommy, are you surprised?" he asked.

"Yes, very surprised."

"I'm sorry I wasn't open and honest, but Hope said that this was a good secret to keep."

Bailey Ann pursed her lips. "But—"

"I know, Bailey Ann," Hope interrupted her before she could start. They were more like sisters than cousins or friends. But she and Mikey were definitely best friends. She looped her arm around his shoulders so companionably. Though they were the same age, she was almost a head taller than him.

Like Sadie and Lem. They were there, standing behind the kids. And JJ was there, with his arm around Melanie Haven's mother, Juliet.

And Darlene was there with Dr. Miner, too, sneaking glances at him as if she couldn't look away from him. He was doing the same with her.

Everyone was coupled up but Marsh, who walked through the crowd alone. He wore his white hat and a deep green shirt. The badge wasn't pinned to his pocket today. He wasn't on duty, but his brothers teased him about responding to a call about disturbing the peace.

The only peace disturbed was Sarah's.

Everyone stepped back as he walked, letting him make his way to the deck. To her. But once he got there, he dropped down to one knee. And Sarah's heart dropped.

"What are you doing?" she asked, panic clawing at her, making her voice squeaky. "You need to get up…" Everybody was staring at them, and heat rushed to her face.

"Sarah, I know this might seem sudden, but I finally understand what my whole family has been blathering about," he said.

His family chuckled.

"When you know, you know," he said. "And I know that you and I and Mikey would have a beautiful life together. You've made me realize what matters most in the world. Love. I love you, Sarah, and I would be so honored and humbled and happy if you would accept my proposal."

She gasped and shook her head. "No. This is crazy. We barely know each other."

"I know that you are the most beautiful woman I've ever met. Inside and out. You care so much about all people and the most about people you love. You would sacrifice anything for the happiness of the people you love, even your own happiness. You don't have to do that, Sarah. If you would be happy with me, please say yes."

There were no chuckles now, but a few people sniffled. Sarah was one of them. Tears spilled out of her eyes. She wanted so badly to say yes. Because, despite what she'd said, she did know him. She knew he was such a good man, maybe the best man she would ever meet. And she wanted to accept his proposal for herself and for her son, who clearly already worshipped the man.

But could she be that selfish?

"Marsh, I don't want to hurt you..." she whispered.

"You'll only hurt me if you say no," he said.

MARSH FELT AS if he'd been down on one knee for a while. And she still hadn't said yes. But she hadn't said no, either.

He should have done this in private, though, he realized now. He'd taken some bad advice from his grandmother on this one.

But then Mikey walked up and put his arm around Marsh's neck. "Mommy, please say yes," he pleaded. "I want this family to be our family."

"It is," Marsh assured the little boy. "Even if your mother doesn't want to marry me."

"I do," she said.

And everyone gasped.

But she didn't look happy about it, with those tears trailing down her beautiful face.

He couldn't stay on his knee any longer. He jumped up and cupped her face in his hands, brushing away those tears. "Don't cry, Sarah, don't cry.

I don't want to make you sad. I want to make you happy."

"I just don't want to hurt you," she said.

"And like I said, the only way you'll hurt me is if you say no," he reminded her.

"But the election…"

"If people won't vote for me because of something that has nothing to do with you or me or Mikey, then I don't want their votes." He stepped slightly aside, so that she could see the backyard full of people. "Besides, with all the votes I have right here, there is little doubt that I will win. But I don't care about losing the election. I just don't want to lose you, Sarah. You and Mikey mean more to me than anything else."

She stared up at him then, with such wonder and awe, like she couldn't believe what he was saying. Like she couldn't believe he loved her. But then she must have seen it in his face because she wrapped her arms around his shoulders and hugged him tightly. "Yes, then, Marsh, yes, I will marry you."

He leaned down and pressed his lips to hers, sealing the proposal with a kiss. And his head buzzed as happiness and love overwhelmed him. He'd never loved anyone so much, and he knew he'd never been as loved.

She'd been willing to sacrifice her happiness for his. She was the most selfless, beautiful soul.

"Hey, cheapskate, where's the ring?" Cash called out.

And laughter followed.

Marsh patted his pocket, and panic flashed through him.

"I got it," Mikey said.

"Of course you do," Marsh said. And he stepped back so that the little boy could squeeze between them.

He opened the box and held it up to his mother. "Isn't it pretty, Mommy? I helped Marsh pick it out."

"Mikey has great taste in jewelry," Livvy Lemmon said with a smile. The little boy had found some items she'd lost in the room that had once been hers and would now be his for a long time to come, until he went off to college.

"It's beautiful," Sarah said, but she wasn't even looking at the ring. She was looking at her son and Marsh.

Marsh plucked it from the box that Mikey held, and he slid the ring with a sparkling oval diamond onto her finger. It fit perfectly. Just like they did.

"I love you," Sarah said.

"I love you."

"You two should get married right now," Mikey said. "Right here."

Marsh chuckled. "Well, we have to get a license first. But I do think this would be a beautiful place for a wedding." In what would be their own backyard.

"Caleb is eating all the cookies!" Hope called out to Mikey. "We have to go get some." Then she reached between them and pulled Mikey away.

Marsh laughed. "She is so much like her mother."

"She's already stealing my son," Sarah said, but she was laughing.

"Are you sure?" he asked her. "I know I sprang this on you…"

"Somehow, I think this was someone else's idea…" She pointed toward his smiling grandmother.

"She helped me get everyone together and work out the timing," he said. "But it was my idea. I can't imagine my life without you and Mikey in it. And I do want to get married as soon as possible."

"Me, too," she said. "I love you."

"I love you."

People rushed up to congratulate them then. They oohed over the ring and slapped his back. And then some teased his grandmother. "What will you do now, Grandma?" Ben asked her. "Take up knitting?"

She laughed, and it was an unsettling laugh. And Marsh had no doubt that she was already scheming.

As MIKEY LOOKED around the backyard full of people, he remembered the first time he'd met all the Havens and Cassidys in one place, at Ranch Haven. He'd been so scared, not of them, though. He'd been so scared that someone would find out he'd set the fire. But he hadn't set the fire.

He'd just been trying to stop one. He wasn't bad. He was good, really good, like the man who was going to be his daddy. Marsh.

"So I hear you're switching to being a lawman now," Uncle Cash said to him, and he touched the white hat that Mikey was wearing.

He nodded. "Yup."

"I'm still going to be a vet," Hope assured him. "Bailey Ann doesn't know yet if she's going to be a doctor or a lawyer."

"She has a lot of time to figure it out," Uncle Collin said with a really big smile.

Mikey loved this family. They were all so cool. But the coolest was probably Grandma Sadie. She'd told him to call her that, and that snicker-doodles were the best cookies. Hope thought so, too, but Mikey wasn't as convinced. He might have to have a few more before he made his final decision.

As he neared the table with all the food on it, he heard Grandma Sadie talking to Grandpa Lem. Something about how all the Havens and Cassidys were happy now, so they could focus on the lemons.

He grimaced at the thought of lemons. He'd

rather have the cookies. But if they were focusing on lemons, that would leave more cookies for him.

Unless Caleb ate them all first...

* * * * *